PRAISE FOR KAREN KATCHUR

RIVER BODIES

An *Entertainment Weekly* new and notable selection

"Deep, dark, and affecting—Karen Katchur's latest will keep you glued to the page."

—*InStyle*

"Karen Katchur's *River Bodies* has it all: a horrific murder, mysteries resurrected from the past, a story line packed with tension, and vivid characters to bring it all to life. A riveting thriller that suspense readers will love."

—Mary Kubica, *New York Times* bestselling author of *The Good Girl*

"Karen Katchur is a master at writing into the dark spaces of our intimate family relationships, and *River Bodies* is her most stunning work to date."

—Mindy Mejia, author of *Everything You Want Me to Be*

"*River Bodies* weaves an engrossing mystery with richly developed characters for an enjoyable, fast-paced read."

—Laura McHugh, award-winning author of *The Weight of Blood*

"With its striking sense of place and foreboding feeling of unease throughout, I wa   omplicated and layered that   t will leave you gasping, *Riv*   ling author

"Dark secrets of the past flow into the present in this emotionally resonant, deeply insightful tale of family bonds, betrayal, violence, and redemption. Part engrossing love story, part riveting murder mystery, *River Bodies* is a must-read."

—A. J. Banner, *USA Today* bestselling author of *The Twilight Wife*

COLD WOODS

"Karen Katchur ramps up the tension and hits every mark with *Cold Woods*, and this second installment in her compelling Northampton County series . . . will keep readers frantically flipping pages late into the night."

—Heather Gudenkauf, *New York Times* bestselling author of *The Weight of Silence* and *Not a Sound*

"Karen Katchur nails it with *Cold Woods* . . . dark and chilling, creepy and emotionally complex—and enthralling all the way to the shocking end."

—Kimberly Belle, bestselling author of *The Marriage Lie* and *Three Days Missing*

"*Cold Woods* . . . perfectly captures the strange insularity of a small town and unravels its secrets with an expert hand. Not to be missed!"

—Marissa Stapley, bestselling author of *Things to Do When It's Raining*

SPRING GIRLS

OTHER TITLES BY KAREN KATCHUR

SPRING GIRLS

A Thriller

KAREN KATCHUR

THOMAS & MERCER

Published by Thomas & Mercer, Seattle

www.apub.com

Amazon, the Amazon logo, and Thomas & Mercer are trademarks of Amazon.com, Inc., or its affiliates.

ISBN-13: 9781542093248
ISBN-10: 1542093244

Cover design by Shasti O'Leary Soudant

Printed in the United States of America

SPRING GIRLS

DROWNING

Drowning is a quiet death. She learns this firsthand, how it's nothing like she's seen in the movies. There's no thrashing, arms flailing, splashing, crying for help. Rather, it's a silent sinking as the water enters her mouth and nose, soundlessly filling her lungs. The rapids whisper in her ears, a harsh lullaby, as the current pulls and tugs her arms and legs, her torso, playing with her, toying with her, dragging her downriver. She doesn't fight or try to resist. A strange kind of calm settles inside her, a dead calm, an acceptance of what is coming, as though she has chosen it herself: a tragic ending to a mostly happy life.

Only once does her head surface, and even then, it's only the top part: her forehead, her eyes. Foam bubbles in fits and rages, but there is a second where she can see, and in that second, time stretches far and wide. She spies the bridge, the pillars, the cold steel rail where the signs post warnings about the dangers of jumping; the lone figure staring down at her.

A flicker of fear ignites, sizzles against her flesh, extinguishes as quickly as it appears. Darkness sweeps in, swirling around her, tumbling, tumbling, tumbling down . . .

CHAPTER ONE

On a rainy spring afternoon, Janey sat with her son, Christian, in the dark movie theater. They were only moments away from the big climactic scene where the family of superheroes takes the villain down and saves the day. She was barely paying attention to the action on screen, having seen this particular kids' movie before. It was a second run, a promotional tool for the upcoming sequel to be released in June. But she'd needed to get out of the house, distract herself from the disquiet she'd been feeling ever since she'd gotten out of bed. She couldn't pinpoint the cause of her unease. It was just there when she'd opened her eyes, much like the heavy gray clouds consuming the sky.

When the movie ended and the credits rolled, they followed the crowd to the exit. She stopped near a wall of video games, searching for her keys in her purse. Christian pulled on her blouse, his fingers slick with butter from the bag of popcorn he'd eaten, leaving grease stains on her last clean shirt.

"I can't see," he whined, and he crawled up her leg and all the way up her body as though he were a spider on the trunk of a tree. He wrapped his ropy arms around her neck. His forearms squeezed her throat.

"There's nothing to see." She tried to loosen his grip where his arm had dug into her larynx. "It's just a video game." It was a game meant for mature audiences, but of course it was more popular among the younger kids. It was full of death and destruction and shooting characters who looked too much like real people, blowing up cars and buildings.

"I want to seeeeeee!" He tightened his grip on her neck.

"Christian." She coughed, grabbed his arms, tried to pull them away from her throat. There were black spots in front of her eyes. For a second, she thought she might pass out. She tried to pry him off. The scent of buttery popcorn filled her nose. Just as she thought she might black out, he released her and jumped to the ground, fell onto his back. Air rushed her lungs.

He stared up at her from the dirty theater floor, eyes wide, accusing. *How dare she?*

"Oh, honey, I'm so sorry." Did she push him? Or throw him off of her? She crouched next to him, reached for his hands to help him up. "Are you hurt? Please tell me you're not hurt."

"You hit me!" he shrieked.

"I didn't hit you," she pleaded. "Christian, please, you were choking me."

"Is everything okay here?" A woman approached wearing a black shirt with the movie theater's logo stitched on the pocket. She bent over, speaking to Christian directly, ignoring Janey.

"He's fine," Janey said, scooping Christian into her arms even though he was six years old and too big to be carried. She didn't give him the opportunity to answer the movie attendant, knowing he'd say his mommy had struck him. "He was climbing on me and fell. That's all."

"Okay, as long as he's all right," the attendant said before walking away.

As soon as they were in the car, with Christian strapped into his booster seat, Janey felt like she could breathe for the first time. Before she started the engine, she looked at him in the rearview mirror. "You can't tell people I hit you when I clearly didn't. You could get Mommy in trouble. It was an accident. You fell."

He stared back at her in the mirror, unmoving, silent. She started the car and pulled from the parking space. It wasn't until they were a mile from home, stopped at a traffic light, that she touched her neck. Her hand was shaking.

She turned onto Eighth Street, parked in front of a modest single-family home in the small town of Bangor, Pennsylvania. The outside was made of brick, the roof made of slate, a solid square structure built to keep the wolves out, where no amount of huffing or puffing could bring it down. She'd bought the home when Christian had turned two years old, sinking every penny she could scrape together into the house: a desperate need for a safe place to raise her son.

They headed inside. Janey set her keys and purse on the kitchen counter. Christian ran into the family room. She followed him. "Do you have to go to the bathroom?" she asked.

He shook his head.

She set him up with his coloring books and crayons. "I'll be right back."

She stood in front of the bathroom sink, splashed cold water on her face, tossed her hair over her shoulder. A black mark was visible on her neck. But perhaps she was imagining it. She did that sometimes: saw things, memories in her mind's eye that refused to stay buried. She pulled her blouse closed, turned away, struggled to trust herself. She'd wear the required collared shirt to work on Monday, but she'd button it up to the top button to cover her neck, just in case there really was something there. She was an assistant manager at a craft store, family owned and operated, closed on Sundays to honor God. She liked her job. She'd taken to arts and crafts at an early age, raised by a mother who taught home economics at the community college and a father who'd taught woodshop in the middle school before he'd retired. She was the product of a small DIY family of three, a hardworking, country-loving,

God-fearing family. She'd knitted Christian's hat and scarves for winter: black and blue stripes, his favorite colors. She'd decoupaged the secondhand coffee table she'd picked up at a flea market and had sewed her own curtains, which now hung in the family room and their two bedrooms. She'd been raised as a good girl, as her mother had told anyone who would listen. *A good girl.* Her mother had made it sound as though Janey were a child and not a young woman. As for being good, Janey didn't even know what that meant anymore.

She made a cup of tea and some finger sandwiches, set the tray on the coffee table in front of the TV. Christian's coloring books were thrown around, crayons scattered on the floor. His favorite magazine, *When Animals Attack!*, was opened to a page where a great white shark bared several rows of teeth. She flipped the magazine closed with her foot, hoping he wouldn't notice. The toys and books he gravitated toward always felt sharp to her, edgy, violent.

She turned on the local news, stared at the reporter standing in front of yellow crime scene tape. A tall cop with broad shoulders deflected the reporter's questions with the typical noncommittal type of answers law enforcement gave when they weren't prepared to release information to the public.

Christian made race car sounds as he ran around the coffee table, coloring the decoupage top with a bright-orange crayon, crashing into Janey's shins on each pass.

She didn't stop him from ruining the tabletop like she should have. Instead, she sat on the edge of the couch, hands tucked between her thighs, unable to move, to look away from the screen. What she'd sensed earlier, the reason for her unease, was playing out in front of her. It had happened again. She could feel it, deep inside her bones. There, behind the reporter and police, she saw the serenity of the lake, the rolling green mountains, the promise of another victim.

CHAPTER TWO

Detective Geena Brassard stood on the shore of the lake. A cool breeze blew across the water. Light rain curled the ends of her ponytail. She'd been tucked under the bedcovers, Codis, her old bulldog, snoring at her feet, when she'd gotten the call around six thirty this morning that a girl's body had been found in Minsi Lake.

Another spring girl.

She was right on time.

Geena pulled her hood up, zipped the front of her state-issued slicker. Small waves lapped against the shore. Ducks floated on the water, flapped their wings. Birds chattered in the trees. Nature continued without any consequence: a constant white noise behind the scene, ignoring the chaos created by law enforcement.

The girl's body had been found by a local fisherman. He'd gotten up early to take advantage of the lifted regulations on the lake. Fishermen were being encouraged to fish as much as possible over the next several weeks. The dam was badly in need of repair, and the Pennsylvania Fish and Boat Commission had secured moneys to have it fixed. But in order to rebuild the dam, the 117-acre lake had to be drained.

Draining the lake had begun last week. The water level was low. In some areas the lake bottom had been exposed, giving the entire place a rich, earthy smell alongside the tang of death.

"I've never seen anything like it before," the fisherman said, shaking his head. He held a fishing pole in one hand, a tackle box in the other. His long gray hair was tied in a ponytail.

"I understand." Geena imagined the poor man's shock when he'd walked out to the water, thinking he'd get an hour or two of fishing in before the excavation crew showed up, only to find something he'd never expected.

The area had been cordoned off with crime scene tape. The forensic unit buzzed around the scene, a hive of worker bees. The parking lot at the top of the embankment, which had been mostly empty in the early Saturday morning hour, was starting to fill up. The local media had gotten word a girl's body had been found. Originally, the call had been sent directly to the state police on a radio frequency unavailable to public scanners. This had bought the detectives some time, but that window had closed hours ago.

News traveled fast in small towns.

Lieutenant Sayres came to stand next to Geena. At six feet four, he seemed to tower over her, even though she was five feet, eleven and a half inches, coming in just under an even six feet. *You're tall for a woman,* she'd heard from acquaintances, strangers, her entire adult life, as though this were the most interesting thing about her.

Nathan, the county coroner, crouched over the victim. Geena and the lieutenant watched silently, collectively holding their breath. Nathan glanced over his shoulder; then he stood, stepped toward them. He wasn't much older than Geena, midthirties, but they'd both seen horrors well beyond their years. His shoulders rolled forward, and his back curved as though he were perpetually hunched over, which she supposed he was a lot of the time.

"It looks like she's been in the water for at least a couple of hours. No clothes. No jewelry. No remarkable birthmarks or scars that I can see. No tattoos. Nothing on her to confirm an ID. Wrists and ankles have some bruising, probably from being bound. There are also marks on her neck, indicating possible strangulation. The autopsy should be able to tell you what kind of ligatures were used."

"No chance it's a drowning then?" Geena asked.

"I'll have Sandra do the autopsy to rule out drowning as the cause of death," Nathan said. "But based on what I'm seeing, this girl was dead before she entered the water."

"Same as the others," Geena said, glancing at Sayres.

"Let's not get ahead of ourselves," Sayres said.

"There's some debris caught around her legs and hair," Nathan said. "It might give us a clue about where she's been. Or it might just be debris from the lake. Hard to tell."

"This is the closest we've come if it's only been a few hours," Geena said, her voice rising, unable to tamp down her excitement about what this could mean. "He could still be close by."

Sayres nodded. Geena had worked the last two cases when the girls' bodies had started turning up: the first one in a pond off Route 191 and the second one in Martins Creek, both located in Northampton County. That was until Sayres had pulled her off the cases, transferred her to the field station. Still, she knew the details of the crimes better than anyone on the team, except for maybe Albert Eugenis, her old partner.

"This is a priority case," Sayres said to Nathan. "Make sure Sandra does the autopsy ASAP."

"Understood," Nathan said.

Sayres turned to Geena. "I've already got the dogs on the way to search the area surrounding the lake and woods. I'll need a team knocking door to door on every house up and down this road. And let's find out if any of them have security cameras."

At this point, they looked up at the light posts in the parking lot. No cameras.

The lieutenant muttered something about the lack of security in the backwoods of the small town; then he added, "Here's your partner now."

Detective Parker Reed signed the log, then ducked underneath the yellow tape, made his way over to them.

Parker's predecessor, Albert, had retired a year ago almost to the date, a few days after the second girl had been found in Martins Creek. Albert had said he'd had enough; he couldn't do it anymore. The idea they were looking at a possible serial killer had put him over the edge emotionally, mentally. He was tapped out. Thirty-five years on the job, four of those years working with Geena, and just like that, her mentor, her partner and friend, had filled out the paperwork, walked out the front door of the Pennsylvania State Police barracks, collected his pension. She hadn't forgiven him for abandoning her. And, not that she'd ever admit this to him, she'd also understood. Anyone working the job as long as he had—well, it was bound to catch up to him. He'd taken up organic farming, tended to a couple of acres of tomatoes, peas, carrots, squash, eggplant, broccoli, and bush beans. Pearl, his wife, had welcomed the change, his new hobby. Pearl couldn't have been happier.

Geena shivered at the thought of having nothing better to do with her day than weed, water, and fertilize, not when her adrenaline was pumping, her senses on high alert. The air was charged as though the forensic unit, the detectives, knew they were getting closer with this one, nearer to the madman behind the crimes. But as Parker approached, the rush that had overtaken her stalled. Sayres was still mad at him for becoming personally involved with Becca, a witness on a case last autumn. And lately, Sayres's anger had tended to spill over onto Geena. It had started around the time of Albert's retirement. For seven long months, Sayres had grumbled about what he was going to do with her. The other investigators already had partners. It wasn't in their budget to promote someone to fill Albert's position. And then in December, Sayres had transferred her to the field station, where she'd become partners with Parker. In some ways she felt as though the transfer had been punishment for Albert's leaving.

"It's about time you got here," Sayres said to Parker.

Parker glanced at Geena, possibly trying to gauge from her what kind of mood the lieutenant was in.

"She'll catch you up," Sayres said before stepping away and climbing up the hillside to meet the media.

"You're not his favorite person," she said as she headed to where the girl's body lay on the shoreline.

Parker followed her. "He sure can hold a grudge."

"Why are you late?" she asked.

"Never heard my phone go off."

"Big date with Becca last night?"

"Something like that." The corners of his lips turned up for a brief second. Parker didn't smile often, and even a hint of one was an improvement over his usual sober expression. He didn't talk much about his relationship with Becca, other than to say they'd been childhood friends. It seemed to Geena that he'd fallen in love with the girl next door.

They stopped near the body. The smell of flesh breaking down, the rot and decay, clung to the air and coated the back of her throat. She pointed to the bruising on the girl's neck and the marks on her wrists and ankles and then filled him in on what Nathan had said about the injuries. Parker's face paled. He seemed to look everywhere but at the victim.

"You okay?" she asked. He'd struggled with looking at dead bodies ever since he'd witnessed a guy blow his brains out in that same case last autumn, when he'd gotten involved with Becca. Geena hadn't been his partner then, but she'd heard he'd shown up at the field station with blood splatter on his clothes.

"I'm fine," he said unconvincingly. A bead of sweat dripped by his temple. He covered his mouth and turned away.

"Get ahold of yourself," she whispered, and she looked around to see if anyone else had noticed. No one was paying attention. "Come on." She grabbed his arm and led him away to the embankment. He wiped the sheen of sweat from his forehead. He appeared to be trying to pull himself together. She couldn't help but think he'd better get past this if he was going to stick with her in homicide. He'd only made detective in the last year: a rookie.

They trekked up the hill side by side. At least he was tall, she thought. She could stand next to him, walk beside him without feeling self-conscious. It had taken her months to get used to working beside Albert, a small man with a barrel for a chest, shocking white hair, twinkling eyes. Short men had a way of making her feel awkward, lanky, a giant with boobs.

Everybody had loved Albert, wanted to talk to him and tell him their secrets, as though they were confiding in their own grandfather. Even she'd confessed her darkest fears, her secrets, taken from the pages of her journal, which she'd vowed no one would ever read. "Diary of a tall girl," Albert had called her confessions during those long nights on the job.

Geena had grown to love Albert too.

By the time she and Parker had reached the top of the hill, a local news reporter was waiting, microphone in hand. The redheaded reporter had positioned herself with her back to the lake so her viewers could get a glimpse of the water and the crime scene tape. The camera rolled as she approached Lieutenant Sayres for a statement.

Geena veered away from the media. Parker stopped, apparently wanting to listen to what the lieutenant had to say. Geena got in her car to escape the misting rain. She tapped her finger on the steering wheel while she waited for Parker to join her. She missed Albert, his suits worn at the elbows, his breakaway glasses that hung from his neck more than they'd ever rested on his nose. The smell of talcum powder on his skin reminded her of her childhood, her own father before he died. In ways, Albert's retiring had felt like a death, a loss she'd had to suffer alone.

Even now, all these months later, she was still trying to find her way, her place, without him.

Once the lieutenant had finished talking with the media, he handed down orders to the team. Bill Henson and Craig Lowry, two seasoned detectives with twenty years between them, took to the streets, walking the back roads near the lake, knocking door to door, looking for witnesses. The tracking dogs had since arrived but hadn't picked up a scent. They had a lot of ground to cover. The rain was making the terrain slippery, muddy, miserable. Geena stayed behind where the girl's body had been discovered and had since been transported to the county morgue awaiting Sandra's autopsy. The dogs' barking was a distant cry. Mostly, she heard the rain striking the hood of her slicker. She kept her eyes on the ground, searching for an article of clothing, a shoe print, anything.

Parker walked parallel to her, using the grid method of searching a scene. He mentioned he'd fished in this lake when he was a kid. Even though he knew the area better than any of them, he was being treated like an outsider. Everyone at headquarters had had their hands in the previous two cases. Parker hadn't joined the team until after the second girl had been found.

Geena empathized with his situation. She understood what it was like to be on the outside looking in, being one of the few women in the academy and later in the troop. It had taken her several months to feel comfortable, to acclimate with the other cadets, and even longer once she'd been assigned to the station in Bethlehem. It wasn't until she'd made detective, partnered with Albert, that she'd finally settled in. And now she found herself back on uneven ground, both figuratively and literally. She glanced at Parker, checked his progress.

He shook his head. He hadn't found anything either.

After another hour of searching that turned up nothing, the team took a break, headed back to the command center, where a tent had been erected. The dogs returned to rest, regroup.

"We're going to have to branch out, cover more of the wooded area throughout these hills," Sayres said.

"He couldn't have carried her far in this terrain," Parker offered.

"You think he drove her here?" Sayres asked.

"It's possible," Parker said.

"With the excavation crew, I bet a ton of vehicles are entering and exiting this place," Geena said. "Tracks are going to be hard to pin down. He could've come and gone relatively unnoticed."

"That's a good point." Sayres turned to Pat, their intelligence officer. "Did anyone get back to you about a missing person?"

Pat held up his phone. "Signal's been spotty all day. Nothing's coming in or going out."

"The mountains might have something to do with that," Sayres said. "All right, Brassard, you're up. Give me the names of missing girls in the database."

The team's eyes were on her, expectant. It was a test. Her eidetic memory was the reason she'd been promoted in the first place. "No new reports have come in that I'm aware of. There is an older case, a girl who went missing a couple years ago. But her description doesn't match our current victim."

There were so many missing girls, so many missing women in the database. It was hard to keep up with all their names and faces. The site was overflowing with people who had disappeared. And yet, ever since the first girl had turned up in the pond, Geena had made it her mission to memorize all the girls in the missing person files in Pennsylvania, their faces like snapshots in a photo lineup in her mind.

Sayres nodded and turned to Bill and Craig. "Get me a list of the names of the excavation crew who've been working the site the last couple days. Check any tire prints against their vehicles. Find out if they've seen anything, feel them out." He looked back at Geena and Parker. "You two head back to headquarters, since it appears we're in a dead zone. I'll let your sergeant know you won't be working out of the field station for this one. And double-check those missing person files again. Something might've come in in the last few hours. We need to get an ID on our victim."

Geena sat in front of the computer at her old desk at headquarters. She shook off her raincoat, tossed it over the back of the chair. The station itself was nondescript with its white floors and gray walls. The small office she'd shared with Albert on the second floor wasn't any different from the rest of the building, especially now that he'd taken his personal items with him. He'd had a plant, some kind of creeping vine sitting on the corner of his desk, its stems reaching around the adjoining wall of their cubicle. They'd often pushed back from their computers, discussed their cases, her dog, his wife, his two kids, who had since grown, moved out, lived in different states. His wedding photo had taken up space at the opposite corner of his desk, along with various family photos. The caricature he and Pearl had sat for at the farmers' fair had been removed from the wall. His desk had sat empty for months. Her only personal effect had been a three-by-four-inch picture of Codis staring up at her from the kitchen floor, his face smushed, his mouth turned up as though he were smiling. He was such a goofy dog. She loved him more than anything. But the photo wasn't here anymore. She'd taken it with her when she'd been transferred. It sat at home in a box.

"We don't have much to go on," she said to Parker. To his credit, he didn't mention the memory test Sayres had given her, and then how he'd promptly sent them to headquarters to check the missing person files anyway. She continued. "Female, youngish. Nathan didn't give me an age.

We'll have to wait for the autopsy. I'm going. It's up to you whether you want to join me." She kept her eyes on the computer screen, giving him an out if he needed one. Technically, they both didn't need to be there, and maybe it was better if he didn't see the body again, outside of photos.

"I'll go," he said about the autopsy. He stood behind her, looked over her shoulder at the computer screen. "Is the other desk mine?" he asked.

"I guess it's yours while you're here," she said. She'd had months to get used to a new partner, but she hadn't prepared herself for someone taking over Albert's desk. Now that they were here, she wasn't ready to have someone sit in his seat. In ways it had been easier to make the adjustment at the field station. There weren't any reminders of her old partner there.

"I could really use some coffee," Parker said, and he got up from the desk. "You?"

"Definitely," she said.

The station was quiet on a Saturday, with most of the team out at the lake. The rest of the troop was out on patrol. The sergeant was off duty, and Geena hoped he was being smart and enjoying time with his family.

She busied herself searching the missing person database while Parker fiddled with the coffee maker. He returned with two mugs, set one down on her desk. She waited for her screen to load.

Her phone went off, the ringtone set to sound like an old rotary phone.

"We got a probable ID on the vic," Lieutenant Sayres said. "Local law enforcement took a call a few minutes ago about a missing girl that matches the description. Her name is Valerie Brown, goes by Val." He filled her in on the few details he had about Valerie's disappearance. Age twenty-three. Reported missing when she failed to come home after going for a walk on the trails after dinner. "I'll need you and Reed to head out and talk to the parents, get them to ID her. The body should've made it to the morgue by now."

Geena hung up the phone, primed herself mentally, emotionally, for the hardest part of the job, talking with Valerie's parents. She'd have to prepare them for the probability that their daughter had been found and then ask them to identify the body. The previous victim had been submerged in water for over a month, six weeks to be exact, the body so badly decomposed, unrecognizable, they'd had to use dental records to make a positive ID. That wouldn't be the case this time around.

Parker stood in front of the whiteboard, where two female victims' names and headshots had been posted. "We're going on the assumption they're connected?" he asked, keeping his back to her.

"Yes," she said. "Two victims in the last couple years. They were bound, raped, and strangled. But it gets a little murky from there. They were found in different locations. One in a pond off Route 191, the other in Martins Creek. Our victim today seems to be the third. She fits the profile—college aged, long hair, alone on the mountain trails."

"Any leads?"

"Nothing that stuck," she said.

It had seemed random at first, two separate attacks occurring three years apart. Added to the fact they hadn't discovered any connection between the victims. Yet there were similarities—their age and the length of their hair, their injuries, how they'd disappeared when they were alone on the trails, with close proximity to a body of water. A pattern was developing.

They had no witnesses. No DNA or prints. *Yet,* she reminded herself. They'd found this latest victim much sooner than the other two. There was a chance they'd get something; she was hopeful the water hadn't washed the evidence away. The cases had become personal to Geena, the ones that had forced her partner into retirement.

"Three victims," Parker said.

"Yes," she said, but what she didn't tell Parker was that Albert had suspected there was a fourth victim, the true first victim, the one who had survived.

CHAPTER THREE

Geena stood in the county morgue next to Mark and Susan Brown, parents of the missing girl, Valerie, third victim of the unsub. Geena didn't say this to them. To put it in blunt terms like that would have been beyond cruel. Right now, it was more important that the Browns identify their daughter. Their questions about how this could have happened and who could have done this would come later.

They stood behind a glass window. She noticed Parker kept his head turned away. The girl's face was uncovered, the rest of her body hidden from view. The belief was that her face would be enough for the Browns to make an ID. The girl's hands and feet had been bagged in hopes of collecting evidence underneath her nails. Her body was bruised and bloated, her skin waxy. It wouldn't do them any good to see any more of their daughter than was absolutely necessary.

Mrs. Brown collapsed into her husband's embrace, made a deep noise within her throat that could only be associated with intense grief, the kind of sound Geena would never get used to hearing. Geena stepped away from the glass, ushered the Browns down the hall.

As soon as it was polite to do so, she extricated herself from the grieving parents. She put a call in to Lieutenant Sayres, told him they had a positive ID on the victim. Then she called the local police and let them know, requested whatever information they had to be sent to her directly. She didn't need the autopsy report to confirm what she'd known when she'd first glimpsed Valerie's manicured fingernails.

They wouldn't find defensive wounds.

Parker comforted the Browns for a little longer, then saw them off, much like Albert used to do, leaving Geena to manage her own feelings and the anger that burned inside that the unsub was still out there, that he'd hurt another girl. The family needed to see Geena as strong, confident that she'd catch whoever had done this to their precious daughter. And that was exactly what she'd give them over the next few days and weeks ahead. But right now, she needed to take a minute to check herself.

Parker came to stand next to her in the parking lot, the Browns' four-door sedan heading down the street.

"They agreed to meet us at the station now for a formal interview," he said.

She nodded. They got in the car. As they drove back to headquarters, she caught him up on everything she knew about the unsub. He listened without comment, drummed his fingers on the armrest on the passenger side of the car.

"We think he used chloroform or another chemical like it, covered their noses and mouths with some kind of cotton rag." Geena suspected the girls had never seen him coming. "To date, there isn't any evidence that the girls tried to put up a fight, no scratches or defensive wounds. It seems possible they weren't even conscious when the assault took place." The unsub was a coward of the biggest kind, keeping his victims bound, possibly unconscious, while he did unspeakable things to them. Her theory was that he'd strangled them before they were fully awake, untied them after they died, disposed of them in the lakes and creeks.

It was the untying of the ligatures that stood out as unusual. Most serial killers wouldn't bother with this detail once their victim was dead. If she could figure out why he'd untied them, she'd be that much closer to understanding him and potentially catching him.

She continued. "The first girl was found after three weeks in the water. The second after six weeks. Valerie is the quickest one we've found to date. Let's hope the water didn't destroy the evidence, like with the others." The freshwater temperatures the last few springs had remained warm, accelerating the decomposition of the bodies, not to mention the feasting that had taken place by aquatic life. The girls' flesh had turned into adipocere, or corpse wax, and then it had been nibbled away in pieces, along with the evidence. Bodies in salt water had a whole other level of decomposition and list of predators. Over time in salt water, a person's head, hands, and feet detached, floated away. It wasn't unusual to find the body part washed up on shore.

They pulled into the parking lot at the station, where the Browns were waiting. Once everyone was relatively comfortable in the interview room, Geena moved her chair closer to Mrs. Brown, leaned in. She'd seen Albert do it a thousand times with witnesses, victims, suspects. "Show them you care. Respect them as a person," Albert had said. "Even the most hardened criminal is still a human being." Geena wasn't so sure she believed it, at least not about the unsub. In her mind, serial killers weren't human, and maybe they weren't in Albert's either. Maybe that was what had broken him in the end.

"I know you don't feel like answering questions right now, but the best way to find out who did this to your daughter is to get all the information we can from you, and the sooner the better," she said.

Mrs. Brown nodded, wiped her nose. She raised her eyes, fixed them on Parker. She may have been a grieving mother, but she still noticed the handsome man in the room. She looked to him to take the lead.

Geena continued leaning in close to Mrs. Brown despite her gazing at Parker. "When was the last time you saw your daughter?" she asked.

Mrs. Brown shook her head. "I . . . I don't remember what time it was."

"It's okay," Parker said. "Take your time."

Mr. Brown spoke up, turning his attention to Parker too. "Last night around five o'clock. She had dinner with us and then decided it was such a nice night that she would go for a walk."

"Was it unusual for her to go for a walk after dinner?" Parker asked.

"No, it wasn't unusual," Mr. Brown said. "She did it all the time. She grew up here. She knows the trails."

Geena had grown up in the city of Bethlehem. She'd taken day trips to hike the mountain trails and ski, but wandering around in the woods at dusk wasn't something she'd ever done. But the locals in the Slate Belt wouldn't think anything of it. The mountains were in their backyards, where they'd grown up hiking the Appalachian Trail, tubing down the Delaware River, four-wheeling, skiing, camping, fishing, and hunting.

"Did she go alone?" Parker asked. "Or was she meeting someone?"

"She was alone. She liked to walk alone. The trails are right outside our house," Mr. Brown said.

"I don't understand how this could've happened," Mrs. Brown said. Fresh tears spilled onto her cheeks.

Mr. Brown kept talking. It seemed to Geena that he wanted to talk, and laying down the facts appeared to be his way of controlling his grief. "We were in bed early, maybe nine o'clock. We just assumed she'd come home from her walk and went straight to her bedroom. It's what she usually does. She doesn't always check in with us. She's an adult." He paused.

Geena could only imagine what was going through his mind—if only he'd gotten up to check she was in her room, called out good night and waited for a response, or had never let her walk alone in the woods in the first place. Maybe he wished he'd made stricter rules, held her tighter, longer, told her one last time he loved her.

Mr. Brown continued. "My wife went to Val's room this morning to see if she wanted to come to breakfast with us, and that's when we found her bed empty. She hadn't slept in it."

"What time was that?" Parker asked.

"Um, I'm not sure. But I called the police right away. I knew something was wrong." He looked at his wife. "I think we both knew."

"We're not bad parents," Mrs. Brown said. "She was living with us to save money while she was taking college classes. We're not neglectful. She's twenty-three. I didn't want to hover." She covered her face, sobbed. Mr. Brown put his arm around her.

After a few seconds had passed and Valerie's parents had collected themselves, Parker asked, "Do you know if your daughter had her phone with her?"

"No, no. You can't get a signal. We sit too close to the mountain."

"Okay," Parker said. "Do you remember what she was wearing?"

Geena took notes, marked down the time Valerie left for her walk, what she'd been wearing, the fact she hadn't been carrying her cell phone. Both Mr. and Mrs. Brown turned their full attention to Parker at this point, talking to him as though Geena weren't in the room and Parker were the lead investigator in the case.

Geena could do nothing but take notes and listen, not wanting to jeopardize the free flow of information. But the fact she'd been dismissed so easily, even by Mrs. Brown, and for no other reason that Geena could see than the fact she was a woman, sent her teeth vibrating.

Men had no idea how good they had it, the instant respect for their authority. Since Geena had joined the state police, she'd had to fight for every inch of that same respect that men on the force took for granted. And now she'd have to take back the lead from Parker? She thought not. It wasn't Parker's fault. She just missed Albert.

It hadn't been a competition or a male/female thing between her and Albert. His grandfatherly appearance and his kind, warm eyes had been disarming. It was natural for people to gravitate toward him, want to talk with him. Geena understood this, accepted it, observed, and listened.

It wasn't like that anymore, not since she'd partnered with Parker four months ago, but there was nothing to be done about it. The bottom line was this wasn't about her. This was about the victims, Valerie and her parents, and she would do her job as best she could to help them, no matter who took the lead.

When the interview was winding down, Geena excused herself from the room. She rummaged through brochures, maps of the areas the team had already covered in the previous two cases, until she found a map of Minsi Lake. She returned to the small room where the Browns and Parker were wrapping up. She spread the map on the table in front of them.

"Which trails would she have taken?" she asked.

Mr. Brown studied the map, pointed to the trails he thought his daughter would've walked. The Browns were sent home, a box of tissues tucked under Mrs. Brown's arm. Geena checked her phone for anything from the lieutenant. Nothing. She searched her pockets for the car keys. She had to get back to the lake and have the tracking dogs take another look around, now that she had a map of the trails Valerie had most likely trekked before she'd been abducted.

Parker brushed off the dried mud still clinging to the cuff of his pants from walking around the lake earlier that day. "We need to get on those trails," he said.

"That's exactly what I was thinking." It was one of many thoughts she'd had since Valerie's body had been found, but she wasn't ready to share them just yet. She was still working on a theory, one with too many unanswered questions. They hadn't been able to connect the victims to each other or to the unsub, which led her to believe he hunted and killed based on opportunity. It seemed possible the victims had simply been in the wrong place at the wrong time.

But why had he chosen Minsi Lake to dispose of Valerie's body? The other two girls had been left in remote locations, and because of that they hadn't been discovered right away. Was it because he'd had more time to think things through with them, and therefore he'd chosen his watering hole more carefully? Or was it luck that Minsi Lake was in the process of being drained and the water level had been too low to hide the body?

She looked at the map again, traced her finger along a trail. Maybe the unsub was getting sloppy—or worse, maybe he was getting brave.

CHAPTER FOUR

Janey collected her purse, then stood from the pew. She took Christian's hand. They fell in line behind the throng of people exiting the church now that Easter Mass had ended. The line moved slowly, Father Perry standing at the door, shaking the hand of each parishioner, touching the foreheads of babies, squeezing the arms of tired mothers, a gesture meant to comfort. *Hang in there.*

Janey felt the crowd at her back, ushering her and Christian outside, where families and friends gathered. A spring breeze blew her skirt across her ankles. The yellow scarf tied around her neck hid the mark she was now certain was on her skin. She hadn't imagined it, like she'd thought initially, not after pressing her fingers against the spot and feeling the soreness of a bruise.

The sun was high in the sky. She shielded her eyes from the glare, searched for her parents. The egg hunt would start in half an hour in the field on the side of the church, where picnic tables had been set up, each piled high with bagels, biscuits, scones, and muffins. Janey had baked two dozen chocolate chip scones, Christian's favorite, dropped them off in the church basement before services. Now they were displayed with the other baked goods. She spied her mother's cupcakes, frosting in the shape of the Easter Bunny done with the skill of an artist.

Janey spotted her father standing alone next to the tables under an oak tree with his hands in his pockets. Her mother stood a couple of feet away with a group of women. The mood was somber. Behind the exchange of pleasantries, murmurs about the girl's body that had been found in Minsi Lake were on everyone's tongues. They were too polite to talk above whispers. *Who was she? Do we know her? Will they catch whoever has done this?*

Janey hadn't been able to think of anything else, not after sitting in front of the TV much of the day and night in the last twenty-four hours since the news broke.

"Come on," she said to Christian, and she led him over to the table with the sign-up sheet for the egg hunt. She signed him up for the six-year-old age group. Not far from where they were standing, a bunch of young girls and boys were running in circles with pink and blue streamers, playing some kind of game.

"Why don't you go play with them?" she said to him. "I'll get your basket from the car."

She gave him a little nudge in their direction, watched as he walked toward them with his head down. Carlyn Walsh, his clinical psychologist, a specialist in children with behavioral disorders, had suggested Janey try to encourage him to interact more with kids his own age.

She walked to the car, unlocked the back door, lifted the basket from the floor. Then she joined her father under the oak tree. He looked older to her, his cheeks hollowed, his skin a little gray. He was worried, she knew. This news about another girl was on everybody's minds.

She wasn't sure how to bring it up, or what she should even say. She asked instead, "How's the project coming along?" He was building something in his woodshop in the garage with Christian. Christian had told her it was a secret project between him and Pop.

"It's coming along just fine," he said.

"Can you give me any hints on what it is?"

"I promised Christian I wouldn't talk about it until it's finished."

"Not even a little hint?"

He shook his head. It seemed to her that he wanted to talk about the recent news, but he didn't know how to bring it up either. It wasn't something they could talk about easily. As it turned out, they didn't have to say anything. They could overhear two women talking about whether the girl in the lake had been murdered or if she could've possibly drowned.

Pop put his arm around Janey. She leaned into him heavily. Silently, they watched the kids playing. Christian stood in the center of the game, trying to karate chop the colorful streamers snapping behind the boys and girls as they ran past. Janey had a feeling they were taunting him, making fun of him, playing some made-up version of monkey in the middle that didn't look at all innocent, not in her eyes. But he had to figure this out on his own, how to interact, to take part in games with his peers. Carlyn had told her it would be hard at first, to have patience. She promised that with a little help, Christian would learn how to play with others. Still, it broke Janey's heart. It took everything she had not to interfere, to grab him by the hand, remove him from the game, protect him from ridicule, from being the kid the other kids thought of as weird.

She fiddled with the handle of the basket, looked at the grass by her feet. She wondered what her father was thinking while he watched her son playing. Someone announced that the egg hunt was starting. The kids scattered in search of their parents and their baskets.

"Here's your basket," she called. Christian ran over to her, took it from her, and went to stand at the starting line with his age group.

Her father kissed her temple, gave her shoulders a squeeze. "It's going to be okay," he said before joining her mother at the picnic tables.

Janey stayed under the tree. The wind picked up, rustling the leaves. Something tickled her ear, soft and feathery, like a whisper. At the same time, she felt the breeze on the back of her neck, sending a chill down her spine. She looked behind her. There wasn't anyone there. It wasn't the first time she'd felt someone around her: a presence she couldn't see. She tried to shake it off and turned back to the egg hunt, hoping no one had been paying attention to her, wondering what she'd been looking at. She noticed some kind of commotion in the field between a couple of kids and their parents.

Please don't let Christian be involved, she thought.

A little girl screamed.

Janey took off in the direction of the cries. She searched for her son.

"What happened?" she asked, breaking through the crowd, stopping next to Claire, one of the mothers from Christian's elementary school. Claire's daughter, Emma, was crying.

"He took my basket." Emma pointed at Christian.

It was hard to argue, given the pink basket was in the grass near Christian's feet, along with several painted eggs, all of them broken. His own basket was full of brightly colored eggs. His head was down.

"He broke my eggs," Emma said.

Janey took hold of Christian's hand. "Apologize to Emma," she said. He looked up at her.

"Christian, I want you to apologize to Emma for breaking her eggs." He continued to stare.

Janey turned toward Claire and Emma. "I'm so sorry. Here, take some of Christian's eggs." She picked up Emma's basket and put some of Christian's eggs in it.

He tried to take his eggs back.

"Christian!" she scolded. He looked up at her again. Big, fat tears rolled down his cheeks. She turned away from him, her hand on the scarf at her throat. "I'm so sorry," she said again to Claire. "I don't know what's gotten into him." Holding on to Christian's hand, she slipped past the other mothers, leading him away from the egg hunt and the mob that had gathered.

It took everything she had not to run.

After leaving the church, Janey spent the day at her parents' house. Her mother busied herself in the kitchen, while her father fiddled in his woodshop. At one point, Janey had turned on the TV in the family room, but her mother had turned it off. "Enough news for one day," she said. Christian played with his dinosaurs and kept to himself. She didn't know if he felt bad for what he'd done to Emma, or if he felt anything at all. She couldn't read his emotions.

Now that they were home, she tucked him into bed, gave him a hug good night, the first hug of the day. She hated herself for counting the number of times she touched her own son. But Carlyn had suggested Janey do just that and report back to her. Hugs from Janey would help Christian become comfortable with physical contact. "Try for two hugs a day," Carlyn had said.

Christian kept his arms at his side, rolled away when she released him.

"Good night," she whispered, getting up from the bed slowly, yearning for the kind of love and warmth that usually existed between a mother and child, if only he'd reciprocate.

She turned out the light, lingered in the doorway, making sure he was settled, quiet, ready for sleep. When he didn't stir, she padded to the kitchen and opened the cabinet, grabbed a glass, and filled it with wine. She turned on the TV and sat at the table, watching the local news. Her mother's words echoed in her ears. *Enough news for one day.* She could feel her disapproval as she stared at the small screen and waited for the girl in the lake to appear.

CHAPTER FIVE

Geena stood in the Browns' backyard with Zach from the K9 unit. They were looking at the map she'd provided, preparing for trail work. They'd run out of daylight yesterday and hadn't been able to start their search as originally planned. In the meantime, they'd learned that the debris that had been caught in Valerie's hair and around her legs was indigenous to the area. The original crime scene was thought to be close by.

A mobile computer-crime lab team had also arrived to gather intel on Valerie. They would collect everything from her social media sites to her emails and online search history to her text messages on her phone. Valerie's laptop was already tucked under the arm of one of the tech guys. He was asking the Browns for Valerie's passwords, but they were shaking their heads. They didn't know. They stood on the porch in what looked to Geena like a state of shock.

"No worries," the tech said. "I'll get around it."

Parker stood next to Geena in the yard. The sun was out, but the grass was wet from the rain the day before. More showers were expected by the afternoon. She wore the same state-issued slicker as Parker and Zach, a bulletproof vest underneath. Zach and his tracking dog started for the part of the woods where the dog indicated Valerie had entered.

They followed a few paces behind him. The dog circled around and backtracked twice. He lost the scent, then picked it up again. It went this way for the next hour until Zach said he believed they were on the right trail this time.

He continued down the path, keeping pace with the dog. The dog stopped and stared into the woods off to their right. Geena and Parker stopped too. Something moved between the trees. The dog sniffed the air, then returned to the trail, indicating a trash scent, a scent that belonged to someone other than Valerie.

Parker pointed in the direction of a small slope where another trail branched off, this one narrower than the one they were following.

Geena saw a flash of orange out of the corner of her eye. "Police!" she called, and she pulled her weapon.

Zach and the dog stopped again. Parker reached for his weapon.

"I see you," she said, every inch of muscle locked, tensed, shot full of adrenaline. "I need you to step away from the tree with your hands raised."

A kid stepped out from behind an oak tree, his hands raised like he'd been told.

She lowered her weapon. Parker lowered his weapon too.

The boy had a homemade bow and arrow peeking out from behind his shoulder, the strap cutting across his chest. He was dressed in head-to-toe camouflage, minus the bright-orange bill of his baseball cap.

"I didn't shoot nothing," he said.

Geena holstered her weapon. Parker did the same. She approached the boy. He couldn't have been any older than twelve. She put her hand on his shoulder. Zach and the dog started walking again, moving farther down the trail.

"It's okay," she said to the boy. "You're not in any trouble," she assured him. "Are you alone?" Parker stood next to her.

"Yes," the boy said.

"What's your name? Do you live around here?" she asked.

"Tim. Just over the hill." He pointed to the sloping hill. "I was shooting at squirrels, but I promise I didn't hit nothing."

"It's okay," Parker said. "I used to play in these woods, too, when I was your age. Did you see anyone else around here today, or yesterday perhaps?" he asked.

He shook his head. "No, sir."

"Okay, now why don't you go on home? We're going to be out here for a while," Parker said.

Tim nodded, took off up the hill.

Geena smacked the back of her neck where she felt something bite her, looked at her hand. She hated bugs.

"Mosquitoes," Parker said. He turned down the path in the direction Zach had headed with his dog.

She wiped her hand on her thigh and picked up her pace to catch up to him.

✻

After another hour of searching the trails, they stopped for a second time. The dog circled an area where the brush was flattened underneath a large maple tree. Not far from the tree was a ring of rocks for a campfire. The dog barked, jumped on Zach, sat, jumped again, speaking a language known only to his handler.

"She was here," Zach said of Valerie, rewarding the dog with a game of tug-of-war.

"We need to be careful where we step," Geena said. The mud underneath the tree had been walked on. There was a partial shoe print from what looked to her like someone with a pretty large foot. She took her phone out, couldn't get a signal. "Wait here," she said to Parker and Zach. She had to follow the trail all the way back to the Browns' backyard before she could get through to the lieutenant. She wasn't able to control the urgency in her voice when she requested a forensic unit.

✻

Within an hour the forensic unit had arrived. They roped off a large area to secure what they believed to be a campsite. And, based on Zach's dog picking up Valerie's scent at the site, it was possibly the scene of the crime. A designated entrance and exit were established to avoid any contamination of evidence. The site was sketched and photographed. Markers were placed next to the holes they'd found, from what looked like stakes where a tent had been erected. The shoe print underneath the tree was photographed and cast. They sifted through the campfire, looking for evidence of the victim's clothes or ligatures or whatever else they might find. When nothing turned up, the team decided a line search was their best option to extend the search farther out into the wooded area. Everyone put on protective gloves and began scouring the terrain.

They took their time, sifting through vegetation, looking for hair, fibers, ligatures, clothing. But after hours of searching, they still weren't finding anything. And then the rain came, adding more frustration to a long day.

Dusk was sweeping through the woods as more storm clouds gathered. Zach returned with his dog after walking the rest of the trails surrounding Valerie's home and the lake.

"Nothing," he said.

The only thing Geena could think of as to why the dog hadn't been able to pick up a clear scent beyond the campsite was the rain. She couldn't remember a spring where they'd gotten so much precipitation, everything from a light drizzle to torrential downpours for days at a time. Water had soaked every inch of this case, destroying evidence. It was another kind of weapon the killer had used against them.

She turned to Parker, feeling disappointed. She said, "Maybe the autopsy will turn up something."

CHAPTER SIX

The smell of a decomposing body overwhelmed the room. It was the kind of smell that stayed on your clothes and hair, seeped into your pores.

Geena spread peppermint oil on the inside of her mask. Parker did the same. The peppermint oil made it a little more bearable. But not much.

Sandra cleared her throat and stood over the body. She'd told Geena once that she didn't notice the smell so much anymore. She'd gone nose blind to it. She'd been doing autopsies for the county longer than Geena had been on the force. She was well liked by the team, respected.

Sandra talked into a recorder, making note of Valerie's hair, which was knotted in what had once been a ponytail. "No braids," Sandra said.

The first two girls had had small braids around the crowns of their heads.

"Maybe he didn't have enough time," Geena offered.

"It's an odd thing for a guy to do, though," Parker said.

"What are you saying?" Geena asked.

"I don't know. Maybe it was a coincidence."

"Maybe," she said. It was possible. But from her experience, coincidences were rare when it came to violent crimes.

Sandra cleared her throat again and continued with her exam.

Toxicology would test for chloroform around the mouth and nose and for any evidence of drugs in the victim's system. The hyoid bone in the neck had been fractured, indicating manual strangulation. The bruises on the wrists and ankles were similar to the wounds on the other two victims. The ligatures hadn't been found in any of the cases, which led to the question as to whether the unsub was using the same ones over and over again.

"Do you see this?" Sandra asked, having turned Valerie onto her side. "She died on her back. You can tell by the lividity, where the blood pooled after death. It's fixed, which means he didn't move her body for at least eight hours." She pointed to a pattern on the skin between the shoulder blades, the backs of her arms, buttocks. "This is the impression of the surface where she died."

The pattern consisted of small squares packed together in a sort of grid.

"It's definitely man made," Parker said. Geena wondered if he was aware that he'd taken several steps backward, putting himself in the corner of the room.

Sandra looked closer. "You're going to need someone in textile fabrics to confirm this, but it almost looks to me like something that was made of a synthetic material, maybe nylon." She pointed to the area by the right shoulder blade. "That looks like it could've been made by a zipper."

"Like from a tent or sleeping bag," Geena said. It explained why they hadn't been able to find much at the campsite. The unsub had packed up the evidence and taken it with him. Still, this was another break in the case. They had a shoe print with a lug-pattern sole meant for backpacking and mountaineering, size eleven. She was getting a clearer picture of the man they were dealing with. He was someone who was big, an outdoorsman, comfortable in the woods. But if he was *living* in the mountains, they were in trouble. Even with an army of law enforcement, it had taken forty-eight days to track and arrest the survivalist charged with ambushing and killing a state trooper in the Poconos. That guy had worn diapers so he could remain stationary for long periods of time. *Diapers.*

"Anything under the nails?" Geena asked.

"Nothing. No signs of defensive wounds." Sandra scratched her forehead with the back of her wrist. Her curly hair was tucked neatly under a cap.

Geena stepped away. She'd expected this, and yet she'd held out hope. If only the girls had fought back, they might've given them the DNA evidence they needed to catch him.

Parker hovered in the corner. One hand pressed against the wall for support. He looked like he was going to be sick. She stepped toward him to see if there was anything she could do to help. He held up his other hand, stopped her from approaching.

"I got this," he said.

"Do you?" she asked.

"Hey, guys," Sandra said, a big smile showing underneath her mask. "We've got semen."

Geena left the autopsy, telling Parker she'd meet up with him back at headquarters. She drove straight to Albert's to tell him they finally had the unsub's DNA. She found her old partner kneeling in the dirt in his garden, a small trowel in his hand. He wore a wide-brimmed straw hat on his head to shield him from the midmorning sun. The gray clouds had finally parted, giving them a much-needed break from the rain.

Geena walked between the rows, careful not to step where seeds had been planted. She stopped slightly behind him and off to the side.

"Pearl said I could find you here," she said.

"You found me." He looked up at her from underneath the brim of the hat. "Well, don't just stand there. Grab a trowel and get down here and get your hands dirty."

She knelt next to him. The soil was dark and rich and wet. It bled through the knees of her pants, soaking the cotton on contact. Albert dropped a couple of seeds into a hole, covered them with care.

"What are we planting?" she asked, searching for another trowel to help him dig.

"Broccoli." He pointed two rows over. "And beans over there."

She didn't mention that she'd never known him to eat vegetables, at least not that she'd ever seen. But who was she to point that out?

"I hear you have a new partner," he said, and he sank the trowel into the ground.

"I do," she said.

He nodded. "I hear he's young. Around your age."

"Your age never bothered me. You know that. And it never bothered anyone else on the team. You're missed, Albert. You were the best investigator we had."

Albert stopped digging, paused to look at her. Then he got up, knelt on the other side of her, continued planting. The skin on his arms that stuck out from underneath his rolled-up shirtsleeves was thin and dry. She dropped a few seeds into the freshly dug hole. She didn't bother to ask whether he'd seen the news recently. She was sure he had. And she was just as sure he knew the reason she was kneeling beside him now.

She touched his arm, stopped him from moving more dirt around. "I need her name, Albert."

He shook his head, went back to digging.

"You can't keep protecting her," she said, reached for his hand.

He scooped up some soil, let it fall between his fingers. "You have to trust me," he said. "There isn't any evidence to connect her to the others. Nothing that's going to help with the case."

"You don't know that for certain," she said, a lump growing inside her throat. "You can't bury evidence."

He shook his head. "There was nothing there to bury."

"Her very existence is evidence." Albert had tracked down Jane Doe after he'd gotten a tip from a source after the second girl had been found.

"Let it go, Geena," he said. "It will only hurt your career at this point if you pursue this."

She considered that, of course, how she'd known about another possible victim and how she'd protected Albert by not telling anyone. But another innocent girl had been murdered. She couldn't stand by if there was evidence out there that could prevent it from happening again. "They'll take your pension. Is that why you won't tell me her name?"

"No," he said. "It's not about money. I have everything I need right here." He nodded at his field, rows and rows of rich earth waiting for the seeds to feed, nurture, grow.

"Then why? What is it about?"

"I told you all this before. If I truly believed she was connected to the case, if she had any information on who he is, if there was anything at all, I would've told you. It would be in the file front and center. But she doesn't remember anything about who he is or what he looks like. Nothing." He went back to digging. "It will ruin her life if it gets out. You know what the public will do to her. They'll blame the victim. They'll crucify her."

Geena understood the potential risk and the reason she hadn't pressured him about it when they'd been partners. She'd seen it happen in other cases, rape victims especially, how the public turned on the woman, said she'd dressed provocatively, had loose morals, brought it on herself. Geena had played out in her mind every night in the last year whether Albert's choice, his decision to withhold Jane Doe's name from her, had been the right one. Each time she'd come back to the facts. How the only survivor couldn't identify her attacker. How the public, the media, would want to take out their anger and fear on the one person who had survived. How she should've been able to point her finger and say, "This man is the killer." And only then would their daughters, girlfriends, wives, their loved ones be safe, and they could all go about their lives as usual.

But Jane Doe couldn't give them what they wanted.

Geena included.

But now they were getting closer to identifying the unsub with the latest victim. They finally had evidence this time. They had a shoe print and DNA. Geena had to know the first victim's name and the information that had led Albert to her. She could be the missing link, the one factor that tied it all together.

"I swear I'll do everything in my power to protect her identity." If he was right and there was nothing there to connect the girl to the other victims, she'd back off, but she'd have to find out for herself. "I'll protect us. All of us."

Pearl appeared by the side of the house, wiping her hands on a towel. "Everything okay?" she asked.

"Everything's fine," Albert called.

Pearl lingered for a moment, then disappeared behind the house again.

"Albert," Geena said. "Listen to me. I need her name. We finally got something this time. We got semen. DNA."

Albert paused, stared at her. Then he put the trowel down, looked toward the sky, the blazing sun. Another minute passed. "Okay," he said, his eyes glassy. "Okay."

UNDROWNED

Her eyes open, close, open again. She is on her back, some kind of bed, a gurney. The overhead lights are bright, fluorescent lights awash with white. The bed is moving, rolling. She is being pushed through double doors. There's someone running alongside her, tubes hanging. She's shivering, tiny tremors along her spine. There are voices. Someone is talking. "You're lucky to be alive," she hears them say.

CHAPTER SEVEN

Janey braided her hair in a side braid to cover her neck where the black mark on her skin had faded to purple. Her shirt was buttoned all the way to the top button. She was warm, feeling sticky under her arms, moving bolts of fabric from one display to another. Students in middle school who were taking home economics had one final project due before the end of the school year. The store would get a crowd of kids and parents tonight. They'd pick out fabric to sew a small tote bag, complete with straps and a hook-and-loop fastener.

She continued moving fabric around. She was tired, having stayed up late watching the news. She hadn't learned anything new about the girl they'd found in the lake. She was thinking how she didn't even know the girl's name as she counted the number of bolts on the display. She was having trouble concentrating, feeling as though someone's eyes were on her. She looked over her shoulder. There wasn't anyone there. This feeling, looking over her shoulder, was a part of her now, something she'd had to live with day and night.

She returned to her work, lifted another bolt of fabric, putting the more popular patterns up front, the ones with polka dots, elephants, flowers, footballs. She moved the striped patterns to the back of the rows, since they were not suggested for beginning sewers when even master sewers had difficulty getting the stripes to align.

She lifted another bolt, one with an Aztec design, struggled to put it on the rack.

Josh walked down the aisle toward her. He managed the store, a nephew of the owners. She was only the assistant manager. "Here, let me help you with that." He took the opposite end of the bolt, heaved it onto the countertop, pushed it to the side.

She didn't correct him, even though she'd meant for it to be displayed on the metal rack next to the other fabrics with similar patterns and colors.

"How was your weekend?" He asked her the same question every Monday, and every Monday she gave him the same answer. "It was good."

"I did a little fishing, caught a couple of small trout out at the lake," he said, even though she hadn't asked. "I spent Easter at my uncle's house. They had this huge egg hunt for my younger cousins. Sometimes I wish I were still a kid, you know?"

She nodded, switched another bolt of fabric around. Josh was four years older than Janey, and he was single, from what she'd overheard from some of the cashiers, the part-time teenage girls they hired when they needed additional help. How they swooned over him.

He leaned against the counter, casual like, arms folded loosely at his waist. His oxford shirt was rolled up at the sleeves, the hair on his forearms light, matching his sandy-blond hair, his light-brown eyes.

"I was thinking about going out after work for a drink—"

Josh broke off when Janey immediately began shaking her head.

"I don't drink," she said, telling a white lie, since she'd gone through an entire bottle of wine the night before.

"Oh, I wasn't suggesting . . ." He paused, rubbed the back of his neck. "Do you drink coffee?"

"I have to pick up Christian from after-school care."

"Okay," he said, trying to shrug off her rejection as though it were no big deal. He pushed off the counter, turned to head down one of the rows of fabric. "One more thing," he said, turning back around. "One of the customers messed up the artificial flowers. They tied them together and then set them down in the wrong bins. Can you get someone to sort them out and put them back in the right bins? I'd appreciate it."

"Of course," she said. It was a job one of the other girls working the floor should have done, not the assistant manager, but Janey wanted to do it herself. She liked sorting, organizing, rearranging displays. Some might construe it as busywork, and she supposed it was, but there was something soothing about it, adding normalcy to the day she didn't otherwise feel.

Janey made it through her entire shift at the store without bumping into Josh again. She collected Christian from aftercare and made her way home to Eighth Street. She pulled behind a dark sedan that was parked in front of her house. She took her time gathering her purse, collecting herself. She glanced at Christian in the rearview mirror before she opened the driver's side door and stepped out. A woman got out of the sedan at the same time. She was tall, thin. Pretty. She was sharply dressed in a pantsuit, her hair tied in a ponytail. Janey recognized her, knew it was only a matter of time before she'd come knocking on her door.

"Janey Montgomery?" The woman said her name as though it was a question.

"Yes," Janey said.

"I'm Detective Brassard." She peeked in at Christian in the back seat. "Is there someplace we can talk?"

"Sure," Janey said. "Let me get my son settled. We can talk inside."

She opened the rear passenger-side door, helped Christian out of his seat. She reached for his hand as they walked into the house.

"Please make yourself comfortable," Janey said, motioning to the chair in the small family room. The detective towered over them, her face unreadable. "I'll be back in a minute," Janey added, and she led Christian to his room. He hopped onto his bed, the comforter covered in footballs, basketballs, baseballs. She'd picked it out when he'd moved into a big kid's bed, a twin bed. At the time he'd resisted the change, demanded his crib, refused to pick out the colors or theme for his new bedding. He'd left her no choice but to select the sports comforter on her own. Looking back, it had been another misstep on her part. She'd found out soon enough that sports weren't his thing after he'd come home with a bloody nose after his first gym class. He'd never lifted his arms, his hands, when the ball had been thrown to him. It had hit him square in the face. The elementary school's gym teacher had called, worried something was wrong with him physically (other than the bloody nose, of course), mentally. "He has no reflexes," she'd said. "He just stood there. Most kids would've raised their arms to try to catch it or at least prevent themselves from getting hit."

"Why don't you play with your toys while Mommy talks to the nice woman in the other room?" she said.

He didn't respond, already picking up his plastic dinosaurs, off in his imaginary world, dismissing her so easily.

Janey returned to the family room, sat on the couch, and folded her hands in her lap. She wanted to say to the detective she didn't know why she was here or what she could possibly want from her. But it would have been a lie. She knew exactly why she was here. "How did you find me?" she asked. "Was it Albert who told you about me?"

"Yes, Detective Eugenis. Albert. He was my partner until he retired. He told me how to contact you."

"He said I didn't have to talk with anyone but him."

"You don't have to talk to me, but I'm asking you to. I'm asking you to trust me like Albert trusts me. He gave me your name, after all."

Janey considered what the detective was saying. "What do you need from me?" she asked, but she already knew the answer.

"There's been another one, another girl about the age you were," the detective said.

She nodded. "What's her name?" she asked.

"We haven't released her name to the public yet."

"Do you think she's connected to what happened to me?"

"I think she could be."

Janey took a couple of deep breaths. She tried to calm her rapid, fluttering heartbeat. She wondered if she was on the verge of a panic attack. It wouldn't have been the first. "Would you like something to drink?" She didn't wait for Detective Brassard to answer. She raced to the kitchen, gulped down a glass of water. The detective followed her, stood by the counter.

"I'm sorry," Detective Brassard said. She stepped closer to Janey, put her hand on her forearm. "I can't imagine how hard this must be to hear." She paused. "But I need your help."

"I told Albert I don't remember anything. Nothing. If I remembered something, don't you think I would've called and told him by now? Don't you think I would've helped if I could?"

"If you could just tell me everything you told him, go over it with me. Let me decide if there's anything there," Detective Brassard said. "Sometimes telling it again to someone who hasn't heard your side of the events can make a difference. It might help shake something loose in your memory."

She wanted to shout at the detective. Didn't she know how hard Janey had tried to remember everything that had happened to her that night? But her memories were elusive, tainted with emotions, some true, others false. Dr. Watson, her psychologist, had explained how her mind wouldn't let her remember. It was her subconscious way of surviving, of being able to get through the day, every day, not only for herself but also for her son.

"You can still be anonymous. No one else has to know. I won't tell anyone. I promise. But I need to know everything you remember about what happened to you."

She stared at the detective. Of course she wanted to help. She wished she could, for the other girls' sakes. She'd been living with their ghosts every day for the last few years. Even now they circled around her and pulsated under her skin. All but the latest girl. She seemed to be taking her time, gathering her strength, only revealing herself in glimpses, a breeze on the back of her neck, a soft voice in her ear.

The detective continued. "He's not going to stop. He's going to continue hurting others. Raping them. Killing them." The way she looked at Janey, just short of pointing her finger at her, as though solving the case was on Janey's shoulders, as though it had been Janey's hands around the girls' throats. She was doing what Janey feared most. She was blaming her for *his* crimes.

Christian appeared in the kitchen doorway, a velociraptor in his fist.

"Christian." She rushed over to him, put a protective hand on his shoulder.

He stared up at the detective. "Bad cop," he said.

"No, not bad," Detective Brassard said. "I'm one of the good guys." She put her card on the counter. "Think about what I said. Call me when you're ready to talk."

CHAPTER EIGHT

"Where were you?" Parker asked when Geena returned to headquarters and plopped down across from him at her old desk. He looked comfortable in Albert's chair.

"I had a couple of errands," she said. Her visit with Janey Montgomery hadn't gone as planned. She was worried she'd pressed too hard too soon. Albert had a soothing, reassuring voice Janey had no doubt responded to, warmed to. It was clear she trusted Albert, felt more comfortable talking with him.

From what Geena had observed, Janey lived alone with her son. She didn't wear a wedding ring. There weren't many photos around the house, only a few of the boy at different ages, but nothing of Janey. There wasn't a wedding picture displayed on the mantel. The house was small, tidy. The furniture looked secondhand, reupholstered with hand-stitched fabric, fresh paint. Janey appeared to be a single mom, stretching the few dollars she brought in. If anything, meeting Janey had strengthened Geena's resolve to do whatever she'd have to do to get the guy who was responsible for hurting these young, innocent girls.

"Sayres was looking for you," Parker said. "Next time give me a heads-up so I can cover for you."

"What did you tell him?" She couldn't tell Parker about where she'd been. She'd made a promise to protect Janey's identity, at least until she had some answers.

"I mentioned something about you heading home to change clothes. Something I should've done as well." He smelled his sleeve. The funk from the morgue clung to his suit. She had since changed out of her dirt-stained pants after visiting Albert in the fields and before talking to Janey.

"There you are," Sayres said, stopping by their desks. "Jonathon's giving a press conference within the hour. Brassard, you're standing with me. It helps to have a woman in these matters," he said to Parker as a way to explain why she'd been chosen and not him. Parker was certainly camera ready but for the stink of his suit, although the viewers wouldn't be able to smell him through their television screens.

Jonathon Albright, the district attorney of Northampton County, stood behind the podium in a conference room in the government center. Television crews were ready, waiting. Reporters were prepared to take notes. Several flashes went off at once, photos to be used for digital and print media.

Jonathon had gotten a haircut since the last time Geena had seen him, which had been exactly three hours and four months ago, but who was counting? Who was she kidding? She was. She was counting. He looked in her direction. Something passed between them, a quick exchange between old lovers. She stood next to Sayres, tried not to blink when more flashes went off. She hoped her face wasn't flushed. Parker was standing slightly behind her and to her right. It was possible he would appear in the corner of the television screen. There but not there.

"As you know, a young woman's body was discovered in Minsi Lake over the weekend," Jonathon said. "The name of the victim will be released shortly. We're treating it as a homicide."

"Do you have anyone in custody?" a reporter asked.

"Not at this time."

"Any suspects?" someone else asked.

"I can't comment on any suspects," Jonathon said.

"Are you saying you don't have any suspects or that you do?" a reporter asked.

"I won't be discussing the details of the investigation at this time. But I assure you, with the help of the state police, we're doing everything possible to identify the person responsible."

"This is the third woman murdered in the spring," a female reporter said. "Are you looking at the crimes as though they're related? Is this a serial killing?"

A rumble spread throughout the crowd, a buzz of fear and excitement, a promising headline.

Jonathon turned to Sayres. "Lieutenant?"

Sayres stepped up to the mic. "We're not ruling anything out," he said.

"What was the cause of death?" the same female reporter asked.

"We're waiting for the autopsy report for confirmation," Sayres said. "But we believe it to be strangulation."

The crowd erupted in chatter. Someone shouted, "Same as the other two girls!"

Sayres continued once they'd quieted down. "We're setting up a tip line, asking if anyone has any information to please contact the number we'll be giving out momentarily." He paused. "I would also like to take this time to address some safety precautions that should be taken until this matter is resolved. I would advise anyone planning on spending time walking the mountain trails to not go alone, to bring someone with you."

"Is that a warning for everyone or just women?" a reporter from the local paper asked. Geena recognized her from having given statements to the press in the past.

"I think it's a good practice for everyone in general, but women should take extra precautions."

"Excuse me." A young woman in a cute skirt and blouse raised her hand. "I don't recognize the gentleman in the back of the room. Are you some kind of expert in the case?"

Everyone turned to look at Parker, including Geena and the lieutenant. The cameras zoomed in on him. To his credit, he kept his eyes forward, the same serious expression on his face. He was like a magnet, drawing attention wherever he went, no matter what his rank or position was in the room or on the streets.

Sayres introduced Parker, mentioning that he worked in homicide in the field station that covered the part of the county where Minsi Lake was located. "Now, are there any other questions?" he asked.

A few more questions were raised about Minsi Lake, the draining, what it meant to the case, if anything. Once the press conference had wrapped up, the tip-line number announced, Sayres ushered Geena and Parker out into the hallway.

"I'm going to stick around and talk with Jonathon," he said. "I'll see you two back at headquarters." He made a point to look at Geena before he walked away. She took the hint. Jonathon had reunited with his estranged wife. It was the reason he'd broken it off with Geena, now four hours and four months ago. Jonathon's wife also happened to be friends with the lieutenant's wife.

The tip line had been broadcast on all the local networks. Calls had started coming in. The team was busy taking information, most of which wasn't helpful. A couple of false leads had Geena and Parker running all over the county, interviewing possible witnesses. So far nothing had broken.

It was almost seven o'clock at night. Geena slumped in her chair at her desk, exhausted, frustrated, but most of all hungry. She'd skipped dinner and hadn't eaten since a takeout burger at lunch. Parker looked just as ragged. His stomach had been growling every few minutes.

She picked up her car keys. "Grab the file copies and let's go. Dinner's on me."

They headed to her car. She took the side streets, pulled into her parking space in front of her condo. She'd bought the corner unit, tucked deep inside one of Bethlehem's city blocks. Most people driving down the busy street had no idea there were condos behind the wall of maple and oak trees. The small units were conveniently located just two blocks from one of the best pizza restaurants in the city, a family-owned ice cream shop, a reasonably priced dry cleaner. Her condo was a mere ten-minute drive to headquarters.

She unlocked the front door, stepped inside to find Codis wagging his entire backside, grunting and prancing excitedly at her feet. She knelt in front of him, kissed his funny face, rubbed his belly.

"Geena, is that you?" her mother called from the kitchen.

"It's me," she called back, standing.

Parker was right behind her. Codis sniffed his shoes, pant legs, lifted his smushed face, begged for a scratch behind the ear.

Codis was thirteen years old. He was deaf and blind. She'd gotten him as a pup and couldn't imagine coming home without him waiting to greet her at the door. He walked into walls, furniture, grunting and farting like an old man, but she wasn't ready to give up on him. The vet had promised Codis still had a good year or two left. Geena hoped it would be longer.

Parker bent over, scratching behind Codis's ears and letting him lick his hand. Geena's mother appeared, slipping on a light sweater over her T-shirt, her head down as she collected her purse.

"He's walked and fed," her mother said about Codis before looking up. "Oh, I didn't realize you had company." Her mother was in her early sixties, shocking long white hair, tall like Geena. She was attractive and could've had any number of men, but she hadn't dated since losing Geena's father.

"Mom, this is my new partner, Parker Reed. Parker, this is my mom, Ingrid."

Her mother's face noticeably brightened when he stood to shake her hand. Her mother was well aware of Geena's one rule about dating: the man had to be taller than her. Geena shot her a look, a warning not to read anything into this. Parker was her partner, a coworker, nothing more.

Ingrid looked back and forth between them. "I'll leave you to it then. Nice to meet you, Parker." She waved on her way out the door.

"She takes care of Codis for me," Geena said by way of explanation. "I think I mentioned before that my dad died. It was about ten years ago, heart failure. Codis here gives her someone to look after." She shared more than she'd intended, but she supposed he'd learn a lot more about her eventually if they were going to stay partners.

"I'm sorry about your father," he said and then asked, "Codis? After the FBI's DNA database?"

"Yeah." She laughed. "I got him when I was in college, and I was considering applying to the FBI when I graduated. So, you know, Codis. But then my dad died, and I wanted to stick close to home for my mom. I ended up at the state police academy instead."

She led him to the small patio in the back, where she had a table and chairs, outdoor grill. She lit the citronella torches to fend off the mosquitoes as dusk barely hung on, giving way to night. She left Parker in the lounge chair with the files containing all the information on the previous two cases while she made a quick pot of spaghetti and heated sauce from a jar. Thirty minutes later she carried a steaming bowl of pasta and a bottle of red wine to the patio.

Parker was bent over a bush, getting sick. The table was covered with the files. She noticed some of the photos of the victims' bodies that had been taken at the crime scenes had fallen to the ground. She set the bowl and wine down. She picked up the photos and then looked at him. He stood upright, wiped his mouth with the back of his hand.

"Some detective I turned out to be," he said.

"It means you care. I'd be more worried if it didn't have any effect on you at all."

They stared at each other, and in that moment, they exchanged a silent understanding. This was between them.

"Bathroom?" he asked.

"In the foyer on the right," she said.

When he returned, he helped her set the table. She sat across from him and picked up her fork. "You know, it might just be a case of PTSD. Maybe if you talked with someone about it . . ."

He was shaking his head. "I'll be fine. It's just been a long couple of days."

She nodded, although she wasn't sure she agreed with him. But what more could she say? Even if she could think of something, it was clear he wasn't ready to listen.

They ate in silence after that. It wasn't until she finished eating that she picked up her glass of wine and leaned back in the chair. She noticed Parker hadn't touched his glass. Codis was curled up at her feet.

"Did you read the BAU profiler's report?" They'd requested a profile of the unsub from the FBI's Behavioral Analysis Unit after the second girl had been found. "She thinks our guy is somewhere between twenty-five and thirty-five years old, somewhat of a loner, doesn't like confrontation, which is why we believe he knocks them out. And killing is incidental. It's something that's necessary but not what drives him. I think untying the victims is our biggest clue into his psyche." The profiler believed untying the victims showed a desire to comfort, perhaps something that had been done to the killer himself after he'd experienced some form of abuse in his past.

"I agree. The untying is unusual." Parker ran his hand over the top of his head, smoothing back the lock of hair that had fallen across his brow. "So, what's the next step? Hike the trails again, see who's been hanging around the watering holes?"

"Maybe. But as you know, there are three hundred thousand people in Northampton County, and I bet half of them have spent time on the mountain in the last few years. And let's not forget that the trails cross into Lehigh and Monroe County too. He could be entering the woods from any number of places over three counties."

"So we wait for toxicology and DNA analysis," Parker said. "What are the chances this guy is in the system?"

"Wouldn't that be something," she said, and she sipped her wine, relaxing in the warmth of the alcohol slowly working its way through her body. The night air was chilly. The stars were out, signaling the end of the rain for now, anyway. She was aware of Parker's eyes on her, as though he was waiting for her to say something more about the case.

She thought about giving him one last piece of information: the tip Albert had received from some source he'd never revealed to her, the one that had led him to Janey. But her promise to Albert, her loyalty to her old partner, held her back from saying anything.

She was reminded of something from her childhood: an image of her father at the bottom of a slide at the local park. She was five years old and had been sitting at the top after taking an inordinate amount of time climbing the ladder. His arms had been outstretched, coaxing her down. "I'll catch you," he'd said. "I promise I won't let you fall." She'd let go, her trust in him unwavering, but he'd turned his head at the last second and she'd fallen, scraping her knees.

Something had captured her father's attention, enough to distract him from his own daughter. Albert had been distracted, too, but by an unnamed source, sending him spiraling down a path of poor decisions. And like on that slide, she'd slid feet first, trusting he'd known what he was doing, wondering whether this time she'd come away unscathed when she reached the bottom.

~*Helen Watson, Psy.D.*
Patient: Janey Montgomery, ID 27112

"*During our last session, I gave you some homework. Were you able to complete it?*" Dr. Watson asks.

"*Yes,*" Janey says.

The doctor watches as Janey pulls a piece of paper from her pocket, unfolds it, and smooths the creases.

"*I've listed at least a hundred reasons under the column heading, 'Things I Love about My Son,'*" Janey says. "*Some are silly things, like the smell of sleep on his skin when he first wakes up, or the way his curls fall across his forehead.*"

The doctor makes a mental note of how Janey has covered her heart and tears have filled her eyes. Then Janey plucks a tissue from the box, wipes the tears away.

"*I'm sorry,*" Janey says. "*I don't know what's come over me.*"

"*There's nothing to apologize for. It's a wonderful list,*" Dr. Watson says. "*It shows how much you love your son.*"

"*I do. I do love him.*"

"*No one questions that,*" Dr. Watson says. But she's waiting for Janey to say something about the other half of the assignment, the one where Janey was supposed to list the things she doesn't like about her son. She waits her out. *Several seconds pass until Janey asks the question, the real reason she is here and why she has called this emergency session.*

"Did you see the news?" Janey asks.

"Yes," Dr. Watson says. "How are you feeling?"

"Guilty, like it's my fault. Like I should be able to stop it."

"You're not to blame for what happened to those girls. It's not your fault."

Janey plays with the dirty tissue in her hands. "A detective came to see me," she says. "A different one. I've never met her before. She said Albert gave her my name. Why would he do that? He promised he'd never tell anyone and that I only had to talk with him."

"You're part of a criminal investigation, whether you want to be or not," Dr. Watson says.

"But I told him I didn't know anything, that I couldn't help him. He promised."

"Do you feel like he betrayed you? That he's not going to protect you?"

Janey sniffs, uses the tissue to wipe her nose. She shrugs.

"This new detective, did you talk to her?" Dr. Watson asks.

"No," Janey says. "I didn't talk to her."

"Why not?"

Janey shrugs again. "I don't know. I mean, I want to. I just don't have anything to tell her that I think will help her. Do you think I do? Should I at least try?"

"I can't answer that for you. That's something you need to answer for yourself. But maybe there is something I can do. How about this? Why don't you practice on me? Pretend I'm the detective. Tell me what you would say to her if she was sitting here right now."

"Okay. Well, I guess I would tell her the same thing I told Albert, that I don't know anything."

"But I think you do know something," Dr. Watson says. "I think you know more than you're willing to admit."

"But I don't! I don't. I can't." She shreds the tissue in her hands, grabs another one, blows her nose. Several more seconds pass.

"What are you feeling right now, this minute?" Dr. Watson asks.

"Scared," Janey says.

"Why are you scared?"

"I don't know," Janey says.

"Why are you scared?" Dr. Watson asks a second time, pressing her to answer.

"I don't know," Janey says again.

"I think you do."

"I'm scared he'll come for me!" Janey screams.

CHAPTER NINE

Janey stood at the kitchen counter in front of a cutting board and two small chicken breasts. Her eyes were puffy from crying in Dr. Watson's office. Her throat was raw. She reached for one of the seven knives from the butcher's block and trimmed the fat around the meat, then placed each breast inside a plastic bag filled with barbeque sauce to marinate before grilling.

The TV on the counter was turned to the news. The police had released the victim's name, Valerie Brown, along with her photo. She looked familiar, as if Janey had seen her before, but she couldn't place where.

Someone banged on the door. Janey jumped, covered her heart.

"Hello! Janey? Christian? It's Carlyn."

Janey rushed to the front door, slid the chain bolt, unlocked the knob. Pop had added chain bolts to both the front and back doors at Janey's request when she'd first moved in. Anything to help her feel more secure, safe. She'd relied on those locks even now, especially now, knowing her attacker was out there somewhere and that he'd struck again.

She tried to pull herself together, put her session with Dr. Watson and Valerie's photo out of her mind, and let Carlyn into the small foyer. Carlyn's hands were typically full of whatever games and props she used in Christian's behavioral therapy. But today she was carrying only a single board game with her.

"I have her. Wait right here," Carlyn said, and she rushed back to her car. She returned with a small bunny tucked inside the crook of her arm. The rabbit was supposed to be a late Easter present for Christian. With everything else going on, Janey had forgotten she'd agreed on getting him a pet.

"If it doesn't work out, I can take her back," Carlyn assured her. "But I'm hopeful this will help Christian with connecting and bonding with another living thing."

The bunny hid its itty-bitty face in Carlyn's forearm. One of its ears lay flat against its back; the other was upright, as though the bunny was trying to decide what it thought of them. Janey didn't know if she could handle taking care of a rabbit now, not with so much else on her mind. But she'd have to find a way, if it would help her son.

She took the rabbit from Carlyn's arms. "She's precious," she said. Both of the bunny's ears perked up at the sound of her voice.

"She's affectionate, as far as rabbits go. She doesn't seem to mind being held and cuddled," Carlyn said. "I thought her personality would be a good fit."

Janey called for Christian. He was in his room. The bunny twitched its tiny nose, nudged its head against her arm. Janey and Carlyn sat on the floor, put the bunny between them.

Christian walked into the family room, a *T. rex* in his hand.

"Look what Carlyn brought you," Janey said.

Christian's eyes narrowed, skeptical as he approached them. He looked at the rabbit on the floor, made no attempt to reach for it, pet it.

"Sit next to me," Carlyn said. She moved over, making room for Christian to sit. He did as he was told. "Here, stick out your hand and let her sniff you."

He stuck his hand out. The rabbit's nose twitched again, sniffed around his fingers. "It tickles," he said.

Janey should've been focusing on her son and the bunny, but she found herself looking to the foyer and the unlocked front door. She wished she'd locked it after Carlyn had walked in with the rabbit.

The bunny hopped closer to Christian, and he pulled his hand away. The sudden movement startled her, and she leaped over Janey's leg, pulling Janey back from her thoughts. The rabbit hopped around the family room, exploring her new home. Christian got up and followed her. He kept his distance, careful not to step on her as they went from room to room. He watched her as though she was a thing of curiosity. The bunny whimpered, tried hopping between his legs. He jumped back, danced to get out of her path.

"What's she doing?" he asked.

"It's okay, Christian. She's just a little frightened. She needs time to get used to her new home," Carlyn said, and then she turned to Janey. "I have a small cage and some grass hay and pellet food to get you started. It's out in the car."

She returned a minute later and set the small cage in the corner of the kitchen. She poured the pellet food in a bowl. She picked up the rabbit and put it in its cage. Christian stayed in the family room.

"It's going to be okay," Carlyn said, keeping her voice down. "Christian just needs time to warm up to her, but I have every reason to believe he will. It will be a good thing for him."

Janey wasn't so sure now, after seeing how tentative he'd been with the rabbit.

Carlyn returned to the family room. Her voice was low, talking to Christian, playing a board game with him, asking him questions, having him high-five her every third roll of the dice. While they were distracted with the game, Janey slipped into the foyer and locked the front door. Then she went out the back door and put the chicken on the grill before returning to the kitchen. She slid the chain bolt on the back door again, even though she knew in a few minutes she'd have to go back outside.

She leaned against the table, looked at the bunny. "We're not so different, you and I," she said, thinking how they were both locked in cages. But hers . . . well, she'd created hers on her own. And it wasn't going to change, ever, not unless she did something about it. She wondered how much longer she could continue like this. She thought about the latest girl, Valerie. Dr. Watson was right. Janey was a part of what was happening, whether she wanted to be or not.

She crossed the kitchen then, and she searched the counter, looking for the detective's card.

CHAPTER TEN

"I'm glad you called," Geena said as she sat across from Janey in her family room. The coffee table between them was covered in a decoupage of pink and white flowers. Someone had taken an orange crayon and scribbled across the top, presumably Janey's son. An Easter program from the local church had been pushed to the side.

"I don't have much time," Janey said. "I already dropped my son off at school, but my shift at the store starts soon."

Janey's feet were crossed at the ankle, her hands in her lap. She was wearing cotton pants, a light-blue polo with the craft store's name stitched on the pocket. She wore her blonde hair in a single braid draped over her right shoulder, like she'd worn when Geena had first talked with her. No jewelry or makeup. Geena made a mental note of these small details, filed them away. You never knew what could be important later.

"I saw Valerie's picture in the news," Janey said.

"Did you know her?" Geena asked.

"No. I didn't know her," Janey said. "But she kind of looked familiar, like I might've seen her around, but I can't remember where."

"Will you let me know if you do remember? It could be important."

"Yes, of course."

"Let's get started, then. I'd like to ask you questions about what happened to you, and with your permission, I'd like to record it."

"No," Janey said, and she shook her head. "This is hard enough. I don't want to be recorded."

"Okay," Geena said. "We'll do it your way." Maybe it was for the best. A recorded interview would be evidence there had been a witness, a victim no one other than she and Albert knew existed. "I'd like for you to start at the beginning. Tell me everything. Don't leave anything out."

"It will be seven years this Thursday," Janey said. "April fifth."

Geena leaned forward, rested her arms on top of her thighs, her hands clasped. "This time of year must be very difficult for you," she said. But the fact Janey remembered the exact date was a good sign. She guessed it wasn't something one could forget. "Do you remember what time of day it was?"

"Early evening. I can't say for sure the exact time. Light enough that I could still see. I was walking a mountain trail not too far from the university where I was going to school. It was nearing the end of the second semester my freshman year. I was still homesick and struggling with some classes. I needed a break, someplace to think and clear my head. I went for a walk."

"Were you alone?"

"Yes."

"What was the weather like?"

"Clear, but chilly. I was wearing a light jacket."

"Do you remember what trail you were walking on?"

"It was a smaller trail, one that runs close to the Delaware River." She had a far-off look in her eyes, as though she were there, walking the trail as she spoke. "I suppose I could show it to you, but it will have to be another time, when I don't have to be at work."

"Did you pass anyone on the trail? See anyone in the woods or on the river?"

Janey shook her head. "No. I was alone, or I thought I was alone."

"What happened next?"

"I was grabbed from behind." She reached her hand around the back of her head. "By my ponytail," she said, and then dropped her arm. "My mouth was covered. I didn't have time to scream."

"Did you hear anything before you were grabbed? Smell anything?"

"No. Nothing. I was deep in my own thoughts. I never heard him come up behind me."

"What covered your mouth? A hand? A cloth or rag of some sort?"

"It was some kind of rag. It covered my mouth and nose."

"Did it have an odor to it?"

"Not that I remember."

"No odor at all? Nothing sweet, like overripe fruit, or maybe like a disinfectant kind of smell?"

"No. I don't think so, anyway."

"Did you see his face? His hair? Was he short? Tall? Fat? Thin?"

"I . . . I don't remember."

"Can you tell me what he was wearing? Sneakers? Jeans? T-shirt?"

"I . . . I don't know."

"Okay. That's okay. What's the next thing you remember?"

Janey hesitated, waited a long second, and then shook her head. "Nothing."

"Can you try? It's important."

"I remember being in the river," she said. "Or at least in my dreams I do. The water is everywhere." Her voice was so soft that Geena had to strain to hear her.

"Do you remember how you ended up in the river?" she asked.

Janey shook her head again. "I was told I fell from a bridge." She didn't seem to be aware that her hands had moved to her throat.

"Did he choke you?"

"Again, this was something I was told. I don't remember it," she said, and her hands fell to her lap.

"Okay. Sure. Well, can you tell me the next thing you do remember?" she asked.

"Nothing. I don't remember anything else."

Geena leaned forward a little more, unsure if what she was about to suggest would be crossing a line, but she was desperate. How many girls would have to die before they caught him? "Have you ever considered therapy to try and recover your memory?"

Geena sat in her car in the parking lot outside headquarters, replaying her conversation with Janey over again. Albert had been right. There wasn't much Janey could tell them. It had been seven years since she'd been abducted, and memory had a way of distorting with time. Another thought crossed Geena's mind about Janey's son. It had to do with his age and whether he could've been born around the same time.

Parker walked out of the building, headed to one of the cruisers. He was wearing another dark suit, striped tie. Geena got out of her car, met up with him.

"There you are," he said. "Sayres wants us to talk to the parents again." He climbed into the car. She got in on the passenger side.

"Did you watch the news this morning?" he asked. "They're calling him the Spring Strangler. And his victims, the Spring Girls."

"I guess they got their headline." She'd heard bits and pieces on the local radio station on the drive to Janey's house.

"I suppose that's the name of our case, then," he said.

"Sounds like it," she said.

Parker took the back roads. He made a slight detour past Minsi Lake, ended up pulling into the parking lot.

"Just curious to see how much they've drained," he said. "And who might be hanging around."

Another three feet of water had been drained in the last few days. Several men in waders lifted nets full of fish. Geena had read in the paper the fish were being moved to another lake in Monroe County. The turtles, however, were proving to be a bit more challenging. Authorities used floating hoop traps to capture them. Snappers and painted and eastern musk turtles had been relocated to a nearby dam. A biologist supervising the trapping and relocation was hoping to capture more of the redbellies in their baited nets, a species of turtle on Pennsylvania's threatened list.

Some of the locals had come out to help or perhaps just to watch the emptying of their beloved lake. They were taking pictures, videos, to be posted on their social media pages. Nothing out of the ordinary. Geena and Parker got out of the car, joined some of the bystanders. The crime scene tape had been taken down, discarded, but that didn't matter. What had happened to Valerie was still on the minds of the community.

"When will the lake be completely drained?" she asked one of the men holding up his phone, taking photos of the fish caught in one of the nets. His camo baseball cap was pulled down low, shading his face.

"Another week or so," he said, and he continued taking pictures.

A guy wearing a similar baseball cap stepped between them. "Hard to believe how fast it can be done." He also held up his phone to get pictures of the fish.

Geena nodded. Parker stood quietly next to her. The two men taking photos discussed the lifted fishing regulations. Every now and again she checked the bottom of her shoes for mud, searched for a better place to stand. After a while, they made their way back to the car. Valerie's parents' home was another couple of miles, on the other side of the lake.

Within minutes, they pulled up to the Browns' house and got out of the car. Mr. and Mrs. Brown were waiting for them at the door.

"Thanks for meeting with us again," Geena said.

They settled in the family room. Pictures of Valerie hung on the wall. More current photos had been placed on the mantel over the fireplace, along with a wedding photo of the Browns themselves. The carpet was worn in high-traffic areas, the furniture scuffed, but the house, overall, was clean. The Browns sat close to each other on the couch, their thighs touching, holding hands, clinging to each other.

"When can we make arrangements?" Mr. Brown asked.

He was asking when their daughter's body would be released to them, when they could bury her. "I'm not sure," Geena said. "It may be a few more days." They were still waiting on the lab work. They wouldn't know if they'd need more samples until the results came back.

Mr. Brown nodded, consoled his wife, who had started sobbing.

"I'm sorry," Geena said. "We're working as fast as we can."

Parker asked the Browns more questions about Valerie, now that a few days had gone by and they were past the initial shock of losing their daughter. Mr. Brown confirmed Valerie had lived at home, worked as a legal secretary while taking night classes at the community college. She had planned to go to law school one day. Geena made a note of the community college and jotted down the law firm where Valerie had worked. She wrote down the names of friends and coworkers the Browns supplied.

"No arguments with anyone recently? Ex-boyfriends? Angry coworkers?" Parker asked.

"No, nothing like that. I think she would've told me if she was in trouble," Mrs. Brown said. "But she was always so independent, so I can't say I knew everything that was going on in her life."

"Do you mind if we take a look in her bedroom?" Geena asked.

"Of course," Mr. Brown said. "It's the first door on the right, down the hall."

The Browns stayed in the family room. Geena and Parker entered Valerie's bedroom and slipped on rubber gloves.

Geena ran her hand over the green duvet, the matching curtains, then looked down at the green oval area rug. "Green," she said.

"Everything's green," Parker said.

"Must've been her favorite color."

There was nothing atypical about the room. Clothes had been flung on a chair. More of the same spilled from the closet. Makeup and brushes and hair ties were scattered on top of the dresser. A full-length mirror hung on the wall. Valerie had been a normal girl making plans for her future. Same as Janey had been seven years ago.

They looked in the dresser drawers, in the closet, and under the bed.

"Nothing of interest," she said.

"Let's take a peek in her car," Parker said.

"Couldn't hurt," she said.

Outside, Geena looked up at the gray clouds. Rain was expected. What a surprise. Valerie's car was parked in the driveway at the side of the house, a small silver sedan.

They searched the glove box, console, underneath the seats, the trunk, finding a half tube of lipstick, an empty tin of breath mints, and a crumpled wrapper from a fast-food restaurant. They were finding only what one would expect from a twenty-three-year-old girl. But then Geena pulled a palm and a church program from the side pocket on the driver's side door. She recognized the program as the same one that had been on Janey's coffee table.

"What is it?" Parker asked, leaning over the passenger side to see what she'd found.

"Nothing," she said. She couldn't tell him what was racing through her mind. She was holding evidence of what was quite possibly a connection between Janey and Valerie.

CHAPTER ELEVEN

Geena sat at her desk at the station, scrolling through case files on her computer. Outside, the thunderstorm had passed, leaving everything wet and soggy. With all the rain they'd been having lately, the grass and trees had turned a vibrant green. Valerie would've enjoyed these weeks, so much of her favorite color on display.

Geena pulled up Mia Snyder's file, victim number one, missing April 9, 2014, found three weeks later in the pond at Polly Acres. She remembered Mia was a Methodist. She and Albert had gone to the funeral, studied the crowds of mourners, looked for suspicious behavior, anyone who stood out, the killer himself. They'd gone to Jessica Lawrence's funeral, the second victim, for the same purpose.

She grabbed a pen, sheet of paper, wrote down the girls' names, along with their faiths. It wasn't a perfect match, with three of the girls being Catholic, including Janey, and one Methodist. It sounded like the start of a bad joke.

She picked up the church program she'd found in Valerie's car. The church was probably where Janey had seen Valerie. What were the odds that two of the victims had attended the same parish? Both girls lived in the same general area. It could have meant nothing, but it was definitely worth looking into further.

She researched the priest who presided over the church. She found a few local news clips about charity work, participating in a local fair, nothing noteworthy. He'd lived in Italy until recently, replacing the former priest, who had passed, and therefore was not living in the country when the first victims had turned up. The church itself was relatively insulated within the small town. Could the unsub be a member? How did one find out who the parishioners were? She couldn't take this to Sayres and the team to get access to tech support and the other help she needed. There was only one person she could take this to.

"Albert?" Geena called as she stepped through the back door into the kitchen. She was struck by a familiar smell, something earthy and full of sunshine, Albert's new scent. The kitchen was bright with its white cabinets, yellow-painted walls. There was a bowl of fruit in the center of a butcher-block table. "Hello?" she called again, expecting Pearl to appear any second. Ever since Albert had retired, Pearl had intercepted Geena, prevented her from spending any length of time with him.

"Back here." Albert's voice came from the other side of the house, where he'd set up what Pearl affectionately called his "farming study." It was where he researched the when, where, why, and how of growing plants and organic vegetable seeds.

She found him at his desk, a book opened in his lap, his computer turned on. He took one look at her and asked, "Did something happen?"

She paced in front of him, the palm and church program in her hand. "Is Pearl home?"

"No, she's at her book club."

She stopped in the middle of the room, held up the palm and the program. "There's a connection between Janey and the latest victim. They both go to the same church. It's the first connection we've found."

Albert kept his eyes on her, watched as she walked back and forth again.

"I went to see Janey," she explained. "She didn't remember much, like you said. But now this." She raised the palm and the program again. "I need access to the church. Maybe this Father Perry can help me. But this is a church, Albert. A *church*. I can't just pound on the front door, asking questions about a murder investigation." She sat on the only other chair in the small room and dropped her head in her hands. "What are we going to do?"

He closed the book in his lap. "What are you thinking of doing?"

"You know I have to look into it. I can't ignore it. But how can I without telling Sayres about Janey? I can't keep covering her up for you."

"Does your partner know?" Albert kept his voice low.

"No. But I'm sure he's wondering where I've run off to." She'd left him at headquarters, skipped out on him without an explanation as to where she was going. All she'd said was that she'd be back.

Albert looked down at the closed book in his lap; his glasses were perched on the end of his nose. "Did you know that certain plants work well together when they're planted next to each other, and others don't? The ones that work well together, they're called companion plants. It sounds nice, doesn't it?" He opened the book, searched for a page, and then held it up for her to see the image, of a row of ripe tomatoes next to some kind of herb, perhaps basil. "Some plants help each other grow; others help repel insects, even diseases."

"Can we get back to what I'm supposed to do about our little problem?"

He continued. "I'm thinking of rearranging my garden around this theory, organizing it by companion plants." He put the book down. "There's nothing scientific about it. Some think of companion plants as folklore. But me, I think there's something to it."

"Okay, this is great and all, but—"

He cut her off. "Partners are like plants. Some are there to help; others are there to hurt."

"What are you saying?"

"Your new partner. Can you trust him?" Albert asked. "Is he there to help? Or hurt?"

"Parker? I don't know. We've only been working together a few months."

"But what does your gut tell you? Can you trust him?"

"I'm not sure." She thought she could. They were still feeling each other out, circling around each other, waiting for something to happen that would expose their true selves, as only the job could.

"It's better you find out sooner rather than later."

"Are you suggesting I tell him about Janey?"

"He's your partner now."

"But you got me into this situation."

"I never stopped you from going to Sayres."

"I had your back. And I have it now. That didn't change just because you left."

"Maybe. But now you need Parker to have yours."

"Why did you quit?" she asked, the question tumbling out along with the hurt, a whiny child questioning a parent's decision when they didn't understand it. "Why did you leave me, and in the middle of this, this shitstorm?"

"Maybe I wasn't your companion plant after all."

Geena's head was swimming. How could that be? They'd worked hundreds of cases together. He was her mentor, a father figure. "How do I explain to Parker what led me to Janey in the first place?"

Albert looked away. "You'll think of something."

"Why are you doing this? Why is it so important to keep on protecting her?"

He shook his head, unwilling to answer.

Geena left Albert in his study. She drove straight home and plopped down on the couch. Codis grunted until she picked him up, put him on the cushion next to her. Albert wasn't himself. The job had gotten to him; that was all. One too many dead bodies to look at, witnesses to interview, suspects to contend with. It had backed up on him. It had nothing to do with her. He'd lost his edge. And now it was her job to protect him. She was trying to figure out exactly how she was going to go about it when her phone went off.

Where are you? Parker texted.

Maybe she'd found her answer. She texted him back, Let's get a drink. She was taking a chance he was there to help her, not hurt her.

Geena picked up Parker at headquarters. Then she drove toward Allentown, wound her way on the back roads to a dive bar she used to frequent with Albert. She purposely avoided Benny's, where the guys in their troop hung out. She didn't want to be around them, not tonight. She didn't want them to hear what she had to say.

She pulled down an alley and parked.

"How'd you find this place?" Parker asked as they got out of the car.

"Albert used to come here. He liked their hot wings."

It was dark inside and nearly empty except for the few regulars sitting at the bar. Geena ordered a pitcher of beer, then carried the pitcher and two mugs to a far corner booth where Parker sat waiting.

"Cheers," she said, and she guzzled the beer until the mug was empty.

Parker watched her. He hadn't even taken a sip from his own mug. She poured herself another full glass and studied him, tried to decide whether she could trust him.

A loud burst came from the bar, a couple of guys arguing over the Phillies game, whether the guy was out at first base or not.

"Are you going to tell me what we're doing here?" Parker asked.

Maybe she was already feeling the mug of beer she'd drunk. Or maybe it was Parker himself, telling her to take a chance on him. She couldn't go knocking on the church's front door without telling the lieutenant. They didn't have any other leads. They were still waiting for the DNA report. She worried the case was growing cold. And then there was Albert. She needed help.

"Her name is Janey Montgomery," she said just as a country song came on the old jukebox, a tale of somebody doing somebody wrong.

~Helen Watson, Psy.D.
Patient: Janey Montgomery, ID 27112

Dr. Watson shifts her position in her chair, crosses her legs. Her notebook sits in her lap. She waits, watches Janey pick at a cuticle. Then she asks, "Why don't we pick up with Christian and the homework assignment I gave you?"

Janey eludes the question and changes the subject, something she does often enough that Dr. Watson isn't surprised.

"The detective came to see me again," Janey says.

"Which detective is this?"

"Brassard. The woman. She suggested therapy to help me remember." (*The irony isn't lost on either patient or doctor.) Then Janey adds, "What about hypnosis?"*

"We talked about this," Dr. Watson says. "We can certainly try it, but as you know, I'm skeptical about the results of this method. Hypnosis can produce false memories."

"Yeah, I know," Janey says. "It's just, I didn't have much to tell her. I don't think I helped."

"I know it must be frustrating. But I really do think we're making progress in our sessions. Don't you think so too?"

Janey nods. "I do. I just wish it was going faster."

"Well," Dr. Watson says. "It will take as long as it takes. We'll get there."

Janey nods again.

Dr. Watson sits back in the chair, relaxes. She opens her notebook. "So, about that homework assignment—"

Janey interrupts her and says, "I had another dream."

"Okay." It's obvious Janey isn't interested in talking about the assignment, and that she has other things on her mind.

"It was a little different from the others," Janey says.

"How was it different?" Dr. Watson asks.

"It's all a bit fuzzy," Janey says.

Janey has started rocking. Dr. Watson knows Janey isn't aware that she rocks whenever she feels threatened. It's a subconscious movement meant to soothe and relieve stress.

"Sometimes it's hard to remember our dreams exactly. Why don't you start from the beginning, tell me what isn't *fuzzy?" Dr. Watson says.*

"It wasn't different in terms of the sequence of events. I mean, it started out the same as the others. I was walking through the woods, but the woods started filling up with water, rising all around me, but I could still stand, like it wasn't deep yet. But it was getting deeper, and I was trying to walk through it, trying to find a way out."

"Why do you think you were in the woods?" Dr. Watson asks.

"Because that's where I was walking before I was grabbed," Janey says. "My feet were on the ground in the dirt, and there were trees. And then I wasn't in the woods anymore."

"Where were you?"

"I was in the river. I was being dragged under. The waves crashed over my head, and I saw, or I think I saw . . ." Janey starts rocking faster.

Dr. Watson leans forward, hands clutching her notebook. "What did you see?"

"A dark figure," Janey says. She shakes her head. "It's not clear. The face isn't clear."

Dr. Watson sits back, crosses her legs. "This is no different than all of your other dreams." Her words are clipped. She scribbles tiny circles in the notebook in her lap. She's certain Janey detects disappointment in her tone. Janey looks down and away. It's the look she wears when she's ashamed of something. Dr. Watson knows all of Janey's looks. She also knows Janey is trying hard to remember. But she's not trying hard enough.

"You said something was different about this dream, but you haven't told me anything that we haven't already covered," Dr. Watson says. She makes a point of looking at her watch. "What is it? What's different about this dream?"

"When I was walking in the woods, I was holding someone's hand," Janey says.

"Whose hand were you holding?"

"My son's," Janey says. "I was holding my son's hand."

CHAPTER TWELVE

"Are you telling me you buried evidence?" Parker asked. He leaned across the small table in the bar, so close that his forearm nearly touched Geena's.

"No, not buried," she said. She'd never admit to wrongdoing, not directly. It was a poor attempt to protect Albert, she realized a little too late. "Albert got a tip from some source. He followed up on it."

"Who else knows about this Janey Montgomery?"

"Albert. Me. And now you."

"Why didn't either of you say anything?"

They were whispering, or at least she was whispering, the kind of talking a person did when they were drunk, which wasn't really whispering at all. She'd finished off the first pitcher of beer by herself. The second pitcher was full and pushed to the corner of the table. Parker was still nursing his first beer, also pushed to the corner next to the pitcher. They were the only two seated in the back booths. Most of the regulars had gone home, except for two older men who looked as though they'd made a career out of drinking here.

"At the time, Albert asked me to trust him. He said it was important that I did. He said nothing good would come from exposing her. He insisted he'd give up her name if he thought she was connected to the case and could help in any possible way. I didn't find out who she was until the other day."

"The other day? And you're just telling me now?"

"Don't make me regret it."

Parker was no longer leaning across the table. His spine was up against the back of the booth. He glared at her. "The first victim is always a big piece of the puzzle, the one that more often than not leads you to the killer, and you know that. Did you check into her friends? Boyfriends? Coworkers?"

"Albert assured me that he did. He promised me that he'd found nothing there."

"And you believed him?"

"I did, yes." She resented his tone, but his questioning her decisions where Albert was concerned would be nothing compared to what Sayres was going to do to her.

"Do you believe him now?"

"Yes."

"Where's Albert's file on her?"

"He never gave it to me."

"We need to get it. Too much time has passed. His notes are going to be important."

Parker was right. Why hadn't she thought to ask Albert for them sooner? *Because he wasn't himself in the last weeks before he retired, and it frightened her.* It was a scary thing to witness the breakdown of someone you admired, looked up to like a father, someone you loved. The weight of her own weaknesses when it came to Albert sobered her. "I'll get it from him."

"We need to talk to Janey."

"I already did."

"Of course you did." He didn't hide his annoyance. "We need to talk with her again. Is there a police report? Medical exam? Rape kit? Anything?"

"Albert told me there was a police report, but it was flimsy. He said they first thought it was an attempted suicide by drowning. She refused to talk, and she was placed under psychiatric care during her stay at the hospital. Eventually, she opened up to one of the doctors. That's all the information he gave me." She paused. "She's scared. We can't just barge into her home and demand she give us what we need." She had tried playing on Janey's conscience, bringing up the other victims and letting her know there could be more, and she needed Janey's help. It had worked and had gotten her back inside Janey's house, but would it work again?

"Let's hope Albert did his job. We're still going to have to talk with her."

"What about Sayres?" she asked. He seemed more concerned about Albert screwing up the case than he was about getting into trouble with their superiors.

"We tell him we jumped on it as soon as we found out about Janey, and we came to him at the first opportunity with the information," he said.

"And how did we find out about her?"

"We found an anonymous tip in the file that was never followed up on. We followed up on it."

"We lie?"

"What other choice do we have?"

"You have a choice. You can go to Sayres right now, tell him everything I told you about what Albert did. If this gets out that he deliberately withheld evidence, and I didn't come forward when I found out what he was doing, it could cost me my career. Yours too."

He nibbled his bottom lip, and Geena noticed for the first time how full his lips were. Such a nice mouth, she thought, then immediately pushed it from her mind. Alcohol affected her judgment when it came to men, especially good-looking ones. The last guy she'd taken home from a bar happened to have been the DA. It was right after

Albert had announced his retirement. She'd gone to Benny's to drink her wounds away. It had been a mistake. A heartbreaking error on her part. The second Jonathon's wife had said she was sorry for leaving and wanted to come back, he'd welcomed her home.

Parker seemed to consider what she'd said, and then he stated, "I'm willing to take that risk."

She thought maybe his decision had something to do with what she knew about him. He couldn't look at a dead body without feeling sick. It was like a surgeon who couldn't stand the sight of blood. She decided whatever his reason, it didn't matter. It was in her nature to be protective, not vindictive, and whatever happened to her and this case, she'd keep his secret.

"There's one other thing. I found a church program in Valerie's car. Janey goes to the same church."

Parker shook his head, clearly irritated. "I want to talk to Albert," he said.

"Now?" she asked.

"Right now."

"Albert." Geena knocked on the door. It was the middle of the night. The house was dark. She knocked again, aware of Parker standing close behind her. She'd argued with him about whether she was sober enough to drive, but in the end, she'd handed over her keys.

A light turned on in one of the upstairs windows.

"Albert," she called again. "It's Geena."

In another minute the outside light turned on and illuminated the front stoop. She shot a look at Parker. His eyes were alert, a lock of hair falling across his forehead. She tasted beer on her tongue. She was sure Albert would know she'd been drinking.

The front door opened to Albert pulling his robe closed, tying it at his waist. His white hair stuck up. His glasses perched on his nose, his face droopy from sleep. Pearl stood behind him. Her face was stiff, her eyes filled with resentment at their intrusion.

"I know it's late. I'm sorry, but this couldn't wait." She hitched her thumb at Parker. "This is Parker Reed. Can we come in?"

"Of course," Albert said, and he stepped aside.

"I'll put a pot of coffee on," Pearl said, padding away in her slippers, pink robe.

"Let's go to my study," Albert said.

Albert sat behind his small desk. The same book he'd been reading when she'd been here earlier sat open next to his computer. More books about plants and vegetables and organic farming were piled around the room. Stacks of gardening magazines teetered on the floor next to his chair. Geena took the only other seat in the room, her long legs stretched out in front of her. Parker leaned against a bookshelf, his shoulder touching the framed certificate Albert had received when he'd retired, the one commending him for years served.

"I told Parker about Janey Montgomery." Geena recognized the look on Albert's face as he gazed at Parker. He was wondering all the things Geena had wondered herself. *Can I trust him?*

"I imagine you have some questions for me," he said to Parker.

"I do," Parker said, pushing off the wall and placing his hands on the back of Geena's chair. "I want to see everything you have on this girl. I'm assuming you kept a file."

"I did," Albert said. "You'll have to forgive me, but it's a paper file. I'm old school that way." He opened a desk drawer, dug around in the bottom of it, pulled out a manila folder, and dropped it on the desk. "Everything you need is in there. Everything but the medical records from her stay at the hospital."

"Where are those?" Geena asked.

"You'll have to get them from her. I believe she has a copy."

She thought it was odd Janey would keep a copy with her. She wondered if she was trying to hide something. "What's in the medical records?" she asked.

"I'm not entirely sure," Albert said.

Pearl walked into the study carrying a tray of coffee mugs. She passed them around. "I didn't know if you liked cream or sugar," she said to no one in particular and then walked out, but not before glaring at Geena first.

Geena sank deeper into the chair, sipped the hot coffee. Albert could be infuriating when he didn't tell her everything, parceled out only bits and pieces of information. He'd said it was all part of her training when they'd first partnered together, to get her to search for answers on her own and to think critically about what evidence she'd found on a case. Working with him had been the best as well as the most frustrating part of the job.

She picked up the file and continued sipping the coffee while she flipped through the information he'd gathered on Janey, which included her phone records, emails, and class schedule. She pulled out the police report from when Janey had been found in the river by a young couple who had been camping along the riverbank. She'd been transported to the hospital, where she was interviewed by a local police officer after she'd opened up to the doctors about what had really happened to her. There was something off about the way the police officer had written his report. It read as though he hadn't believed Janey. Nonetheless, a rape kit was requested, but there wasn't any indication whether it was done.

"Did you find a rape kit?" she asked Albert. If Janey had endured the exam, it was possible the kit was sitting in the evidence room at the local police station.

"I looked for it at the station. They don't have it."

"Okay." She thought maybe it hadn't been done, then. She passed the report to Parker. "The local police in Portland handled it. Mia

Snyder didn't turn up until three years later, at Polly Acres. It's not surprising nobody made the connection between the two."

Parker looked over the report and scowled. "Toby Bryant was the investigating officer."

"Do you know him?" she asked.

"Yeah, I know him from the case last fall. He's the chief now. Looks like he was the deputy when this was filed. It's pretty flimsy, like you said. Doesn't look like he did any investigating at all." He handed the report back to Geena. "I'm not surprised it was missed either," he said.

Albert stayed quiet during Geena and Parker's exchange. He looked old sitting behind his desk, his robe frayed at the collar, his skin gray under the white light. They shouldn't have come here in the middle of the night. They should've waited until morning. She put her coffee cup down. "Is this everything?" she asked. "There's nothing else?"

"That's everything," he said, and he looked to Parker. "Don't judge me too harshly. If I had found any evidence that would've helped find this guy, I would've said something."

Parker didn't say anything. He eyed Albert curiously, stared at him in that intense way he had whenever he was sizing someone up.

Geena closed the file and stood.

Then Parker reached out and shook Albert's hand. "Thank you for the coffee," he said.

"I'll call you," Geena said to Albert and then left him sitting alone in his study. Pearl appeared in the hallway and walked them out.

At the front door, Pearl touched Geena's arm. "Leave him out of this case," she said.

"I'll do my best," Geena promised, and she turned to go.

"And Geena," Pearl said. "Don't come back here again."

CHAPTER THIRTEEN

Janey ushered Christian into the bathroom to brush his teeth, comb his wavy hair. She was up and moving, trying to function as though it was just another day. She was forcing herself to put one foot in front of the other when all she really wanted was to hide under the bedcovers and disappear. She'd expected to feel stronger, braver after talking with the detective, but instead all she felt was a sense of shame, as though she'd let her down. She knew the information she'd given the detective hadn't been enough. She'd needed more from her. So much more than she'd been able to give.

She checked her phone for the time. She was going to be late for her shift at the store if she didn't hurry Christian along, but rushing him wasn't always an easy thing to do. If she wasn't careful, she'd push him into a meltdown, and then she was sure to be late.

She squeezed the toothpaste onto his toothbrush, hoping beyond reason that she'd applied it in a straight line so he wouldn't make her do it again. And again. And again. Sometimes she believed he was messing with her just to see how far he could push her.

"Here you go," she said, and she handed it to him.

He wouldn't take it. She was trying hard to be patient with him. It wasn't an easy thing to do on good days. But with everything else she was trying to cope with, it was even harder now.

"Please take your toothbrush," she said. This time he took it from her.

She'd read all the books written by so-called experts on how to handle tantrums, meltdowns, a strong-willed child. She'd tried them all, had given him choices (which only exacerbated the situation, if you asked her), left shopping carts full of groceries in the aisles, walked out of parks, theaters, church. Nothing she'd tried had worked. It was best to leave him to his fits and rages, except when she was late for work. She could lose her job for being late again. It would be the third time this month.

She thought about trying to brush his hair while he cleaned his teeth, or would that be pushing it? She decided to let it go. She'd run a quick brush over his head when he finished.

Christian had been seen by four pediatric neurologists and had undergone a series of tests by the time he was three years old. She couldn't get the doctors to commit to a diagnosis. Was it autism or Asperger's, OCD, ADD, ADHD? She'd all but begged, "Please give me something to work with here." In the end, they hadn't believed he was on the spectrum, although they had agreed he'd exhibited some mild dissociation. Their solution was medication, which she'd refused. She'd have to live with the fact that he was just a difficult child. He was smarter than most kids his age. Maybe the trouble was with *her*. She'd bought more books by more experts, this time telling her how to raise a *gifted* child, which she then read in search of answers. Nothing seemed to work, and she had all but given up. It hadn't been until Christian was accused of bringing a plastic gun to school in early December that the guidance counselor had suggested she consider behavioral therapy for him. Since he hadn't been given a medical diagnosis, she wasn't able to obtain an IEP. But seeking a private therapist for her son outside of school was something she could do on her own. But again, without a diagnosis, insurance wouldn't cover it. *Fine.* She'd found a way to pay for it out of her own pocket.

The incident with the plastic gun had been a blessing in disguise. Never mind that Janey had no idea where Christian had even gotten it. She didn't have toys like that in their home. But no matter, because it had brought Carlyn to them, someone who truly believed Christian could be helped, shaped into a manageable young boy without losing his sense of who he was, his smart, mischievous ways.

Janey was tired. The pressure of the last few days was wearing on her.

When Christian set his toothbrush down, she reached for the hairbrush. She went to comb the top of the unruly waves, which had gotten too long because she'd been putting off taking him for a haircut. The last woman who'd tried to cut his hair had insisted it wasn't an accident when Christian had kicked her between her legs from his high position in the chair.

But Janey knew her son. It hadn't been intentional. He was flailing his legs in a tantrum.

"No," Christian said, and he pushed her hand with the brush away from his head.

Janey should have been firmer with him, disciplined him when he acted out, but she didn't have it in her this morning. She had fifteen minutes to get him to school and then herself to the store, which was normally a twenty-five-minute drive. Consistency was the key to changing his behaviors, Carlyn had said. If you want to brush his hair in the morning before school, you have to be firm and consistent on getting it done. It made sense, but it was hard to do. Maybe Janey just wasn't strong enough to be his mother. She blamed herself, a pattern Dr. Watson had pointed out.

The bunny was getting used to her new home, hopped around by their feet. Janey had started calling the rabbit Bunnie. It wasn't a very original name, but nothing else had come to mind. She scooped Bunnie up, kissed the top of her head, held her out for Christian to do the same.

He did. She noticed he'd started petting Bunnie when he thought she wasn't looking. At least it was a sign he was warming up to their pet.

She carried the rabbit to the kitchen, cuddled her, then set her back in the cage and hoped she wouldn't be too lonely until they returned home later that evening.

They were on their way. Christian was in the back seat, looking out the window at the houses, trees, and buildings as they passed. His hair stuck up in tangles.

She pulled into what was supposed to be a line of cars of parents dropping their kids off at school, but today there wasn't a line. They were running late. She parked. She'd have to walk him inside. She got him out of the car and took his hand. He didn't seem to mind this, holding her hand when she walked him into school, into the house, into church. Other times, he'd pull away, refuse to let her hold his hand when they crossed the street. She accepted this part of him. It was his choice of when he wanted to be touched, handled. He'd only just allowed her to give him hugs, and then only at nighttime before bed. Two hugs a day, she reminded herself. She'd have to work harder for the second one.

A man was walking down the sidewalk toward them. Janey squeezed Christian's hand, hurried him along. Was it Janey's imagination, or did the man seem to pick up his pace? She tugged Christian's arm. "Hurry," she said quietly. The man was coming up behind them. She heard his footsteps on the sidewalk. He was getting closer. She scooped Christian into her arms and raced for the elementary school's door, pressing the buzzer with her finger several times, more times than necessary.

"Can I help you?" the tinny voice asked.

"I'm dropping my son off," she said, aware she sounded frantic. The door was unlocked and she raced inside, out of breath, heart hammering. The buzzer sounded again. In the next second, the man who was following her walked into the school.

"Is everything okay?" he asked.

She saw him clearly for the first time. He was an ordinary delivery man, dropping off a package at the front office.

"Everything is fine," she said, setting Christian down. She was shaking as she led him down the hall to his classroom. She was embarrassed for allowing her fear to get the better of her. She had to get ahold of herself.

"Good morning, Christian," Mrs. Mitchell said. "Why don't you hang up your jacket and join the other kids on the carpet for a special circle time?" She was older, maybe sixtyish. Her glasses were thick, like her waist. She was kind, good with the kids. Everybody said so. She'd been teaching kindergarten for the better part of twenty years. Christian had started kindergarten this past fall. He'd turned six in January. He was one of the older kids in his class.

Christian hung up his jacket. He never looked back at Janey, who blew him a kiss.

"I wonder if I could have a word with you?" Mrs. Mitchell asked.

"Of course," Janey said, and she checked the clock on the wall. She was going to be late for work.

"One of the other moms asked if I could speak to you about a situation."

"I know what this is about." It had to be *Claire* making trouble for her over the stupid broken Easter eggs. "I assure you, I had a long talk with Christian." She hadn't, because at the time, he'd refused to speak to her. "He knows what he did was wrong. He's sorry."

"Yes . . . well, yes," Mrs. Mitchell said. "Claire, Emma's mom, has asked that we keep Christian and Emma apart as much as possible throughout the day. She has some concerns that Christian is bullying Emma."

"Bullying Emma? That's what she said?"

"I want to assure you we haven't seen any such behavior here in the school. As far as we're concerned, he hasn't displayed any aggression toward Emma. If you ask me," she said, "quite the opposite is true.

Christian isn't bullying anyone, because he's not interacting with them. But you know this. We've talked about it. Is he still getting help?"

"Yes," Janey said, heat creeping up her neck.

Mrs. Mitchell patted Janey's arm and said in a low voice, "I'm sure we won't have a problem, but I wanted you to be aware of the situation." She turned then and addressed the class.

Janey had been dismissed. Before she walked out, she glanced into the classroom and found Christian at the far end of the carpet, away from the other kids, playing with his shoelaces.

She turned away from him then, and rushed back to her car. She jumped inside, making sure to lock the doors.

CHAPTER FOURTEEN

Geena shoved the file on Janey underneath some paperwork on her desk at headquarters. She'd gone through it several times with Parker last night. There wasn't much there. Janey was an only child, and no one in her small circle of friends seemed suspect. And the police report had only added more questions than answers.

Parker walked in carrying a cup of coffee. "Briefing is starting," he said.

She picked up her coffee from her desk and followed him and the rest of the team into the conference room. Sayres was already there, shuffling papers around. To his right was a whiteboard with the photos of the Spring Girls. Their brief bios were written underneath: age, approximate location of where they were believed to have been abducted, and where they were ultimately found, including dates and times. The team filtered in, taking their seats, leaning back in chairs, coffee mugs in hand, phones and folders containing notes on the investigation placed neatly in their laps.

There was a certain smell to a room that was packed with men. It was a blend of morning, coffee, and cologne or aftershave, but most prominently, it was the sharp scent of testosterone. She was the only woman on the eight-man team. Parker sat next to her. He'd been shaving regularly since they'd been working out of headquarters. When they'd worked out of the field station, he'd often shown up with a day's growth of stubble.

"I'll keep it short," Sayres said. "I know some of you have been here all night covering the tip line. We'll get to that in a minute. First, the autopsy confirmed Valerie Brown died of manual strangulation. They didn't find water in her lungs, so drowning was ruled out. The ligatures used on all three victims' wrists and ankles are believed to be a quarter-inch diamond-braid nylon rope. Who's checking the stores in the area to see if anyone made a similar purchase in the last few weeks?"

Bill Henson raised his hand. "Nothing so far," he said.

Sayres continued. "We got the toxicology report. Trace amounts of chloroform were detected on Valerie's lips and nose and on the skin around her mouth." He looked around the room. "No other drugs or alcohol were found in her system. It doesn't appear any of the victims were injected with anything. According to the autopsy reports, there weren't any needle marks on any of them, so we can rule that out.

"The tech team is working on scrubbing Valerie's computer and phone so we can determine who she'd been in contact with in recent weeks, what sites she'd visited, and so forth. What we do have is a shoe print at the camping location. This is the only evidence we've gotten from the site. It seems he's packing up the rest of the evidence and taking it with him—his tent, sleeping bag, ligatures, et cetera. This could most likely be his murder kit. The fact that all three victims were found without any clothing or jewelry raises the question as to whether he's keeping the items as trophies." He nodded to Craig Lowry, Bill's partner, confirming this was his theory and one he agreed with. "We should get the DNA report sometime today or tomorrow. Let's hope this guy's in the system." He paused. "Now, what have we got in terms of tips? Anything from the security cameras in the area? Tire tracks?"

Craig spoke up first. "I've got a woman claiming she saw a guy fishing alone on Minsi Lake around the time Valerie went for her walk on Friday night. The call came in first thing this morning. She claimed she left early Saturday morning for her sister's place across the state for the holiday. She didn't return until yesterday and called when she saw the news and the tip line."

Sayres nodded. "Check it out. Anyone else?"

Someone mentioned another tip about a "suspicious-looking character" walking the Appalachian Trail late Saturday afternoon. Although it was several miles from the crime scene, it still would have been possible for the unsub to cover the distance on foot. Craig would look into the AT guy too.

"We didn't find anything on the security cameras, other than a couple of raccoons making the rounds in garbage cans," Bill said.

Craig added, "And the tire tracks match the excavation crews' trucks."

"Okay. There's one more thing I forgot to mention," Sayres said. "Since all three victims were college students, although we've determined they attended different schools, I want someone to check with campus security at each location and see if there are any reports of someone suspicious hanging around the students. And while you're at it, check the victims' class schedules, housing, friends, see if there are any connections there."

"I'll look into it," Bill said.

"All right. I think that's everything, unless someone has anything else?" Sayres asked.

Geena tapped a pen on her thigh, a nervous habit and one that used to drive Albert crazy. She was aware of Parker sitting up straighter in the seat next to her. When she didn't mention Janey or the church program, she half expected him to. It wasn't right to keep it from Sayres and the team. But she still felt the need to protect Albert, at least until she had all the answers where Janey was concerned. Albert had never let her down before, and she had to believe he wouldn't this time either. Her loyalty to him was unshakable. Parker seemed to understand this, accepted her silence on the matter, kept his face blank, unreadable.

"You're blinded by who you want him to be rather than by who he is," her mother had said when Geena had confided she was concerned about Albert's handling of the case.

"What do you mean by who I want him to be?" she'd asked.

"You only see him as you want to see him. It was the same with your father. You're loyal to a fault."

They were back to this again, her mother's jealousy over Geena's close relationship with her father. She'd accused Geena of building her father up into this wonderful man, when in fact her mother had insisted he'd been flawed just like everyone else. Geena had rebelled in childlike fashion, unwilling to accept that her father had been anything less than perfect. Even after his death, the rift between mother and daughter that he'd unintentionally created hadn't fully closed. And that's where Albert had come in. Geena's relationship with him had grown inside that crack.

When Sayres dismissed the team from the conference room, Geena and Parker returned to their desks. Neither one brought up the reason they hadn't mentioned Janey's name during the briefing. He could've easily told the lieutenant everything Albert had done, including her part in it. But he hadn't. And for this, she felt a certain closeness to him she hadn't felt before. They had another secret between them, if she included his little problem with looking at dead bodies.

"I want to talk with Janey and get her medical file. And I want to double-check with her to see if this rape kit was ever done or not. But I want to talk with her alone." She knew it must have been difficult for Janey to talk about what had happened to her. Having to expose herself, her vulnerability, to a man, and not knowing if he would judge her, surely added a whole other layer of discomfort.

"Why do you want to go alone?" Parker looked at her in that intense way he had, the same way he looked at witnesses and suspects. They were trained to make eye contact, to speak with directness, to observe.

"It will be easier for her to talk with a woman. She won't feel as though she has to justify her actions or explain herself, like it was somehow her fault. Which it wasn't. At all."

"Of course not. It's not something I would ever do," he said. "But I'm still coming with you. I'm in this just as deep as you are now."

They stopped talking when Sayres walked into the small office they shared. He looked back and forth between them; then he tossed the folder he was carrying onto Geena's desk. "DNA report. Our guy's not in the system," he said and then walked out.

CHAPTER FIFTEEN

Janey heated water on the stove for a cup of tea. What she really wanted was a glass of wine, but she needed a clear head for what she was about to do. Christian was in his room, occupied with his dinosaurs. He often played in his room after school, closing his door, wanting to be alone. She didn't mind, savoring the small window of time to unwind before dinner. She'd been busy at the store most of the day, her mind not able to settle on any one thought, bouncing between talking with the detective and Christian's troubles at school. And then she'd gotten a text message from the detective. She'd meant to get back to her, but she'd been putting it off. She didn't have anything new to tell her, and she didn't want to disappoint her any more than she already had.

The kettle whistled. She removed it from the burner and poured the boiling water into a mug. She carried the steaming tea and her phone to the bathroom and set them on the counter next to the sink. Next, she opened the medicine cabinet and took out the stopwatch. Then she turned on the water to fill the tub, setting the stopwatch on the ledge where she could see it. While she waited, she sipped her tea. The herbal blend was soothing.

When the tub was full, she dropped her clothes onto the floor and slid into the warm water. Her breathing slowed, in and out, for several long minutes. Once she was feeling calm and relaxed, she turned on the stopwatch, took a big, deep breath, and slipped underwater.

Janey almost drowned the night she'd been dropped from the bridge into the river. And then, sometime after Christian had been born, she'd read an article about free diving. Something about it had appealed to her. Being able to hold her breath underwater for minutes at a time was a way she could feel as though she was taking back some control. What she found was if she could put herself in a meditative state through breathing exercises, she could hold her breath for long periods of time, and her stress and anxiety lessened. There was freedom in having control over this one thing where she'd had none before.

She continued holding her breath, relaxing her body even as the pressure inside her chest was building. It was during this relaxed state she remembered where she'd seen Valerie before. Palm Sunday. At church. A week before she was found in the lake.

Her eyes opened suddenly. She had a strong urge to breathe, to open her mouth in search of oxygen. She tried to stay under for one or two more seconds, to remain in control, but she couldn't risk passing out. What would happen to Christian if she was found unresponsive in the bathtub?

She sat up abruptly, water splashing onto the floor, and gripped the edges of the tub, gulping large amounts of air. She looked at the stopwatch. Five minutes exactly. It was the longest she'd ever held her breath. A personal record.

She trembled as she stepped out of the tub, reached for her phone, and texted the detective, telling her where she'd seen Valerie. The detective texted her back almost instantly, asking if she could stop by. Okay, she replied. Shivering, she grabbed her robe. She was slipping it on when she heard what sounded like Christian crying.

"Christian!" she called, racing down the hall to his bedroom, finding it empty. "Christian!" she called again and then ran into the kitchen. He was sitting on the floor, wiping his eyes. The rabbit's cage was opened. Bunnie was hiding underneath the table.

"What happened?" She bent down, scooped the rabbit up, smelled something burnt, noticed the bottom of her furry feet were singed. A sense of dread moved through her as she glanced at the stove. The burner had been hot from when she'd heated up the water for tea.

"Did you put Bunnie on the hot stove?" she asked.

Christian didn't answer. Instead, he got up and ran from the room.

She looked at Bunnie's feet under the light. She didn't see any lesions or blisters. She wouldn't need to go to the animal hospital, but she shouldn't hop around too much until they healed. Janey put the rabbit back in the cage, gave her fresh pellets and water.

She found Christian in his room. "Christian." She sat on the edge of his bed. "Do you want to tell me what happened to Bunnie?"

He stared at the ceiling and wouldn't look at her. She felt as though this was somehow her fault. She'd been distracted lately. Maybe she wasn't paying enough attention to him, and this was his way of acting out.

"Why was Bunnie out of her cage?" she asked.

"I heard her scratching," he said, but he still wouldn't look at her.

"Did you think she wanted to get out?"

He nodded.

"Why did you put her down on the hot stove?" she asked.

He turned his back to her. "I didn't mean to hurt her," he said.

"It was an accident?"

He nodded into his pillow.

"You didn't know the stove was hot?"

He shook his head.

"Okay," she said. "It's going to be okay." She wrapped her arms around him, pulled him to her, the first hug of the day. His shoulders shook as he cried. "Shh," she said. "It was an accident. And accidents happen." She held him tightly, rocked him. "It's going to be okay," she said again. She continued to hold him until he cried himself out and eventually fell asleep.

By the time she'd gotten up to leave, she'd had to wipe her own tears from her cheeks. She tried to convince herself the injury to Bunnie had nothing to do with the pressure she was under. It was like she'd told him. It had been an accident. She pulled a blanket over him. She'd let him nap and wake him later when dinner was ready. She lingered in his doorway. His small body was just a bump underneath the cover, his sandy-blond hair splayed on the pillow. All she could think was how peaceful he looked, like an angel.

CHAPTER SIXTEEN

"Thanks for meeting with us." Geena sat in the pink and yellow flowered chair. Janey sat across from her on the matching couch. Parker sat on the arm of the chair next to Geena. He was leaning forward, his legs spread, his elbows on his thighs, his hands gripping a manila folder. He was too eager. Geena sensed it. Janey was eyeing him suspiciously.

"He's my partner," Geena said. "He wants to catch whoever did this to you and to the other girls as much as Albert and I do. But we still need your help."

"I don't see how, but I'll try." Janey wore her blonde hair in another single braid over her right shoulder. Geena noticed a small mark on Janey's neck, yellowish in color, a fading bruise.

"Albert said you have a copy of your medical records from when you were in the hospital. We need to see those records," Geena said. She couldn't get a warrant to get the records from the hospital, since no one was supposed to know that Janey existed.

"Why?" Janey asked.

"We think it will help with our investigation."

"You don't know what you're asking of me," Janey said.

"We're asking for your cooperation," Geena said. "We need your help to catch him before he hurts someone else." She was working the guilt angle again, scraping away at Janey's resistance a little at a time.

Parker jumped in. "I brought a couple photos with me," he said. "I'd like for you to take a look at them. Maybe you'll recognize the girls. Maybe you've seen them around, like you did with Valerie." He put a manila folder on the coffee table, opened it, and pulled out pictures of Mia and Jessica. He'd downloaded the images from the girls' social media pages.

Janey touched each photo with the tips of her fingers, tracing the outline of their faces. It was weird the way she fixated on the images as though she was in a trance. Eventually, she turned her gaze away. She shook her head. "I haven't seen them before, not outside of the news. Valerie is the only one who looks familiar. I saw her at church sometimes with her parents, but even then, not that often. She's probably more of the holiday churchgoer," she said. "But that's really all I know. I don't know anything else about her."

"Okay," he said.

"I'm sorry I can't be of more help," Janey added.

"But you can be," he said. "You can help us by letting us see the medical records." His tone was gentle, but Geena heard impatience in it.

This time it was Geena's turn to jump in. "Have you ever heard of a rape kit?" she asked.

"Yes," Janey said. "It was done when I was in the hospital."

"Okay," she said. So the exam had been done, but Albert hadn't been able to locate the kit at the local police station. It wouldn't be the first time evidence had gotten lost. She was frustrated. It was an imperfect system. But it was still possible the results of the exam would be mentioned in the medical file. She would still need to see Janey's medical records. She didn't feel she had a choice but to tell Janey the truth. "We don't have the results of the exam they did on you. It's possible they're lost. But they still could be mentioned in your medical records." She kept perfectly still, waiting for Janey's reaction.

Janey seemed to consider what she was saying. She peered at the photos again, touched the edge of an image of Mia laughing at whoever had taken her picture.

"There could be evidence there that could help us," Parker said. "We won't know unless you show us those records."

Janey closed her eyes briefly, as though she finally understood. "Okay," she said. "Wait here." She stood and left the room. When she returned, she handed a stack of papers to Parker. "They're copies. I'm guessing you'll want to keep them."

"Yes, thank you," Parker said.

"Thank you," Geena said, and she took the papers from Parker.

"Are people going to know about me? Are they going to find out I'm one of them?" Janey asked.

"You're one of who?" Parker asked.

"One of the Spring Girls," she said.

"We'll protect your identity as best we can, but we can't make any promises." Geena thought about how hungry the public was for answers. "Janey, have you told anyone about what happened to you? Family? Friends? Coworkers?"

"Just my parents," she said.

There was a noise in the hallway, footsteps.

Janey's face drained of what little color she had, her skin as pale as cream, her eyelashes so blonde as to almost be white. "Come here," she said, coaxing her son out of the hallway. "This is my son, Christian. I believe you've met him before," she said to Geena.

"Right. I'm the good cop," Geena said.

"What does that make me then?" Parker said with a wink and stood, offering his hand for Christian to shake, but Christian only stared up at him.

The sun had set, the blue sky faded but for a wisp of clouds. Geena and Parker were sitting on the patio in the back of her condo under the outside lights, going through Janey's medical records.

"Bruises were found on her neck, wrists, and ankles. Same as the others," she said. "She suffered a dislocated shoulder and fractured clavicle, the injury consistent with a fall. I guess that happened when she was dropped from the bridge."

"Uh-huh," Parker said, but she could tell he wasn't listening. He was sifting through the stack of papers.

"It's here," he said, and he pulled out a sheet of paper. "A copy of the written report from the results of the rape-kit exam." He scanned it. "There was evidence of sexual assault, some abrasions."

"Okay," Geena said. "Anything else?"

"Nothing was collected in terms of anything like hair or semen," Parker said. "The exam wasn't done until forty-eight hours after she was admitted to the hospital. I guess that was because they first thought it was attempted suicide. She was probably cleaned up in that time and any evidence washed away."

"Who was the forensic nurse who did the exam?" she asked.

"Angie Dunham," he said.

Geena picked up her phone. The closest thing she had to a girlfriend these days just happened to be the very same Angie Dunham. They'd met on a prior case Geena had worked before being assigned to homicide. She'd been involved in a high-speed chase on Route 22. The driver, a middle-aged white man, had stolen a minivan and then opted to flee from police. He'd eventually exited the highway, stopped the vehicle in a residential area, fled on foot. With the aid of a helicopter tracking his movements, he'd been apprehended, cuffed, and put into the back of a cruiser. As they'd continued to process the scene, Geena had opened the back of the stolen minivan, finding a twelve-year-old girl huddled on the floor, clothes torn, bruises on her tear-streaked face.

Angie had been the forensic nurse who had handled the case. She was short, with soft rolls on her stomach and arms, the kind of cushion on her body that made you want to curl up against her for comfort and warmth. Her voice was tender, yet her presence was strong. She had an air about her that said nothing would hurt you, not while she was here. She was a natural with kids, victims. Geena thought Angie would make a great mother one day, but so far, Angie had stayed married to her job, much like Geena was married to hers.

She texted Angie, asked if she could meet with her about a case she'd worked, get her thoughts on it. They tried to get together every couple of weeks, but it was hard with their erratic schedules.

"This is curious," Parker said, and he passed another report to Geena. He pointed to the last paragraph. *Patient refused the morning-after pill for religious reasons.*

"Oh, that is interesting," she said, wondering about Christian. He was the right age. And just because they didn't find semen during the exam didn't mean there hadn't been any there. Women who were raped had the same chance of becoming pregnant as any other woman. But how many women who'd been raped kept their babies? Very few, she'd say. Adoption was a more common choice for women who opposed abortion. But she supposed anything was possible. "What do you make of her son?" she asked.

"I'm guessing he's around five or six. Shy. He kind of looks like her, but then again, he kind of doesn't."

Christian's hair was a darker shade of blond, his eyes light brown, where Janey's hair was so blonde to almost be white, her skin pale, her eyes blue. The only dark coloring she possessed was the smattering of freckles across her nose.

"Maybe her reluctance to give us these reports was never about her. Maybe she's been trying to protect someone else this entire time," she said.

"What are you saying?" Parker asked.

"I'm saying it's possible Christian is the Strangler's son."

CHAPTER SEVENTEEN

Janey had moved through the house as though she were running with scissors, expecting at any moment to fall on the sharp point, the scissors piercing her heart until she was bleeding out on the cold tile floor, and the only witnesses—the ghosts of the Spring Girls. They'd followed her, hissing into her ear, ever since she'd talked with the detectives earlier. It was as though her actions had stirred them up, excited them. She'd felt them before, of course, lingering over her shoulder, a faint breeze blowing through her hair, shivers on the back of her neck, teeth marks on her flesh. Sometimes they took over her dreams, calling to her, clawing, scraping, tearing at her skin. She'd wake up covered in scratches down her arms, across her torso. Some nights their faces appeared as clear as though she were looking at her own reflection in a mirror.

Mia, in particular, visited more often than the others. Mia's lips were dark, her hair silky, her nose turned up at the end, a beautiful girl, but it was the expression in her eyes that scared Janey. It was as though Mia had known all along what had been coming, how her life would end in tragedy, and whose hands had been around her neck. *You should be with us,* she accused. Janey was one of them. She should've died as they had died. Who was she to cheat death?

But the latest girl, Valerie, had come at her without warning, forcing her way into Janey's thoughts with so much anger that Janey was left hollowed out, her body beaten and bruised. They were relentless in their haunting, driving her mad with guilt.

Today Janey had taken a step toward self-preservation. It was a reflexive action, a natural instinct, a breathing thing inside of her, this will to live, this need to survive. She'd given the detectives what they'd wanted from her. She'd done it willingly, and she would've said happily, if it weren't for Christian. It took everything she could muster not to fall to her knees, beg him for forgiveness. She'd tried to protect him all these years, keep him safe from harm, from the truth. He would be singled out even more now than he already was, picked on by the other kids, and maybe by some of their parents, for being the son of a monster.

Christian wasn't like other boys his age. He'd never asked once who his father was, why his father didn't live with them. Since the day he was born, it was as though he'd come with the understanding it would always be just the two of them, Janey and Christian, Christian and Janey.

Whatever the Strangler had taken from her, her small little life, he'd still given her Christian. And her son was a gift. How could she see him any other way? She didn't expect anyone to understand her decision to keep her baby. How could they, unless they were faced with the same hard choice?

Christian splashed in the tub as he made a dinosaur jump through the air before dropping it into the bubbles to strike the unsuspecting dolphin riding the waves below. He played as she washed his hair, the wet locks sliding through her fingers. She made a mohawk out of his long bangs, the silliness of it making her smile. He roared, picked up another toy, cut through the mountains of suds, off in his own world as though she weren't there. When the water temperature cooled and goose bumps covered his body, she pulled the plug and had him stand up, swathed him in a soft dry towel. With him wrapped in the warmth of the cotton, she had him sit on the toilet seat while she attempted to cut his toenails.

"Please keep still," she asked for the tenth time. She was worried about cutting him, hurting him. His nails were long, jagged. He kept squirming, and without warning, he kicked her in the jaw. Hard. She fell backward, landing on her butt on the linoleum floor. Stars burst behind her eyes from the pain.

Christian laughed. "Mommy is so funny."

Later, after he'd changed into his pajamas and had had a snack, she entered his bedroom to say good night, hug him. She crept across his room, slipping into the bed next to him. He rolled to his side, grabbed her cheeks in his hands, touched his forehead to hers. His breath smelled sweet from the grapes he'd eaten, mixed with the minty toothpaste from brushing his teeth. He stared into her eyes as though he was searching for the truth, what was in her heart. She tried to look away, not wanting him to see the betrayal she was certain was reflected in her gaze, the words *I'm sorry* on her lips. He pressed her cheeks harder, her jaw screaming in protest.

CHAPTER EIGHTEEN

Geena paced around the small patio, thinking about all the possibilities of what it could mean to the case if Christian was the Strangler's son.

Parker put the reports on the table. "It's definitely worth checking out," he said.

"Definitely." It must've been why Albert had finally given up Janey's name. It was because they'd been able to get the Strangler's DNA. They now had the evidence that could definitively link Janey to the other girls, or at least to Valerie Brown, bringing them another step closer to catching him. What everyone in law enforcement knew but the public didn't was that there were anywhere from twenty-five to fifty active serial killers in the United States at any given time, and most of them wouldn't be caught. Albert knew these facts, and maybe that was why he'd been so reluctant to toss Janey and her son into the middle of an investigation, into the public's eye, not unless it was absolutely necessary and he could prove without a doubt that she had been the first victim.

Geena returned to her chair. Albert had had his reasons, but Geena realized he was wrong. He never should've hidden the evidence from her or the rest of the team. And she'd been wrong to go along with him, blinded by an implicit trust. She hated that her mother was right. She only saw Albert the way she'd wanted to see him. He wasn't infallible, as she'd believed.

"If Christian is his son," Parker said, pulling Geena away from her thoughts, "what kind of life will the boy have once the world knows his father is a serial killer?"

"Not an easy one, that's for sure."

"You do know we have to go to Sayres with this," Parker said.

"Yes," she said, but first she wanted to call Albert, tell him she understood why he'd done what he had, even though she didn't agree with it. She wasn't angry with him. But she was mad at herself for going along with his decision for as long as she had. She picked up her phone. It was half past eight and still early enough to call him on his cell. She began talking before he had a chance to say hello. "I know why you did it," she said.

"Geena? It's Pearl."

"Oh. Is Albert there?"

"He can't talk to you." Pearl's voice was cold, even for her. "He's in the hospital. He had a stroke," she said and then hung up.

Geena sat on a hard plastic chair in the waiting room at the hospital. She'd watched doctors, nurses, social workers, janitors come and go for the last hour. She wasn't the only visitor in the waiting room. A mother and daughter sat three chairs down from her, both staring at their phones. An elderly couple sat across from her. The man was in a wheelchair, tubes running from an oxygen tank to his nose. In the corner of the room, a large family had gathered, ten people of varying ages, waiting for news on a loved one.

Geena's head hurt, a dull ache at her temples. She longed to let her hair down, release it from the hair tie that held it back in a ponytail. She checked the time. She'd left Parker at her condo over an hour ago, made him promise to wait a little while longer before they talked with Sayres. It was going on ten o'clock when Theo, Albert's son, stepped into the waiting room, found her sitting there. His hair was longer than she remembered, pulled back in a man bun. He wore a flannel shirt over a white T-shirt, cargo shorts, sandals. She stood, hugged him. His eyes were red, puffy.

"Thanks for coming," he said.

"I came as soon as I heard," she said. "When did you fly in?" Theo lived in Colorado, and by the looks of him, he'd embraced the laid-back, eco-friendly mountain lifestyle.

"My mom called around two a.m. last night, after she'd taken him to the hospital. I took the first flight home. They've got him in a room now. You can go in if you want, but the nurse will probably kick you out if she catches you. Visiting hours ended at eight."

"I won't stay long. I'd just like to see him."

Theo nodded, stuffed his hands into his pockets as they made their way to the elevator, rode it to the fourth floor. When they got off, he stopped her and said, "He doesn't look good. And he can't talk. They're hoping with therapy his speech will come back."

She touched Theo's arm. "Your father is strong. He'll get through this."

Theo nodded. His sister, Megan, stepped into the hallway and gave Geena a hug. "Thanks for coming. Dad will be happy you're here." Megan hadn't changed since the last time Geena had seen her. She was small, like Pearl, her hair straight and to her shoulders, a no-nonsense look about her features, a stiffness to her spine. She appeared to be holding up better than Theo. Geena couldn't help but think that women always did.

She walked into the hospital room. Albert lay in bed with plastic tubes in his nose. More tubes ran from his arm to the pole next to the bed. The only sound was the steady drone of beeps from the heart monitor. Pearl sat in a chair next to him, her hand covering his. The look she gave Geena wasn't warm or welcoming.

"You have five minutes," Pearl said, and she got up. She left the room without saying another word.

Geena sat next to Albert, touched the mess of white hair on his head. "What happened?" she asked. Memories of sitting beside her father after his heart attack flooded her, her tongue thick and swollen with the words, *You can't leave me too.* She sat quietly, searching Albert's face. His eyes opened. His gaze fluttered around the room as though he was unable to focus on any one thing, including her. He closed them again. She took his right hand, held it.

"I understand why you did it, but you were wrong," she said. He gave no indication whether he'd heard her. A container by her feet was filling with urine, draining from the catheter they'd inserted. The room smelled of antiseptic and sickness, the same odors that had clung to her hair, her clothes after spending hours visiting her father. She'd believed he'd be joining them at home after two weeks in the hospital, but he never did. He'd never come home, and she hadn't forgiven him.

Pearl walked back into the room. Geena rose, whispered to Albert that she'd be back to see him tomorrow. Pearl followed her out.

"Give us a minute," Pearl said to Theo and Megan. Albert's kids slipped back into his room, leaving Geena and Pearl alone in the hallway.

"I don't want you talking about the case with him," Pearl said. "You're not to bring it up. Ever again. This whole business with these girls and this, this Strangler . . . it just about killed him, and I won't have you coming around here bothering him with it. Do I make myself clear? You keep this case away from him." Pearl marched into Albert's room, closed the door behind her.

A nurse called to Geena. "Excuse me," she said. "Visiting hours are over. I'm going to have to ask you to leave."

"Yeah," Geena said. "I'm going."

⚜

Parker was gone by the time Geena returned home. Codis greeted her with grunts and snorts, his back end wiggling with excitement. She sat on the floor and put her back against the couch. She rubbed his belly. "I can't imagine anyone ever being this excited to see me." She kissed his head.

When cuddle time was over and Codis had curled up on his pillow, she went to the kitchen for a drink of water, found a note from Parker on the table. Who leaves written notes anymore when you can text? She found it sweet. *Hope Albert is okay. Get some rest. We'll strategize first thing in the morning.*

Next to the note, he'd left the file on Janey. Geena opened it, flipped through the records Albert had kept on his investigation, followed the small pinched lines of his handwriting where he'd written in the margins. *What happened to you, Albert?* She wasn't the only one who had seen the changes in him in the last year. Pearl had noticed. She'd made that very clear when she'd asked Geena to keep the case away from him. Pearl had always been polite to Geena but she'd never liked her, although Geena hadn't taken it personally until now. Pearl had made it known how she'd resented Albert's job, the hours he'd spent away from home, from her and their kids, especially when Megan and Theo had been little. She'd taken jabs at Albert, digs about how he'd loved the job more than his own family, and she'd done it in Geena's presence. To Albert's credit, he'd shaken it off, made light of it. "Nonsense," he'd said and then grabbed Pearl by the waist, planted a big kiss on her lips.

Albert was a good man who loved his wife and kids. Geena had only ever wanted a piece of him: a partner, a mentor, a father figure. Maybe it was this last piece Pearl had sensed and felt threatened by.

She closed the file, her eyelids heavy with sleep. She made her way to her bedroom, removed her gun, placed it on the nightstand next to her badge. She stripped down to her underwear, dropped onto the bed, vaguely aware that tomorrow morning when she finally told Sayres about Janey, she might lose her job . . . or, at the very least, she could be suspended from doing what she loved to do. Her identity, her purpose in life, was ingrained in her career. How could she separate the two? Who would she be if she wasn't Geena Brassard, homicide investigator?

~Helen Watson, Psy.D.
Patient: Janey Montgomery, ID 27112

"Do you still check the locks before you go to bed at night?" Dr. Watson asks.
Janey looks tired. There are dark circles under her eyes.

"Yes," Janey says. "I check the locks on the front and back doors. I check
the windows."

"Does it make you feel safe, this ritual of checking the locks and
windows?"

Janey doesn't answer. Dr. Watson can tell Janey is working up the nerve
to tell her something by the way she fidgets with her fingers in her lap, crosses
her legs, uncrosses them. She waits her out.

"I put a chair against the outside of Christian's door," Janey says finally.

"You locked him in his room?"

"Yes," Janey says.

"Why didn't you want him to get out of his room?" Dr. Watson asks.
Janey is rocking, although the doctor knows Janey is unaware she's doing it.

"It was the only way I could get some sleep," Janey says.

"You can't sleep unless you lock your son in his room?"

"He hurt the rabbit," Janey whispers.

"I'm sorry, but I couldn't hear you," Dr. Watson says. "Could you repeat
that?"

"He hurt the rabbit," Janey says louder, covers her ears.

"You have a rabbit?"

"Yes, we just got it. I don't know. Maybe it wasn't a good idea."

"What did he do to the rabbit?" Dr. Watson leans forward. She can't wait to hear what Janey says next.

"He put the rabbit on top of the stove." Her rocking is faster. "When the burner was hot," Janey says.

"I see. Do you think he did it intentionally? Do you think he wanted to hurt the rabbit?"

"No. It was an accident." Janey rocks faster, violently. "He didn't mean it."

CHAPTER NINETEEN

Janey lifted Bunnie out of her cage and set her on the floor. Her feet seemed to be okay. She was hopping around the house with the speed and agility of a normal rabbit. *So quick,* Janey thought. How she admired the rabbit, her ability to change direction, to leap out of harm's way. What Janey wouldn't do to have that capability.

"Christian!" she called. He'd been quiet all morning, grumpier than usual. She found him in his room, lying in bed. She lingered outside his bedroom door, holding a laundry basket full of clean towels. "What's wrong?"

"I don't want to go to school," he said.

"Why?" she asked.

"I don't like it," he said. "I want to stay home."

"I'm sorry you don't like it. But Mommy has to go to work, and that also means you have to go to school."

He got up from his bed and crossed the room. "No!" he shouted and then slammed the door in her face.

She was stunned, stood facing the closed door, unsure what had just happened. She knew she should probably open the door, demand he apologize. But instead, she carried the laundry basket full of towels to the closet and put them away, believing she deserved his anger. One day he'd learn she was the one who'd told the detectives about his father, how she was the one who was responsible for changing the course of his life.

She fixed her hair in another braid, pulling a few strands loose to frame her face in an attempt to cover the bruise on the side of her jaw. It wasn't enough to hide the purple mark. She then applied concealer, telling herself that she could handle this kind of behavior from her son. Not wanting to go to school was normal.

Most kids didn't like school. Although she didn't remember not liking it until she was a teenager. She'd been shy. She'd gotten good grades. She'd had a few close friends in band. She'd been a pretty good flutist, playing in high school and during her first and only year in college. She hadn't been popular, by any means, but she'd always believed being popular was overrated.

But she'd lost touch with any friends she'd had after the attack. She'd sold her flute to a secondhand store. She'd become withdrawn, only stepping out of the house on Sunday mornings for church and for whatever part-time job she'd managed to find while she'd been pregnant. It wasn't until she'd started working at the craft store that she'd gained a little more confidence, reentered the world as much as a single mom in her position could.

She knocked on Christian's door before opening it. She leaned against the doorjamb, arms folded. Christian was lying on his bed again, but this time he was surrounded by his toy dinosaurs and *When Animals Attack!* magazines. She diverted her eyes from the image of a grizzly bear baring its teeth and claws. Outside on the street, several car doors slammed, voices carried. She didn't think anything of it. It was probably just the neighbors, delivery trucks, the hustle of a weekday morning. She checked the time.

"Christian, we have to get moving."

He shook his head.

"I'm going to gather your things, and when I come back, I expect you to get up." She rushed through the house, picked up his backpack, stuffed a pack of crackers inside for his snack. She didn't have time to argue about which snack she'd chosen. She was worried about being late again. Then she grabbed his lunch bag from the refrigerator and put it and the backpack by the door.

She found him lying on his stomach in the same position she'd left him in, her frustration growing, her voice stern when she said, "Get up. We have to go." When he still wouldn't budge, she slipped his sneakers on with him lying there, ran her fingers through his hair as best she could. Reluctantly, he sat up, swung his legs to the floor. She hesitated before bending down to tie his shoe, remembering the kick to her jaw. She tied his shoes without incident. Then she took his hand and led him to the door.

As soon as they'd stepped outside, a woman with too much makeup rushed up to them, shoved a microphone in Janey's face. The woman was followed by a small man carrying a large camera on his shoulder, the lens pointed at her and Christian.

"How do you feel about being the only surviving victim of the Spring Strangler?" the woman asked.

Janey stumbled backward as though she'd been hit. Then she pushed the woman's microphone away. "Get away from me!" she hollered. "Leave me alone." She was confused from the shock of what was happening. And she was feeling something else, something close to foolishness. The detectives had said they'd try to keep her identity hidden. Well, they didn't try hard enough. She should've known they wouldn't.

She'd always been too trusting. It was the reason she was here in the first place. She'd read a blog online once, followed it in the weeks after she'd been released from the hospital, where victims shared their stories, their fears, asked the same question over and over again. *Why me?* Someone had posted a list of traits that made certain women easier targets than others—petite, long hair, walking alone in a deserted area, vulnerability in their stride or on their face, smiling at strangers, emanating kindness, *trusting*. The list had gone on, as though it had been her own fault she'd been attacked, as though she'd brought it on herself by behaving or looking a certain way.

It had made Janey sick.

She pushed past the reporter, trying to get to her car, Christian's hand warm and sticky in her grip. Another reporter came out of nowhere and butted up against Janey's side. More reporters surfaced, as though they'd been waiting, springing from the cracks in the sidewalk, pointing cameras in her face, yelling questions at her.

"Are you working with the police? Did you give them any leads to the identity of the Strangler?"

"Get away from me. Please. I have to get to work." She pushed through the crowd that had gathered, flashes of familiar faces all along Eighth Street, neighbors she'd waved to in passing, chatted with about the weather, the elderly she'd helped with their groceries. They'd come out, stood in the road, on the walkways, gawking at the news vans, reporters, the commotion surrounding Janey's yard, her house, her car.

"Please," she said again, and she opened the rear passenger-side door, strapped Christian inside. She ran around the front of the car to the driver's side, where the same woman with too much makeup was waiting.

"Is there anything you want to say to the Strangler?" she asked.

Over the years, Janey had imagined confronting him, asking him that all-consuming question, *Why me?* There were other times when she'd had too much wine (the entire bottle, to be fair), when she'd pretended her circumstances had been vastly different, and she'd be sitting across from him at her kitchen table, talking with him as though they were a normal couple, facing ordinary problems raising their son. Other times she'd slip into darker thoughts, wandering through the closed door she'd created in her mind and never wanted to open again. Behind that door, she was grabbed from behind, a rag had been shoved in her mouth, her tongue pushing against it, trying to force it out, her screams sticking in her throat. But never in her dreams, nightmares, had she imagined having a conversation with him meant for public consumption. Her secrets would not be aired on television for scrutiny. What Janey had to say to him would be private, between him and her alone.

She opened her mouth.

The crowd grew quiet, intent on listening.

"No comment," she said.

Janey's hands were sweaty on the wheel. She could barely concentrate on the road. A car horn blared, a man yelling obscenities at her out his window. She looked in her side mirror. She'd driven through a stop sign, one she'd known was there from driving down this street, this neighborhood, a hundred times over.

She glanced in the rearview mirror at Christian. He must have had questions about what all those people were doing outside their house. He must have been confused, maybe even a little frightened. Yet he looked out the window like he did every day on the way to school, his expression unreadable.

She tried to focus on driving and the road ahead. It would be stupid to get in an accident. It would draw more attention to her. In another few minutes, she was helping Christian out of the car, walking him into the school. She stopped before they'd reached his classroom door, knelt in front of him. "We'll talk about this later, okay?" She stood and watched as he walked into the room while Mrs. Mitchell greeted him.

"Is everything okay?" Mrs. Mitchell asked her.

"Everything is fine," Janey said, and then she rushed back to the car. She pressed her hand to her chest, her tongue thrusting as though a rag had once again been stuffed in her mouth, forcing the scream down her throat.

CHAPTER TWENTY

Geena walked into headquarters the next morning, the file on Janey in her hand. Someone had leaked Janey's name to the media. The best she could figure was that it had come from one or both of Janey's parents, or possibly Albert's unnamed source who had led him to Janey originally.

Geena was headed straight to the lieutenant's office. There was no getting around it. Her badge was in her pocket, her gun on her hip. She couldn't imagine not having them on her anymore. They were as much a part of her as her arms and legs.

Bill greeted her. He was carrying his favorite Yankees mug. He wore a baseball cap with the Yankees insignia whenever he was off duty. He was a diehard fan. You would think he'd be a Phillies fan, coming from eastern Pennsylvania, but that wasn't always the case. Some of the smaller towns around the county were closer to New York than Philadelphia, and the locals had grown up watching New York stations, rooting for New York teams.

"I'm not sure what's going on, but your partner's in there," Bill said, motioning to Sayres's office with his mug.

Sayres had an open-door policy. This morning the door was shut. It wasn't a good sign. She felt the team's eyes on her as she walked down the hall and knocked on Sayres's door.

"What is it?" he asked, his tone gruff.

She poked her head inside, noticed Parker sitting in a chair in front of the lieutenant's desk.

"Have a seat, Brassard," Sayres said.

She entered the office and sat next to Parker, but not without closing the door behind her first. Parker didn't acknowledge her, kept his gaze straight ahead. The vein in Sayres's forehead bulged.

"Parker tells me we have another victim, a survivor. But he didn't have to tell me, because I saw it on the news this morning before I even made it in to work. Do you want to tell me what the hell is going on?" He slammed his hand down on top of the desk.

"It's complicated—" she'd started to say when Parker cut her off.

"We discovered late yesterday that Albert had gotten a tip from an unnamed source after the second girl was discovered, right before he retired. He'd interviewed Janey Montgomery, collected some intel on her, but didn't find anything that supported the case. It was in the file, but no one pursued it further."

"And how did you two find it? Brassard?" Sayres asked.

"Like I said, it's—"

"Complicated. Yeah, I got that. Simplify it."

She wouldn't contradict Parker, but she wouldn't allow Albert to take the hit on this, not without confessing her role in it. "I knew about some source who had contacted Albert. I knew Albert had interviewed Janey, but that was all the information I had until Parker and I discovered she might be of greater interest to the case than Albert originally thought."

"Why is this the first *I'm* hearing about it?" Sayres's tone told Geena how much he was trying hard to stay in control and not lose his temper with her.

"Albert and I made a mistake."

"Albert doesn't make mistakes," Sayres said.

It was a dig she didn't feel she deserved. She'd worked too hard to overcome her *femaleness*, having to prove she was just as good a cop as any man on the team. She believed she'd done just that with Sayres, but apparently not. He'd immediately assumed it was her mistake. But it was Albert who had made the decision to bury the evidence, not revealing Janey's name to her until a few days ago.

"Why don't you tell me what's really going on here?" Sayres asked. "Or do I have to bring Albert in and get it straight from him?"

"You can't do that." She put the file on Janey on top of Sayres's desk.

"And why not?" he asked.

"Albert had a stroke."

Sayres ran his hand over his shaved head. "When?"

"I found out last night."

"How's he doing?" Sayres asked.

"It's too soon to tell. He's not able to talk."

Sayres leaned back in the chair, scratched his chin with his knuckles. "Who tipped off the media?"

She glanced at Parker. He shrugged. "Maybe her parents. Or maybe the same source who tipped off Albert," she said.

"Who is this source?"

Geena shook her head. "He never revealed the name to me."

Sayres picked up Janey's file, then slammed it back down. "I can't do anything about Albert now," he said. "But maybe I should pull you off the case for not showing me this sooner."

She shot out of her chair. "You can't do that. I've been working too hard and too long on this one. I know this case better than anyone. And we're getting close to catching him. You can't take me off now."

"Sit. Down. Brassard."

She sat.

"If I may interrupt," Parker said. "I think taking Geena off the case would be a mistake."

"Oh, you do, do you?"

"She's a woman."

"I'm well aware of that," Sayres said. "What's your point?"

"Janey is more comfortable talking to a woman."

"And you know this firsthand?"

"We talked with her as soon as we learned she might be of interest," Parker said. "She seemed more at ease talking with Detective Brassard than myself."

"Go on," Sayres said.

"She doesn't remember much," Geena said. "All she remembers is that she was grabbed from behind by her ponytail. A rag covered her mouth and nose. She said she never had time to scream. The police report says she was pulled from the river by a young couple camping on the riverbank. They believed she'd jumped off the bridge, attempted suicide. But the medical records confirm there were bruises on her neck, wrists, and ankles."

"Okay, sounds like our guy. Similar MO."

"That's not all," Geena said. "Janey has a son. We think there's a possibility he could be the Strangler's son. If we could get the boy's DNA, we could find out for sure and link the cases. And the boy, he kind of looks like her, but it's obvious he has some of his father's traits. We could develop a facial composite with an age-progression feature, make a virtual lineup, give the public a face. Maybe something will break." She'd come up with the idea after she'd decided it was time to talk with the lieutenant about Janey. She only wished she'd gotten to him first on her own terms rather than having him hear it from the media.

Sayres held up his hand. "Let's not get ahead of ourselves. Did you even ask her who the father is?"

Geena said, "We didn't think to ask until we discovered she'd refused the morning-after pill seven years ago, after the assault. Her son is about the right age."

"And you're sure about this?"

"Yes."

"Do we know why she refused the pill?" he asked.

"Religious reasons."

"What are our chances of getting her to agree to a cheek swab on the boy?" he asked.

"I think if the request comes from me, we can get it," she said. "There's one more thing I should mention. Both Janey and Valerie went to the same church." She'd been so focused on what they'd learned from the medical reports that she'd almost forgotten this detail. "We can go through the files once we get the intel on Valerie, see if anybody's name jumps out."

"Janey said she didn't know Valerie, only that she saw her at church on occasion," Parker added.

Sayres rested his elbows on the armrests of the chair, fingers steepled in front of him, while he looked them over. "You've put me in a really tough position, Brassard."

"Yes, sir."

He took a moment before speaking again. It took all of Geena's strength to sit patiently and await her fate.

"I'll bring the team up to speed. In the meantime, neither one of you will make a move in this investigation without my approval. You clear everything through me. Every thought, phone call, every crumb you find goes through me before you do anything. Do you understand?"

"Yes, sir," both Geena and Parker said.

Sayres pointed at her. "You've got one more shot before I pull you off this case permanently. Don't screw it up."

"Should we send a unit out on the trail by the river? I know it's been a long time, but maybe we'll find something," Parker said.

"It's been how many years? No," Sayres said.

"But—" Parker started to protest, but Sayres cut him off.

"I'm not wasting manpower on this until we confirm the two are connected. Get me that DNA on the boy."

Geena stood and reached for the file on Janey that she'd set on top of Sayres's desk, but he put his hand on top of it. "Not until I go through it first," he said.

She left his office and strode back to her desk, pulled the chair out hard, and sat. Parker was behind her.

"Do me a favor," he said. "Don't ever put me in that position again. If you're hiding anything else, now's the time to tell me."

She shook her head. There wasn't anything else.

"How's the old guy doing?" Parker asked.

"I talked with his son this morning. There's no change," she said. "Thanks for telling Sayres that Janey was more comfortable talking with me." He must've thought about what she'd told him earlier, how hard it was for a woman to talk about these kinds of things with a man, not knowing whether she'd be judged.

"Well, you're welcome," he said.

"What about this leak?" she asked.

"It could be her parents. You don't always know what goes on inside a family."

"I suppose," she said. "We may have blown her trust in us. There's only one way to find out." She grabbed her jacket.

Sayres stepped out of his office, motioned for everybody to join him in the conference room. The team gathered around.

Sayres said, "We've got what appear to be human remains out at Minsi Lake again."

CHAPTER TWENTY-ONE

"Where are you?" Janey's mother asked.

"I'm in my car." She was still parked outside the elementary school. She'd frozen after having what she believed to be a panic attack, unable to drive, to move forward. The thing she feared most had happened. Her secret was out. It was only a matter of time until her son was dragged into the media frenzy.

"I can't go in to work today," she confessed.

"Oh, honey, I'm so sorry," her mother said. "Your father and I are here for you and Christian. You know that."

"Can I come over?" she asked.

"Of course you can," her mother said.

Janey pulled from the curb, drove straight to her parents' house, parked in the driveway. The garage door was open, the space inside transformed into her father's woodshop. Power tools abounded. He was standing behind the table saw in protective glasses. He wore earmuffs to block out the screeching sound as he cut a piece of wood. He didn't see or hear Janey pull up. She got out of the car. The scent of sawdust filled the air. It was at once familiar and comforting. It smelled like home.

Her mother opened the door and motioned her inside. She greeted Janey with a warm hug.

"It was all over the news this morning," her mother said, stepping out of their embrace. She searched Janey's face. Whenever she looked at her this way, she wondered what her mother hoped to see: the girl her daughter used to be, the good girl she'd raised, or this new one, ashamed by circumstances out of her control.

"Sit," her mother said. "Let me get you something to eat."

"I'm not hungry."

Still, her mother busied herself in the kitchen, filling a basket with croissants, spreading butter and jam on toast.

Janey sat at the table, shrinking down in the chair. She closed her eyes and wished she could disappear. She thought about the time she'd spent two weeks at church camp when she was fourteen years old. While the other girls in her class had spent the month of July at the public swimming pool chasing after boys, Janey had been at camp singing in the choir, practicing her flute, preparing for the myriad of skits she'd perform for her parents on the last day at Holy Mountain campground in the Poconos. She remembered one particular rainy afternoon, sitting in front of a microscope. They were identifying the various bugs they'd come into contact with during their time outdoors. Janey had welts on her legs from mosquitoes and one or two from the deerflies around the lake. She'd approached the microscope but couldn't bring herself to look through the lens at the small bug flattened on the slide. She'd felt sorry for it, to be reduced to nothing more than a specimen, its little bug body magnified for viewing. Janey felt like that tiny bug now, her face plastered on the TV screen, her life exposed, laid bare for all to see.

The doorbell rang. Her mother rushed to answer it.

Maeve, one of her mother's churchgoing friends, walked in carrying a breakfast casserole. Maeve was short and stout like the teapot described in the nursery rhyme. She was quick with a joke. She had a laugh so contagious she once had the entire back row of parishioners giggling during a particularly boring service with Father Perry. If a person wanted to be cheered up, Maeve was the one to call.

"How are you doing, honey?" Maeve asked, but Janey noticed she couldn't quite meet Janey's eyes.

The doorbell rang again. Several more of Janey's mother's friends arrived. They gathered in the kitchen, each bringing a covered dish or some kind of baked good. Janey's mother hugged them, passed around coffee mugs, reveled in the attention, the sympathy she'd garnered for her daughter's situation. They all agreed how brave Janey was, what an awful thing to have happened, how lucky she was to have escaped.

Janey left the kitchen when she couldn't stand to hear one more time how lucky she had been. They were too polite to ask too many questions in front of her. They'd wait until they were alone with Janey's mother to ask her whether she knew who he was or what he looked like. How did she get away? She wouldn't deny her mother her support group. It was the longest secret her mother had kept in her life. A small part of her mother must have been relieved to finally have it out in the open.

Janey slipped into the garage, where her father was working. He handed her a sanding block and pointed to a piece of wood he'd recently cut. She was grateful for the chore, for not having to talk. After some time had passed, he wiped his hands on an old dirty towel.

"She needs her friends," he said of Janey's mother.

"I know."

"What happens now?" he asked.

"I'm not sure," she said.

There were twenty-six messages on Janey's answering machine when she returned home after picking Christian up from school. Most were from the media. A couple of female callers hadn't identified themselves, wanting to know why Janey had waited so long to go to the police, and they all but accused her of not wanting the Strangler caught. Three calls were from Josh. "How are you?" he'd asked each time, not "Where are you?" or "Why didn't you show up for work?"

The last message was from a man asking if she'd liked it, being raped, choked.

She dropped to her knees on the kitchen floor, cried into her hands to muffle the sound. Christian was watching TV in the family room, some inappropriate cartoon where the dismembering of a character's limb was meant to be funny. Eventually, she pulled herself up, found her footing on the tile floor. She put her finger on the delete button to get rid of the messages, but she knew the woman cop and her partner would be interested in the last one. She didn't believe the Strangler would call her. Something told her he wouldn't be so careless. She convinced herself it was just some random pervert with mental health issues. But she was so tired, and it was only day one. There was only so much a person could take before they crumbled.

She took Bunnie out of the cage, stroked her soft fur, then carried her to the family room. She pulled the curtain aside and peeked out the window. Carlyn stood behind her car with the hatch up, where she kept her props for therapy sessions. She was talking to Dr. Watson, which didn't make sense. What was Dr. Watson doing outside Janey's house?

Words were exchanged, followed by Carlyn nodding her head, getting back in her car, driving away. Where was Carlyn going? They had a session scheduled. Janey wanted to ask her what she should tell Christian about why there'd been reporters outside their home earlier that morning. Should she say anything at all? She needed Carlyn's help, her advice.

By then, Dr. Watson had walked to the front door, knocked.

"Janey," Dr. Watson said through the closed door. "I'm here to help you and your son."

CHAPTER TWENTY-TWO

Minsi Lake was nearly dry but for a few large puddles amid the dirt and rocks and plant debris. Most of the fish and turtles had been salvaged and transported to nearby lakes and streams. A smattering of spectators lingered on the concrete embankment that had been submerged in water just two weeks before. Fifty yards in from the same embankment, at the bottom of the lake, an excavation worker had noticed something odd about the arrangement of what he'd thought were rocks. On closer inspection he'd discovered they weren't rocks at all but bones.

Local law enforcement was the first on the scene. Two black and white cruisers were parked in the lot in front of an outdoor porta potty. The officers were standing around, waiting for instructions.

Geena leaned against the car, watched Parker tighten the laces on his hiking boots. Then he rolled up his shirtsleeves, sprayed his arms with bug spray. "The sun is out and the air is wet and humid. It's the perfect conditions for flies," he said, and he passed the can to Geena, who made a face and handed it back.

"You'll be sorry," he said. "The horseflies are the worst. Their bites leave big red welts the size of quarters. If they get infected, they get these nasty puss-filled centers."

"Lovely image," she said. "But I can't stand the smell of bug spray."

"It's unscented," he said, and he showed her the can. When she hesitated again, he said, "Okay, but don't say I didn't warn you."

"Fine," she said, and she took the can, sprayed her arms. She really did hate bugs. A bead of sweat dripped between her shoulder blades. It was hot standing in the open parking lot. So much for spring. It felt more like summer in July. It would only get hotter, standing underneath the glaring sun in the middle of the empty lake.

Lieutenant Sayres had taken over the scene. Access to the public parking lot had been cordoned off. "Reed. Brassard. Follow me," he said.

Geena and Parker walked a pace or two behind Sayres, trekking over mud and rocks, walking around patches of lily pads rather than through them. It was all too easy to get tangled in the plants and trip. With each step the air became heavier, weighing on Geena's shoulders, the pressure building in her lungs, tightening her chest the way only approaching a dead body could do. No one had told her it felt like this when she'd first been assigned to homicide. And then there was her eidetic memory to consider. Once she'd seen the bodies of victims, she could never unsee them. The images were imprinted on her mind's eye forever. Albert had warned that her memory could be an asset or a liability, depending on how she chose to process what she'd seen. At the same time, he'd led her straight into the center of her first homicide, where a woman's body lay twisted in an unnatural position at the bottom of a stairwell, and he'd done it without giving pause as to whether he should have.

They reached the area where the crew member from the excavation team—a heavyset man with a potbelly, his gray shirt soaked through with sweat—had said he'd found the bones. They stopped and stood shoulder to shoulder. From the shape of the skull, the teeth, there was no mistaking that they were looking at human remains.

Sayres squatted, pointed to a cinder block and some rusted chain. "It looks like the body was weighed down." He inched closer. Flies buzzed around the bones, the horseflies Parker had mentioned, along with a few greenheads and the occasional dragonfly. So far, Parker hadn't shown any signs of distress from looking at the remains. She supposed it was because the body wasn't fresh.

"Might not be the Strangler," Sayres added. "It doesn't fit his MO. He doesn't weigh the bodies down. We'll need to get Cheryl out here." Cheryl Leer was their regional forensic anthropologist. She'd worked with Geena and Parker on their previous case, when bones had been found deep in the mountains off the Appalachian Trail.

Parker slipped on rubber gloves and crouched next to the lieutenant. He touched around the eye sockets of the skull. "Cheryl will have to confirm this, but I believe the victim is female. She told me you can tell by the orbits. If they're round and the upper border is sharp like this one, it's a female."

Sayres stood, started walking back in the direction of the parking lot. "Make sure no one gets close to this area." He pointed to the ground. "And find out if these shoe prints are from the crew. I want every print matched to a person," he said.

Geena had no problem keeping stride with both the lieutenant and Parker, her long legs matching their six-foot-plus height. Once they'd reached the embankment, Sayres stepped away and made a few calls, requesting a forensic unit along with Cheryl.

Nathan had arrived while they were out on the lake. "I'm going to take a look," he said.

Sayres nodded. "Reed, go with him. Brassard, talk to the fishermen and the excavation crew. Take down their information. I want to know who they are and what they're doing here."

Geena headed in the direction of the walking path where a group of fishermen was hanging around. She was most interested in them. It wasn't uncommon for the killer to return to the scene and watch the commotion he'd created. If the killer had known the lake was to be drained, he'd expect the body, or in this instance the bones, to be found.

She took out her notepad, a pencil. "Hey, guys. Any of you happen to walk out on the lake? There are a lot of shoe prints out there."

"Sure, I went out, but I didn't get too close," one of the fishermen said.

"And your name?" she asked.

"Chip Connolly."

"Where do you live, Chip?"

"I live off Bangor Vein Road."

She wrote his information down.

"Does this have anything to do with the Strangler?" Chip asked.

Geena looked up from her notepad, more interested now in Chip Connolly. "What makes you say that?" she asked. He was middle aged, overweight. He wore a wedding band, camouflage shorts, tan vest. He was a regular guy. There was nothing special about him. Most serial killers appeared ordinary.

"I have no idea," Chip said. "It's just not right, all these young girls turning up dead in our fishing holes."

"I agree with you. There's nothing right about it. Where do you work, Chip?"

"Oh, I . . . uh, I'm on disability. Bad knees. Worked for a plumbing contractor for fifteen years."

"Which contractor?" she asked. He mentioned a name she'd never heard of, and she made a note to look into it. "What about you?" She went down the line, questioned three other men. Nothing suspicious about them. The last guy on the end came up to her, stood too close for her comfort. "Please, step back for me," she said.

He did as she'd asked. His name was Josh Wheeler. He said he was here because he'd never seen a drained lake before and wanted to check it out. If she had to guess, she would've said he was in his late twenties, possibly even thirty. His hair was light, wavy. She was taller than he was, and it made her feel as though she had a slight edge over him. He answered her questions freely.

"Thanks," she said. She headed toward the excavation crew and went through the process a second time. When she finished with them, she rejoined Sayres, Parker, and Nathan in the parking lot. The forensic unit had arrived. Their van was parked next to the cruisers. They were already flitting around the remains with the flies. A tent was in the process of being erected for central command.

"Cheryl should be here soon," Sayres said.

They turned when a black sedan pulled into the lot and parked in a spot not far from where they were standing. Jonathon got out of the car and made his way over to them. It wasn't unusual for him to show up at crime scenes in high-profile cases. But she had a feeling his presence here had more to do with the recent news about Janey Montgomery. Any missteps on their part could have a negative impact on the case when and if it came up for trial.

Jonathon nodded at Parker, and then he turned to her. "How are you?" he asked.

"I'm fine."

He gazed at her for what felt like a long time. Then he said to Sayres, "What have we got?"

"Skeletal remains. It looks like the body was weighed down. We're waiting for Cheryl to get here," Sayres said.

"Do we know if the victim is male or female?"

"Female," both Nathan and Parker said.

Jonathon nodded and then said, "I saw the news this morning. Why didn't we know about this Janey Montgomery before?"

"Would you like to answer that, Brassard?" Sayres asked, and then he said, "Never mind. Why don't you go check on missing persons and get out of my sight for a while? Reed, go with her."

"Lieutenant," Geena said. She flipped through the mental images of missing girls from the database that she'd memorized. She didn't neces-sarily agree with him that this current case might not be related to the Strangler. In the initial report they'd gotten from the profiler, she'd said you can't rely solely on MO. "We've had victims in the Strangler case every couple of years for the last seven years."

"Your point?" Sayres said.

"I think we should start with missing persons in those years in between. I mean, depending on the age of the bones."

"Are you thinking he weighed some of the bodies down and not others?" Parker asked.

"Possibly," she said.

"Why not weigh all of them down?" Parker asked.

"I don't know," she said. "But whether this is related to the Strangler or not, I'm thinking this girl could be Amy Kaplan. She disappeared in 2012. Her car was found abandoned a couple miles from here."

"She's right," Jonathon said. "I remember the case."

Sayres looked at them, scowled. Ever since he'd learned they were involved with each other several months back, he'd tried to keep them apart. He'd called her into his office, sat her down, asked if she was trying to jeopardize her career. "Of course not," she'd said, her embarrassment reaching new depths. But it hadn't mattered, because her relationship with Jonathon had been over almost as soon as it had begun.

"Get out of here and get me everything we have on her," Sayres said.

Geena and Parker headed for their car.

"What's the story with you and the DA?" Parker asked once they were out of earshot of the others.

"No story," she said. "Why?"

"I'm not blind," he said. "Do you want my advice?"

"Not really."

"Don't shit where you eat."

"It's a little late for that."

135

Back at headquarters, Geena handed Parker her notes on the men she'd interviewed at the scene. He put the names into the system to see if anyone on the list had any prior criminal records.

"Pay specific attention to the ones with the asterisk by their name," she said.

She sat at her desk. While Parker typed away on his computer, she logged into the missing persons database. It took only a minute to find the girl who had stood out among the others she'd stored in her mental photo album. Amy Kaplan, age twenty, a New Jersey resident, attended a New Jersey college. It was a different school from the other victims, but she was the right age. She'd gone missing in early May 2012. Her car, a silver Kia with Jersey plates, had been found on Blue Mountain Drive with a flat tire not two miles from Minsi Lake. Her cell phone had been discovered close by with a dead battery. The local police searched the area, the woods, the lake, but had come up empty. They'd gone on the assumption Amy had gotten a ride from someone.

And disappeared.

Geena now believed a different scenario had taken place. She shared what she'd found with Parker. "What if our guy happened to be hiking the trails, saw her on the side of the road, offered to help, dragged her into the woods, panicked because it wasn't part of his routine, and lost control? It's possible he kept her longer than the others in his heightened state. Then he puts her in the lake, but only after it's been searched." This showed a level of disorganization when compared to his organized MO, but she knew of some documented cases of similar occurrences happening with other serial killers.

"But why does he weigh her down? What's different about her?"

"Maybe she was the one who fought back. Maybe he was worried there'd be evidence underneath her fingernails or somewhere else on her body."

"I guess it's possible."

"Maybe things don't always go as planned for the Strangler . . ." Her voice trailed off. If the Strangler was worried about leaving evidence behind, wouldn't he consider Janey evidence? "Hey, Parker. What if he didn't know Janey survived? What if he saw her on the news this morning?"

"Are you thinking he might go after her?"

"She's our biggest lead. And her son," she said, and she picked up her cell phone. "We should put someone outside her house, just to be safe." She called Sayres. He answered on the first ring. In the background she heard the echo of voices, insects buzzing. She told him what she'd found on Amy Kaplan and requested protection for Janey Montgomery. After she'd hung up with the lieutenant, she said to Parker, "Anything on the fishermen?"

"Nothing so far," he said.

She copied all the information they had on Amy and added it to the file. "He knew Valerie would be found quickly, with so much activity surrounding the draining of the lake," she said, thinking out loud. "He knew eventually we'd find another victim in the same place."

"And?" Parker asked.

"It's been seven years. There are four, possibly five, victims that we know of. He thinks he won't get caught."

CHAPTER TWENTY-THREE

Janey closed the front door. She turned to face Dr. Watson, who stood in the small foyer off the family room. The doctor wasn't much taller than Janey, and Janey was considered short, at five feet two. The doctor's hair was straight, about shoulder length, the color of 1970s wood paneling. There was nothing remarkable about her, an average thirtysomething woman, if you didn't count her Ivy League education, according to the degree hanging on her wall in her office, or the numerous publications in psychology journals that she'd mentioned on more than one occasion but Janey had never read.

"I've been worried about you. I've been trying to reach you all day," Dr. Watson said.

"You saw the news," Janey said.

They went into the kitchen and sat across from each other at the table. Janey didn't recall hearing a message from the doctor on the answering machine. Her cell phone had been turned off most of the day.

"Yes, I saw the news," Dr. Watson said. "Why didn't you call me?"

"Everything happened so quickly." The day had been a blur. It had started with the media outside her house, and then she'd had the panic attack while sitting in her car outside the school. Eventually, she'd ended up at her parents' house.

"I bumped into Christian's therapist outside. I told her I'd be taking over from here," Dr. Watson said.

Janey was confused. "I didn't think you worked with kids," she said.

"I'm a family counselor," Dr. Watson said. "And with the recent news, I want to make sure you and Christian have the right kind of support during this time. I think Christian is going to need someone who is better qualified to handle more than just some of the behavioral issues Carlyn was treating."

Janey was having mixed feelings about switching Christian's therapist. She liked Carlyn. She trusted her with Christian. But Dr. Watson had been treating Janey for several years now. Janey trusted her too. "Okay," she said. Bunnie hopped into the kitchen, stopped near Janey's legs. She picked the rabbit up, cuddled her. "This is Bunnie, the rabbit I told you about."

"Yes, I see that," Dr. Watson said. "How are her feet? Is she healing?"

"Yes, she's better." She put Bunnie down. "So how is this going to work?" she asked.

"I'm going to continue to see you in my office. I think it's best if we don't make any changes in your current treatment plan at this point. I don't want to disrupt the progress we've been making there." She set a bottle of pills on the table. "We can talk about what happened today at your next session. In the meantime, I thought you might need a refill to help you sleep."

Janey reached for the bottle. "Thank you," she said.

"Now, as for Christian, I'd like to work with him here in his home environment. The more comfortable he is, the more headway we can make."

"Okay," she said. Maybe this really was for the best. She did feel better just having the doctor here with her.

"It's settled then," Dr. Watson said. "Now, I think it's time I meet your son."

❦

Christian sat on the couch. His hands were in fists in his lap, while Janey tried to explain to him why Carlyn wasn't coming anymore.

"You didn't do anything wrong," she said.

Dr. Watson entered the room and walked right up to him. She didn't wait for Janey to introduce him.

"Hello, Christian," Dr. Watson said. "My name is Helen." She stood over him, taking up a position of authority. Janey braced herself for his response. It could be anything from silence to screaming and thrashing, with very little in between.

"Hello," Christian said, meeting the doctor's gaze. Janey was shocked. It had taken Carlyn three weeks before Christian would even acknowledge she was in the room.

Dr. Watson sat next to him on the couch. He angled his body toward her. His fisted hands opened. It was so strange to see him engage with somebody, anybody, in this way. The two had locked onto each other, not speaking, or it seemed as though they were having a private conversation without words. Their gazing lasted several long seconds, to the point of making Janey uncomfortable. She cleared her throat.

Dr. Watson kept looking at Christian as she spoke. "Janey, why don't you wait for me in the kitchen. I'm talking with Christian now."

"Oh, sure, okay." She returned to the kitchen. She was embarrassed, as though she'd been scolded by a parent and chased from the room. Bunnie hopped around her ankles. She picked her up and put her in the cage, gave her fresh water, pellet food. She didn't know what to do next, so she picked up her phone out of habit and then laid it back down. She stopped herself from checking her social media sites. She didn't want to know what people were saying about her, or if they blamed her for not being able to identify the Strangler.

In the next room, Dr. Watson and Christian talked in low voices. She couldn't make out what was being said.

Thirty minutes had passed, maybe more, when she heard Dr. Watson say to Christian, "I'm going to talk to your mom now. I want you to stay in here and play until we're done. Is that clear?"

"Yes," Christian said.

Dr. Watson joined Janey in the kitchen. They sat at the table.

"You never said how much you charge for house calls. I'm assuming it's more than your hourly fee?" Janey asked and then added, "I can't afford much."

"Whatever you were paying Carlyn will be fine. I suggest meeting with Christian two times a week at a minimum, at least until things with the media settle down. We'll go from there as to whether it needs to be more or less. Does that work for you?"

She nodded, although she was wondering where she was going to come up with the extra money for two sessions a week. But if it would help Christian, she'd figure something out.

"Maybe we can make things a little less formal between us, since I'll be coming into your home. How about you start calling me Helen?" she said. "It will be less confusing for Christian."

"Okay." She wasn't sure she was comfortable with this. She'd been calling her Dr. Watson since the beginning of her treatment.

"I want to ask you a few questions about Christian, if I may. I just need some background information for my file. I know some things about him that we discussed in *your* therapy, but I need to know more about *him* personally."

"Sure. Whatever I can do to help."

"When did you first notice Christian wasn't like other children?"

She was taken aback by the question. She'd expected the usual inquiry about Christian's behavior. How well did he play with other children? How did he respond to change? How did he express anger? How did he react in stressful situations?

Helen leaned forward. The expression on her face wasn't one Janey recognized, and definitely not one the doctor used in Janey's therapy. It was a look that said, *I don't have time for games. Tell me what you really think.*

"I think I've always known, even before he was born. I guess that sounds crazy."

"Not to me it doesn't," Helen said. "Why did you think he was different?"

"When I was carrying him, it was like I could feel this energy inside of me. Sometimes it frightened me. I wasn't sure I was strong enough to handle it, or if I was even worthy."

Helen was pressed up against the table. It seemed as though she couldn't pull the information out of Janey fast enough. "What kind of energy? Why did it frighten you?"

"It's not something that makes sense to anyone but me."

"Try me." Helen put her hand on Janey's arm, stopping her from rocking. She hadn't even realized she'd been doing it. "It's safe to say it to me," Helen added. "I'll understand."

Several seconds passed before she finally said, "He was the bright spot in the eye of a terrible storm."

CHAPTER TWENTY-FOUR

Twenty-four hours after the discovery of another victim in Minsi Lake, Geena knocked on the front door of a colonial-style house in the small town of Columbia, New Jersey, home of Amy Kaplan's parents.

A middle-aged woman in her fifties stood in the open doorway. The expression on her face told them she knew they were cops, and they weren't here with good news.

"Mrs. Kaplan," Geena said. "I'm Detective Brassard, and this is my partner, Detective Reed. We're with the Pennsylvania State Police." She produced her badge. The woman barely glanced at it.

"May we come in?" Geena asked.

Mrs. Kaplan stepped aside. They followed her to a small family room decorated in various shades of blue, from the blue carpeting and walls to the blue and white striped furniture that looked custom made, or perhaps it had been purchased from IKEA. Geena wasn't a good judge of the cost of home furnishings, having bought most of her furniture online at discount prices in overstock warehouses. Mrs. Kaplan sat on the edge of the couch cushion. Geena sat in the chair opposite her. Parker stood next to her. A glass coffee table covered with magazines and two remote controls separated them.

"Would you like to call your husband?" Geena asked.

"No," Mrs. Kaplan said, leading Geena to believe there was turmoil in the marriage. It wasn't all that unusual in cases where children went missing, or in this case a young adult, but still a child in the parents' eyes. The strain of not knowing what had happened to a loved one sometimes proved too much for a family to bear. They broke apart. Their lives crumbled.

There was no easy way to say it, and in Geena's experience from sitting through enough of these situations with Albert, it was best to say it in a straightforward manner, as though you were ripping off a Band-Aid. "We found your daughter."

Mrs. Kaplan covered her mouth, her hand shaking. Parker was quiet. They'd agreed on the ride over that Geena would take the lead.

She continued. "An excavation crew was draining a lake in Pennsylvania when they found her."

"How do you know it's her?" Mrs. Kaplan asked. "How do you know it's my Amy?"

"We used the dental records you filed with missing persons."

"Oh." She cried.

Geena got up and sat next to her on the couch. She put her hand on Mrs. Kaplan's back. She stayed like this for a few minutes, giving Amy's mother time to grieve and collect herself.

"Mrs. Kaplan," Parker said in a gentle voice. "Do you know why Amy was on Blue Mountain Drive in Pennsylvania?"

"She was visiting her boyfriend. She was thinking about transferring to the same college where he was going, some university in the Poconos. I told her I didn't think it was a good idea. She was only finishing up her sophomore year. A lot can happen in two years. I told her to wait, and if she was still dating him after college, then they could maybe look for a job in the same town. But she wouldn't listen. She was twenty years old. What was I supposed to do?"

Geena didn't have an answer for her. She'd read the reports in the missing persons file. No one among Amy's family or friends, including the boyfriend, were suspects. Amy wasn't Catholic. She had no affiliation with a specific church.

"It's really my Amy?" Mrs. Kaplan asked, her hands clenched in her lap.

"I'm so sorry," Geena said in a soothing tone. She went on to explain that they hadn't confirmed the cause of death yet. Mrs. Kaplan had questions, of course, but mostly she cried. She eventually called her husband. Parker talked with him on the phone.

When there was nothing more either she or Parker could do, she left her card on the table. "We'll be in touch," she said. They showed themselves out.

⚓

While Parker sat at Albert's desk and finished researching the fishermen and excavation crew Geena had interviewed at the lake, she sat at the long table in the conference room going through the files on each of the Strangler's victims. She opened Amy's file from missing persons. She printed a copy of Amy's photo and taped it to the bulletin board with the others. She was going on the assumption Amy was another Spring Girl. She disappeared in spring. The location where she'd disappeared fit with what they knew about the other girls. Her age and the length of her hair also matched the profile.

Geena stood and walked over to the map on the wall. Janey was the first known victim in 2011, when she was pulled from the Delaware River. Mia Snyder (2014) was found in Polly Acres Pond. Amy Kaplan (2012) and Valerie Brown (2018) were both found in Minsi Lake. And Jessica Lawrence (2017) was found in Martins Creek. They had been bound, raped, strangled, discovered in lakes and creeks within fifteen miles of each other. And every assault had occurred in spring. Why spring? The nice weather brought people outside to hike the trails, spend time in nature. Springtime was also the start of fishing season.

Maybe the Strangler liked to fish. She thought there had to be a reason he'd chosen springtime specifically, and it had to have been something that was personal, meaningful to him.

She returned to the table, continued scrolling through Amy's file. The boyfriend, Jason Whitmore, had had a solid alibi. Several witnesses confirmed he'd been in their presence at his apartment, playing video games well into the night after Amy had left his place and subsequently disappeared. Her vehicle was discovered later that evening by a local resident who happened to be driving home from his night shift as a security guard at the new branch of the hospital that had been built off Freemansburg Avenue. He'd pulled over when he'd noticed the passenger-side door of Amy's car had been left open, the interior light on, but there hadn't been anyone around. He'd noticed the flat tire and Jersey plates, thought maybe the person or persons had wandered into the woods and were possibly lost. He'd called 911, and the search for Amy had begun.

Geena put together a timeline from when Amy had left her boyfriend's house at three p.m. and from when her vehicle had been discovered on the side of the road close to one a.m., a total of ten hours. It was a lot of time for the Strangler to spend with his victim. But why hadn't they found her body when they'd searched the lake? Where had he hid her before he'd weighed her down? There were too many missing pieces.

She rubbed her eyes. She'd been staring at the files for the last few hours. Her coffee had gone cold. She checked her phone. She'd called Janey twice, left messages on her voice mail, but Janey hadn't returned either of her calls. They needed to get the cheek swab from Christian for the DNA test and ask her if it was possible her parents had talked with the media. There was a text message from Geena's mother letting her know Codis had been fed, walked. She replied with a quick Thank you as Parker walked into the conference room.

"What's the one thing all the Spring Girls have in common?" she asked, and she stretched. She didn't wait for him to reply. "They're all college students."

"Go on," Parker said. He pulled out the chair next to her and sat.

"Maybe we should dig a little more into the colleges, look at faculty, maintenance, commuters." The victims had appeared random at first glance. It wasn't so random now that they'd identified four girls, Amy possibly the fifth, all college students. Last she'd heard from Bill, he hadn't come up with anything in the girls' backgrounds that connected them. They had different majors, traveled in separate crowds. Two were members in Greek organizations, one in an honor society, the other a sorority. Nothing was matching up. Campus security hadn't even given them any leads. Even the church lead wasn't panning out. She'd gone through the recent intel in Valerie's file. She couldn't find any links to a church member or to Janey.

"We might not need to," Parker said. "I found a connection between Janey and one of the fishermen."

She sat up straighter. "Which one?"

"Josh Wheeler. They're coworkers. They also went to college together."

Now that got her attention. "Show me."

Parker used his smartphone and pulled up a photo of a guy in his late twenties or early thirties. He looked familiar. He was the guy who had stood too close to her. She'd had to ask him to take a step back.

"I saw a couple of photos on his Instagram account," Parker said. "Janey's tagged in some of them."

She supposed it was possible Janey could have been working with the Strangler and not even known it, since she didn't remember anything about him. And if Janey had been knocked out with chloroform, as Valerie had, then the chemical's effects on the brain could very well be the reason she had no memory of the event beyond the initial abduction.

Geena examined the photo again. His hair was sandy blond, a shade closer to Christian's color. "We need to talk to Janey and look into this Josh guy," she said.

"I'll fill Sayres in," Parker said. "Text Janey we're on our way."

Geena picked up her phone.

CHAPTER TWENTY-FIVE

Geena sat in the passenger seat next to Parker. They were on their way to Janey's house. He had one hand on the wheel, his right arm resting on top of the console. The sky was a hazy shade of gray. Drizzle dotted the windshield. He flipped on the wipers.

She checked her phone, listened to a recent voice mail message from Theo explaining that Albert had been stabilized and they would be moving him into a rehabilitation facility. There was a hitch in Theo's voice. She understood. She was worried about Albert too.

She shut off her phone, sitting with her thoughts about Theo's message. When they were closer to Janey's house, Parker asked, "How do you want to play this?"

"We get a sample of Christian's DNA first, and then we find out what she knows about Josh Wheeler."

"Agreed," he said. "Who's taking the lead on this?"

"I am," she said. "I've taken the lead since the beginning. I don't want to confuse her by switching things up. I want her to feel comfortable. We'll stick to our routine. I open, you close."

Parker pulled alongside the curb in front of Janey's house. An unmarked cruiser was parked farther down the street. They got out of the car and waved to the trooper as they made their way to Janey's front door. Parker pressed the doorbell.

Geena noticed the curtain move in the family room window. "Janey?" she called. "It's Detective Brassard and Detective Reed."

Janey opened the door. She looked weary. The single braid she wore over one shoulder had come undone. The elastic band holding it together had slipped and clung to a few stray ends. Her mouth opened as though she was going to say something, but rather than saying whatever was on her mind, she stepped aside and let them in.

"Thank you for seeing us," Geena said.

"Why did you tell them about me? There were reporters outside my house harassing me." Janey sat on the couch, hands in her lap.

"I'm sorry about that," Geena said, taking her position on the chair opposite Janey. "I don't know how the media got your name. I was hoping you could tell us. It didn't come from me or Detective Reed. I can promise you that."

"Then how did they find out?" Janey asked.

"Do you think your parents might've talked with them without your knowledge?" she asked.

"No," Janey said definitively.

"Okay, well, we're here for another reason. It has something to do with what we found in your medical records. And it has to do with your son," Geena said.

Janey stared at her hands in her lap. Christian's voice carried from one of the bedrooms down the hallway. "I was just trying to protect him," she said.

"Why do you feel you have to protect him?" Geena asked, although she was pretty sure she knew the answer. She moved to the edge of the seat cushion, eager for Janey's response. Parker had since moved to the arm of the chair. His body posture appeared relaxed, but she sensed the tension emanating from him.

"I think you know why," Janey said.

"I think I do. Is there any chance you were pregnant before the assault? Or perhaps you got pregnant soon afterward?"

"No," Janey said. "It was my first time. And last."

Geena let out a slow breath. Janey had been a virgin when she'd been raped. Geena flipped through the information they'd collected on the other victims in her mind, that photographic memory coming into play. The other girls hadn't been virgins when they'd been attacked, based on the background information they'd amassed.

"Are you telling us Christian is his son?" Parker asked.

Janey nodded.

Geena got up and sat next to her on the couch. "We're going to need a sample of Christian's DNA. The test is painless. I promise. We can swab his cheek. It won't take more than a second. We'd like to do it now. Right now."

"I think you need to hear something," Janey said, and she stood. Geena looked to Parker for some explanation as to what had happened, why Janey had suddenly seemed to change the subject. Parker shrugged. They followed her to the kitchen.

"I have twenty-six messages on my voice mail. Reporters wanting to talk with me. But there was one message that was different."

"What do you mean different?" Geena's pulse ticked up.

"It's creepy," Janey said. "It scared me."

"Play it for us," Parker said.

They listened to several messages from the local media asking for exclusive interviews and for the information Janey had provided to the police about the Strangler. But then a man's voice filled the room. It was deep and hoarse and sounded as though he was out of breath, asking if Janey had liked being raped, choked.

"Do you recognize the man's voice?" Parker asked as he jotted down the date and time of the message.

"No," Janey said. "I've never heard it before. It doesn't sound like anyone I know, if that's what you're asking."

"Do you know Josh Wheeler?" he asked. Geena shot him a look. They'd agreed to bring up Josh only after they'd gotten the DNA sample from Christian.

"He's my boss," Janey said.

"How well do you know him?"

"I only met him when I started working at the store," Janey said.

"How long have you worked at the store?" Parker asked.

"I started when Christian was two, so it's been about four years now."

"You didn't know him in college?"

Janey shook her head.

"What can you tell us about him?"

"Not much. He's a good boss, nice to work for."

"Ever see him outside of work?"

"No. Why?"

"Just making conversation," Parker said. "We're going to need to take your answering machine. Do you have another one you can use in the meantime?"

"No."

"Let's get you another one, then." He touched her arm reassuringly. "You don't need to be scared. We put a trooper outside your house. He's been there since yesterday."

"Since yesterday? Why? Do you know something? Am I in danger?" Janey's voice rose.

"It's just a precaution," Geena said, but she wasn't so sure now. What if the man on the tape was the Strangler? In a high-profile case in California that had been in the news recently, the killer had terrorized his victims by calling them on the phone.

151

"What about Christian?" Janey asked. "I don't want anyone to know who his father is."

"We'll do our best, but maybe you should prepare yourself," Geena said. "The media might not be far behind in making the connection."

Janey closed her eyes for a moment, nodded.

Parker said, "We really need Christian to do that DNA test now."

Janey said, "He's in his room."

~Helen Watson, Psy.D.
Patient: Janey Montgomery, ID 27112

Helen watches as Janey enters the office and sits in the chair across from her. She opens her notebook, writes the date and time. Janey wipes her eyes with a tissue, although her eyes are dry. Helen makes a note of it, how Janey doesn't seem to know when she's crying and when she's not.

"Have the reporters been bothering you again?" Helen asks.

Janey shakes her head. "No, no one's bothered me since the other morning."

"That's good, isn't it?"

Janey nods.

Helen decides to take the session in another direction, since the media doesn't seem to be Janey's concern at the moment. "Do you remember the homework assignment I gave you a few weeks ago? I asked you to write down all the things you love about Christian and all the things you don't love about him."

"I remember," Janey says. Her voice sounds stronger than it had in their last session, but Helen hears a falseness to it, a kind of strength Janey does not emanate otherwise.

"We already discussed the things you love about him. They were lovely."

"Thank you," Janey says. "They were all true."

"Why don't you tell me about the other half of the assignment? Why don't you tell me about the things you don't like about him? It's okay not to like everything about a person, even when they're your own child. It doesn't mean you don't love them."

Janey plays with the tissue in her hand, folding it, unfolding it. "I didn't write anything for that part of the assignment. I couldn't think of anything that I don't love about him," she says.

"But I saw that you wrote something down. Why don't you tell me what it is?" Helen asks.

Janey continues to fold and unfold the tissue. "I should get rid of the rabbit," she says. "I should find her a better home." She hesitates before adding, "A safer home. But I don't want to. I'm being selfish. I'm only thinking of myself and what I want."

It isn't unusual for Janey to switch topics, and Helen has learned to go along with it. She understands Janey better with each session. Janey doesn't like to tackle hard questions head on. She circles around them, talks about something else that on the surface doesn't appear to be related but in fact is. It's as though Janey cushions the blow in her own mind before delivering the bomb, a coping mechanism she's acquired, borne from tragedy.

"And what is it you want from the rabbit?" Helen asks.

"Something to cuddle. To love me back."

"Who do you think doesn't love you?"

Janey tears the tissue until there is nothing left but a pile of threads.

When Janey doesn't reply, Helen says, "Wanting someone to love you back doesn't sound like someone who is selfish. It's human nature to love and want to be loved in return."

"I should've seen it coming. I did see it coming. And I still didn't give the rabbit up."

"What did you see coming?"

"I told you. He put her on top of the hot stove. He says it was an accident." Janey pulls another tissue out of the pack, folds it into a small square.

"Who are we talking about? Who is he?" Helen asks. "I want you to say his name."

"Christian," Janey says.

"Christian told you it was an accident. But you don't believe him?" Helen asks, and she scribbles circles in her notebook. On the outside she is calm. She's far too skilled to show any emotion during a session. But inside, her heart is thumping. Her palms are sweaty.

"I do believe him," Janey says. "I do."

"Are you sure? You don't sound sure."

"It's not his fault. I'm the one who is selfish."

"Did he hurt the rabbit again? Is that what you're telling me?"

Janey shakes her head. "It's those detectives. They came back. Who do they think they are, anyway? They can't stop him."

Helen isn't certain who Janey is talking about here. She decides to sit and wait to hear whatever it is Janey says next. Although it's getting harder and harder to remain quiet and not interfere. Now, while she waits for Janey to continue, she's almost holding her breath, knowing she's getting closer to the truth of what Janey does and doesn't remember about that night.

"But I can. I can stop him," Janey says.

"Who are we talking about? Who can you stop?"

Janey hugs herself and starts rocking. At first her movements are slow, but they gain speed with each second that passes until she's shaking frantically in the chair.

Helen is running out of time. She will lose her soon, in part to Janey's mind shutting down, a protective reflex.

Helen leans in close. "Who can you stop?" she asks again.

Janey's rocking slows. "You were right," she says. "I did write something down in the other part of the homework assignment."

Helen is frustrated that Janey has shifted gears once again, but she tries hard not to let it show when she says, "Okay. Tell me, what don't you like about your son?"

Janey whispers, "He doesn't love me back."

CHAPTER TWENTY-SIX

Janey strapped Christian into the booster seat. She was exhausted from her late-night session with Helen, but she was up and on time this morning, ready to go back to work. She'd missed two days since the news had broken about her connection with the Strangler. She couldn't afford to miss another day. She glanced at the unmarked police cruiser parked across the street. She hadn't noticed him until the detectives had pointed him out when they'd swabbed Christian's cheek. She couldn't make out what he looked like. The interior of his car was darkened by shadows, the sun not fully up over the mountaintop.

She dropped her keys, watched as they skidded underneath her car. She had no choice but to get down on her hands and knees and pick them up. Every movement she made was under the watchful eye of the cop. His presence was supposed to make her feel safe, but instead it made her feel as though she'd done something wrong. She picked up her keys and scanned the street one more time, looking for signs of the media. They were nowhere in sight. She got into the car. Perhaps he'd chased them away. She should be so lucky.

She drove Christian to school, dropped him off without any trouble. Finally, she arrived at work, shoved her purse in the back room. She slipped down an aisle in which picture frames of assorted colors and sizes were displayed. She was sneaking around, hoping to avoid Josh.

Sometimes the way he looked at her made her uncomfortable. There was something in his eyes that she'd seen before in other boys she'd dated back in high school and during her brief year in college. She could tell he liked her. Seven years ago, she might've been flattered. She might've even welcomed an opportunity to date him. She couldn't deny he was cute, maybe even kind, but for his eyes. What did she see in his eyes that frightened her? Perhaps it was desire. She wasn't someone he could touch in the intimate ways a man touched a woman. Not now. Maybe not ever. Besides, she had Christian to consider. It would take an exceptional kind of man to put up with her son, to accept and love him for who he was.

Her mind flipped back to the detective's questions. Why had he asked her about him? Was he really just making conversation, like he'd said? She reached the end of the aisle, turned, and walked down another aisle, this one lined with wall paintings. The store was empty. She rounded the corner of another aisle and stopped. Josh was walking toward her. She couldn't turn around and say she hadn't seen him. She couldn't move forward. All she could do was stand there, watching as he came toward her.

"I was looking for you," he said. "There's a call for you in the office. It's the guidance counselor from the elementary school. She couldn't reach you on your phone."

She took a step back and pulled out her cell phone from her back pocket. Three missed calls from Christian's school. She mumbled, "Thanks," and rushed to the office at the back of the store.

"Mrs. Delacorte," she said. "Is Christian okay?"

"Yes, he's fine. But I'm afraid you need to come to the school right now. There's been an accident."

"What kind of an accident?" The room seemed to tilt. She steadied herself against the desk.

"We'll talk when you get here," Mrs. Delacorte said, and she hung up.

Josh was standing in the doorway. He smoothed his hair back from his forehead. He looked concerned.

"Everything okay?" he asked.

"I have to go," she said. "Something happened at school with Christian."

"Okay," Josh said, and he took a step closer to her. "Look, Janey, we need to talk."

"Not now."

"It's about the store, our customers . . ."

"I have to go," she said again and then brushed past him. She walked fast and then broke into a jog. She was running by the time she'd reached the door to the parking lot.

Janey sat in a plastic chair in front of Mrs. Delacorte's desk. The room was cluttered with books and pamphlets and the odd toy. A corkboard showcased pictures of Mrs. Delacorte with various students throughout the years, along with primitive drawings they'd made for her covered in hearts and rainbows and big yellow suns.

Christian waited outside the door, in the hallway. Papers and crayons were spread on the floor to occupy him while Mrs. Delacorte and Janey talked in private.

"I'm afraid we have a situation involving Christian and one of the students," Mrs. Delacorte said.

"Emma?" Janey asked.

"No," Mrs. Delacorte said. "Another little girl, Bella."

"What happened?"

"We're not entirely sure, but Bella and Christian were on the slide together. Bella fell."

Janey couldn't move. *Here it comes.*

"Bella said Christian pushed her. Two other little girls claim they saw him do it. Now, I understand this is coming from five- and six-year-olds. Neither I nor Mrs. Mitchell saw what happened," she said. "But I'm sure you can understand our concerns. It's not the first time Christian has been aggressive with the other children."

"I don't know what to say."

"That's not all. Bella's mother called a few minutes ago. Bella's arm is broken."

"Oh." She touched her neck.

"She wants Christian removed from the school."

"But that's not up to her, is it?"

"She's threatened to file a lawsuit if he's not removed."

"I'm sure it was an accident."

"Other parents have expressed their concerns."

"What are you saying?"

"Honestly, I'm not sure. I'm not sure what action we should take here," she said. "But I don't want to make any rash decisions. Let's wait for everyone to settle down a bit."

"And then what?"

Mrs. Delacorte pressed her lips together. "We'll have to decide what's best for everyone involved, but I am considering some kind of in-school suspension."

"I know my son, and I'm sure it was an accident. Can't we just finish out the school year?"

"Is he still getting outside help?"

"Yes." Her words came out in a rush. *Helen.* "He's seeing a new therapist. She can help him. She *is* helping him."

Mrs. Delacorte didn't look convinced, but she said, "Let's take some time to breathe. We'll reevaluate the situation when emotions aren't running so high. Once everyone has had a chance to calm down, we can decide where to go from there." Her lips pressed together again. She looked as though she wasn't sure if she should say anything more.

Then she added, "I know you said Christian is getting help, but are you getting help?"

"I told you I have someone coming to the house."

"I meant for you. There's been some talk among the teachers, parents."

So that was what this was really about—the Strangler. The rumors had started. And she had a strong suspicion the gossip around the school about her and her son wasn't good. Janey stood. She'd heard enough. "I hope Bella will be okay," she said, and she opened the door. She found Christian on the floor among the coloring books. "Come on," she said. She took his hand.

They headed down the hall to the exit.

Mrs. Delacorte called after them, "We'll talk in a few days."

Janey didn't break stride, clinging to Christian's hand. "Don't look back, baby," she said. "Just keep walking."

CHAPTER TWENTY-SEVEN

Geena scrolled through her notes on Josh Wheeler, although she didn't need to review them. All the information she'd dug up on him was imprinted in her memory. But she looked through them for something to do while she waited in the conference room for the rest of the team. Parker stood in front of the map that had been hung on the wall. Red pins identified the locations of where the girls' bodies had been found.

"His hunting grounds are within a fifteen-mile radius," Parker said.

"Yes," Geena said. "What are you thinking?"

"I'm thinking he's got to live nearby."

Bill entered the conference room and sat at the table. He was good at research, finding information and people, known on the team as their unofficial tech guy. Geena was thinking about their problem with the leak. Maybe Bill could help. It wasn't like she could ask Albert, in his current condition.

She'd stopped at the rehabilitation center where Theo had said they'd moved him. She'd had to talk the nurse at the front desk into letting her see him, promising she'd stay a few minutes and no more. She'd wanted to avoid bumping into Pearl during regular visiting hours and the possibility of another confrontation. Pearl was scared, angry, and she'd lashed out at the first person she could find, which just happened to have been Geena. Pearl had finally gotten what she'd wanted all these years, to get Albert away from his job and to stay at home with her, and now this had happened. Having Geena turn up had only exacerbated an already stressful situation.

Geena had sat by his bedside, held his hand. He'd struggled to find his words, but he'd signaled for her to talk, to tell him about the case. He wanted to *know*, which was what Pearl had feared. But Geena had told him where they were in the investigation, the DNA sample taken from Janey's son.

She had barely gotten the last bit of information out about her potential lead when Pearl had pushed the door open, mumbling, "I forgot my phone," stopping cold when she saw Geena in the room. "Get out," she'd said. "Nurse!" she'd called.

"I'm leaving," Geena had said. She'd squeezed Albert's hand and left.

Now Geena looked to Bill. "We still don't know who leaked Janey's name," she said. "She seems certain it's not her parents. I'm thinking it could be this unnamed source of Albert's."

"Say no more. I'll dig around," Bill said. "See what I can find out."

Lieutenant Sayres walked in and took his place at the podium. The rest of the team filed in behind him, taking their seats at the tables, chatting about the baseball game the previous night. The smell of coffee was strong.

"Listen up," the lieutenant said. "We've got the DNA sample from the boy. It was sent to the lab. Once it's confirmed he's the Strangler's son, we'll get a photo and use the software with the age-progression feature. As for Amy Kaplan, we're going on the assumption she's also one of the victims. Her remains are under the care of our resident forensic anthropologist. I'm going to let Brassard fill you in on a possible suspect. Brassard."

Geena stepped to the front of the room. Albert had always addressed the team for her, even though she'd been more than capable. He'd been the senior detective, and it had been out of respect that everyone had deferred to him. But Albert was no longer here. And he'd made too many mistakes with this case. She was ready to take the lead. She tacked an enlarged photo of Josh Wheeler onto the board.

"Our suspect is Joshua Wheeler, goes by Josh. He's thirty years old, born and raised in Easton, Pennsylvania. He graduated from Easton High School in 2007, attended college in the Poconos from the fall of 2007 through spring 2011, graduated with honors with a degree in business. He played baseball all through high school and college, enjoys fishing. He's lived in Northampton County his entire life. He's a local boy, homegrown, familiar with the geography, mountains, lakes, and river."

She glanced around the room. Everyone was listening. She continued. "We know of a connection to at least two of the girls." She paused. This was where it got interesting. The first victim was typically someone the killer knew or someone he'd seen during his regular day. "Janey Montgomery, the first victim and only survivor, not only went to the same university for one year, but they are currently coworkers at a local craft store in Easton."

"What's the likelihood she'd still be working with him if he was the one who assaulted her?" Craig asked. He was leaning back in the chair, tapping a pencil on the tabletop.

"Right. But as we know, she doesn't remember anything about who assaulted her."

"That's a good point," Sayres said.

She nodded. "As it turns out, the fourth victim, Jessica Lawrence, also attended the same college for one semester before transferring, although she wasn't there at the same time as Mr. Wheeler." She'd found this second connection after leaving Janey's and looking further into Josh. "But that's not all. Mr. Wheeler was also one of the fishermen at Minsi Lake when Amy Kaplan was discovered."

"Returning to the scene of the crime," Craig said.

"Who's bringing this Wheeler in for questioning?" Bill asked.

"This one's Reed's and Brassard's. They found him," Sayres said. "Does Wheeler have any connection to the girls' church?" he asked.

"Not that we found," she said.

Sayres nodded. "Let's get it confirmed. In the meantime, we'll keep digging into the victims' backgrounds and colleges and look for other leads. Make sure we get a list of every single employee on those campuses. Faculty, staff, volunteers, cafeteria workers, janitors, everybody."

"I thought we were focusing on Wheeler?" Geena asked.

"We are. But I'd feel better if we did our due diligence on this one. We can't take any chances and grab the wrong guy. There's too much at stake."

Geena and Parker sat behind the building of the craft store in the area where employees parked, waiting for Josh Wheeler. She checked the time. "Where is he?"

No sooner had she asked the question than a black jeep was pulling into the lot, the kind with a roll bar and soft top. Josh got out of the car.

"That's him," she said, and both she and Parker exited their vehicle.

"Mr. Wheeler," she called, her strides long and purposeful, as though she expected him to run. Instead, he waved as she approached. Apparently, he recognized her from the other day at Minsi Lake when she'd taken down his information.

"Hi there," he said. "What can I do for you?" He was smiling, looking back and forth between the two detectives as though he hadn't a care.

"This is Detective Reed," she said.

Josh nodded at Parker.

"We need you to come down to the station with us and answer a few questions," Parker said.

"What's this about?" he asked. "I have to get back to work. I manage the store," he said, panic creeping into his voice.

"We have some questions about one of your employees. We can talk here, or we can talk in private at the station," she said.

"One of my employees? Does this have something to do with Janey?"

Parker nodded. "Shouldn't take too long," he said.

Josh looked back at the store, hesitated, and then agreed to go with them to the station.

They rode to headquarters mostly in silence, commenting on the weather, the forecast for more rain tonight, whether the Phillies game would be postponed. They kept the conversation casual and friendly.

When they reached headquarters, they immediately escorted Josh into one of the interview rooms. Geena sat across from him, while Parker got him a cup of coffee and a bottle of water. They were trying to put him at ease.

She let him know the interview was being recorded. Josh's eyes darted around the room, caught sight of the video camera. He rubbed his palms on the top of his thighs.

"What can you tell us about Janey?" she asked.

"Did something happen to her?"

"What do you mean?"

"I've been following the news. And then I heard about her son on the radio about an hour ago, when I was out for lunch."

Geena stiffened. She and Parker had been focused on collecting information on Josh and picking him up. They hadn't heard any news.

"What about her son?" Parker asked.

"Is it true? Is Christian the Strangler's son?"

"Why don't you tell us?" Geena asked.

"I have no idea. I never asked Janey about Christian's father. I just know he's not in the picture," Josh said.

Parker's phone went off. He checked it and then said, "Excuse me," and left the room.

"Have you talked with Janey today?" she asked.

"She was at the store earlier this morning. But then she got a call from the school about Christian, and she had to go."

"Did she tell you what the call was about?"

"No, but she looked upset about it."

"How close are the two of you? Do you talk to each other outside of work?"

"We're not that close. Janey mostly keeps to herself."

"Does that bother you?"

"No," he said, a little too defensively.

"How would you describe your relationship, then?"

"Coworkers. Maybe friends. That's it. We've never dated, if that's what you're asking."

"But you'd like to date her?" she asked.

"Look, I'll admit I'd like to get to know her better, but it's okay if she's not interested. I'm not mad about it."

"How long have you known Janey?"

"She was a freshman my senior year in college, but I didn't really know her then. I mean, we never hung out or anything. We traveled in different crowds."

"But you did know her?"

"Yeah," he said. "A couple years after I graduated, she came into the store looking for work. I hired her. I knew she'd had a kid and needed a job. And I'm glad I did. She's good with the customers, and the kids love her craft workshops during the summer months."

Geena wasn't getting anything from him that seemed out of the ordinary. He was extremely nervous, but even that wasn't unusual for someone who had never been questioned by a detective before.

"How do you know Jessica Lawrence?"

"I don't know her."

"She went to the same college as you." She pretended to check her notes.

"I don't know every girl who went to the same college as me."

"But you know most of them?"

"No. I didn't say that."

She pushed a photograph of Jessica Lawrence toward him. "Does she look familiar to you? Take your time."

He studied the picture, shrugged. "No, she doesn't. I've never seen her before."

"Okay," she said, and she put the picture back in her file.

"What about this girl?" She took out another photo, this one of Valerie Brown.

"Oh yeah," he said. "I've seen her picture in the news."

"That's right," she said. "Ever see her around before?"

"No."

She took Valerie's photo and placed it back inside the folder. Either he was an exceptional liar or he was telling the truth. "Where were you on Friday, March thirtieth?"

"Good Friday? I was visiting my uncle for the holiday. I was with family. I got up early Saturday morning to drop a line in the water. It was opening day for trout season."

"Where was this? Someplace local?"

"A bit north from here," he said. "Lake Harmony."

"And your uncle will confirm you were with him the whole time?"

"Yeah. And so can my parents, cousins, and aunt. I told you I was with family."

"All night?"

"Yeah. All weekend. What's this about anyway?"

Parker popped his head in. "Can I talk to you for a minute?" he asked.

"Sure," she said. "Hang tight," she said to Josh. "I'll be right back. Can I get you anything?"

"No." He sat back in the chair, his brow furrowed.

She picked up her file and left the interview room.

"What's up?" Geena asked Parker now that they were back at their desks.

"Janey called. She was hysterical. Apparently, Josh was right, and someone leaked to the media about her son being the Strangler's kid."

Geena dropped into the chair, frustrated. But she supposed it was only a matter of time before someone in the media put it together.

"Do you think Albert's source also knew about her son?" He leaned against her desk. "Because if not, who else could it be?" He pulled himself up straight when Sayres walked in.

"I guess you heard," the lieutenant said.

"Janey called a few minutes ago," Parker said. "She's pretty upset with us."

"We've got Bill looking into it," Geena added.

"Where is this Josh Wheeler?" Sayres asked.

"I've got him sitting in an interview room."

"Is he our guy?"

"If he is, he's one heck of a liar."

"Get him to agree to a DNA test. Let's end this thing."

Geena got up, headed for the interview room where Josh sat waiting. Parker followed her. She had already established a rapport with Josh. Parker would step in if she needed him.

She opened the door to find Josh slumped over, head down, hands clasped between his legs. "Thanks for waiting," she said, and she sat across from him.

He looked up. She sensed he had something he wanted to say, so she waited for him to speak.

"I like her," he said. "I've always liked her. She's smart. And pretty."

"Who are we talking about here?"

"Janey," he said. "But I'm not some creepy stalker. I'm not that guy. I'm not the Strangler."

"Okay," she said. "There's a simple way you can prove it."

"How?"

"Provide us with a DNA sample." She didn't give him an opportunity to interrupt. "The test is simple. A swab of your cheek, and you can be back to the store in a matter of minutes." She passed the consent form across the table. "What do you say?"

He looked at the form. "Why should I agree to this?"

"I can't think of a reason why you shouldn't."

He signed the form.

She stood. "I'll be right back with the kit, and then you can be on your way."

CHAPTER TWENTY-EIGHT

Janey was still shaking after hanging up the phone with Detective Reed. She'd been ambushed by a reporter when she'd returned home from the elementary school. She couldn't believe the reporter was the same woman she'd watched on the small television in her kitchen while she'd cooked dinner. The woman on TV, the one with the red hair and green eyes, was compassionate. She had a knack for teasing the story out of a person, tugging at your heartstrings. But to have this same woman coming to Janey's home, lurking outside on her sidewalk, wanting to ask her questions, was something completely different. This wasn't some two-minute clip about someone else's problems.

This was Janey's life.

She stood off to the side of the family room window and peeked around the curtain, looked out at the street. It was empty, minus the police officer who was supposed to be protecting her. So far, he'd gotten out of his car once, when a male reporter had gotten too close to the house, and Janey had screamed at him to get off her front lawn. The officer had jumped out of his cruiser and guided the man off her property, restored order. The media had hung around for a little while after that, lingering on the sidewalk but not coming any closer before they'd climbed into their vehicles and driven away.

And Christian. He'd watched the scene from the same family room window with nothing more than a vague interest.

She pulled the curtain closed. "Do you want to watch TV?" she asked.

She wasn't about to try to leave the house again, even though the news van had long gone. She'd called the store and told them she wouldn't be returning to work today. She had no idea as to what she was going to do with Christian tomorrow, because she wasn't sending him back to school anytime soon. How could she after the news about who his father was had been broadcast for the whole town to hear? But Janey couldn't call off work tomorrow. She needed the money. And her mother was teaching classes at the community college and couldn't babysit. Janey thought about calling her father but instead found herself calling Helen.

There was a knock at the front door. A quick glimpse out the window told Janey what she needed to know. She rushed to unlock it and pulled it open.

"Helen," she said, not bothering to hide how relieved she was to see her.

"What happened?" Helen asked, and she followed Janey into the kitchen. She put her purse on the counter and dropped her keys alongside it.

Janey's shoulders relaxed. Help was here. "Everyone knows who Christian's father is. It was all over the news. And . . . and I got a call from the school. He got in trouble." What a relief to say it out loud without judgment.

"Yes, I heard the news. But what happened at the school?" Helen asked in her no-nonsense voice, one that said she would take control, handle the situation. All Janey would have to do was leave him in Helen's capable hands.

"He pushed a little girl off the slide."

"I see. Did the little girl get hurt?"

"She broke her arm." Janey covered her mouth, unable to say anything more.

Helen nodded, then entered the family room, where Christian sat on the couch. Janey followed her but stopped in the entranceway, hanging back to listen.

"Hello, Christian," Helen said.

"Hello," he said.

"Mind if I join you?" Helen sat next to him and turned off the TV. He didn't scream and holler or pitch a fit that she'd shut off his program. *Amazing.*

"Your mom tells me you got into a bit of trouble in school."

He didn't respond, staring into Helen's eyes, unblinking.

"Did you push a little girl off the slide?" Helen asked.

"No," he said.

Helen looked past Christian at Janey.

"Why would your teacher think you did?" Helen asked, returning her focus to him.

"I don't know," he said.

"Did the girl say or do something you didn't like?"

"No."

"Was she teasing you or not being nice to you?"

"No."

"Then why did you push her?"

"I didn't."

"You can tell me the truth. I won't be mad."

He didn't say anything.

"Are you sorry she got hurt?"

He shrugged.

"Is that a yes or a no?"

"I don't know."

Janey turned her back on them then and walked into the kitchen. She turned on the faucet at the kitchen sink and rinsed out a cup, drowned out their voices. Bunnie hopped around her cage. She gave her some water and leafy greens. Christian wasn't sorry Bella had gotten hurt. Saying he didn't know if he was sorry felt like an admission to her that he really did push the little girl off the slide.

Helen talked with Christian on the family room couch for a long time. Then she picked up her car keys and purse off the kitchen counter. She told Janey not to worry. She would handle everything, and she would see her later. She left without saying anything more.

After Helen had gone, Janey and Christian ate dinner in silence. She'd finished cleaning the last dish when her cell phone went off. She'd had every intention of ignoring it, assuming it was another reporter looking to tell her side of the story. Although most of the calls she'd received all afternoon had come in on the landline. She no longer had an answering machine, so no one could leave a message. The detectives had taken the machine with them. She suspected they'd be back, maybe with a new machine, definitely with more questions.

She recognized the store's number on her phone and answered before it went to voice mail.

"I don't know what to say other than I'm sorry," Josh said.

She closed her eyes, said nothing. Her stomach worked itself into a knot. The little food she'd eaten at dinner backed up in her throat.

"I'm sorry to be the one who has to tell you this, but it's best you don't come in to work tomorrow."

"I don't understand," she said. But she did understand. She understood perfectly. It was what she'd feared. Friends, coworkers, and the community were turning their backs on her and her son, blaming the victim. "It's about what happened to me, isn't it? And Christian?"

"We had reporters camped out in front of the store most of the day. I mean, that's what I was told. I wasn't there. Do you know where I was?" His voice grew louder. "No, of course you don't."

"I can't afford to miss work," she blurted, ignoring what he was telling her. "You know I need the money."

"We didn't make one sale today. Not one customer came into the store to buy something. And those that did venture inside, they came in to . . . well, I don't know what they came in for. Maybe to be nosy. I don't know. But I had to do something. I called my uncle. He thinks you should take some time off, not come into the store for a while. Maybe when things calm down, you can come back."

"You're letting me go?" She couldn't believe Josh had called his uncle. His uncle had stores up and down the East Coast.

"I'm afraid I don't have a choice," he said. "I really am sorry."

CHAPTER TWENTY-NINE

Geena pushed the food around on her plate. She was starving but found she couldn't eat. Codis curled around her feet, his head on the top of her sneaker, her shoelace hanging from his mouth. Ever since he'd been a pup, he'd had a taste for shoelaces. She'd come home after a long day of classes and find her shoes scattered throughout the apartment, the laces soggy and wet and frayed. Now, he sucked on the ends more than he chewed. She supposed it was out of habit, or quite possibly a form of comfort now that he was old. She leaned over, patted his head. He grunted in appreciation.

The clock over the kitchen sink ticked softly in the silence. The light of the moon slipped between the cracked blinds. The drizzle that had coated the streets and lawn had stopped. The sky was clearing. The night was bright.

She got up from the table, scraped the half-eaten chicken salad into the garbage, dropped the dish in the sink. Her phone lit up.

Bill had sent a group text to the team. He was at headquarters, after most of them had gone home. He texted, The creepy caller on Janey's answering machine looks to be a dead end. Just some wacko getting his rocks off. We raided his house, picked up his computer and phone, but it's not looking like he's our guy.

She replied, thanking Bill for the update, suggested he head home. Say hi to Amanda for me, she added. Bill had been married for sixteen years. She'd gone to their anniversary party last summer, a small cookout with the other investigators on the team. When she thought back to the last few years, the get-togethers, whether it was kids' birthdays or anniversaries or just the occasional summer barbeque, she realized all her social interactions were with cops. She couldn't remember the last time she'd gotten together with a girlfriend, or at least not one who worked outside law enforcement.

She checked the time and then changed into her workout clothes, picked up the handouts she'd printed about self-defense and safety awareness. Once a month she volunteered at the community center, teaching basic self-defense classes to women and teenage girls. Teach them how to fight, flee, in hopes they could avoid becoming another statistic.

She drove to the center, parked, and entered the building. A group of six women and two sixteen-year-old girls were waiting for her in one of the fitness rooms. She introduced herself and for the first fifteen minutes talked about safety awareness. "Never walk and talk on your phone. If you need to take a call, find someplace safe to put your back against the wall. Always be aware of your surroundings. And don't wear headphones on the street. You'll never hear if someone comes up behind you. Always have your keys out and ready. The last thing you want to do is waste time fishing around in your purse or pockets. It leaves you vulnerable to an attack." She rattled off a dozen more tips, then passed around the handout, which highlighted everything she'd just said.

For the last forty-five minutes of class, she showed the group basic self-defense moves and what to do if they were grabbed from behind, if their hair was pulled, if they were being choked. "Use your voice if you can," she said. "If you have no other option but to fight, you must commit to it. Make the strike count."

"Anaya," she called to one of the women who had taken the class a few times before. The more you practiced the techniques, the more they became instinctual. "What body parts are we aiming for again?"

"Eyes, nose, ears, throat, knees, and—my personal favorite—groin." She grinned.

Everyone laughed.

When class ended, she thanked the women for coming, asked them to come back and to bring their friends with them.

Afterward Geena felt invigorated, as though she'd taken back some control after a long few days. She hoped the group was leaving with the same feeling. She was packing up her bag when her phone went off. Angie, the forensic nurse who had examined Janey, was finally getting back to her.

The next morning, Geena sat across from Angie at their favorite coffee shop on New Street in Bethlehem. It was seven a.m. The doors to the small corner shop had just opened. They were the first customers, but soon the place would be a bustle of activity, with morning commuters ordering their favorite liquid drug to kick-start the day.

They took their usual spot, a table near the window so they could watch the comings and goings not only inside the shop but also on the street. Geena liked to have an open view of her surroundings, preferring to sit with her back against the wall, just as she'd suggested in class. She looked around, noticed a young guy who had walked in with his dog, a pit bull mix. The coffee shop was a dog-friendly business. A mother and child walked in behind him. The little girl's cheeks were smeared with jelly. The mother wore slippers. Nothing unusual for the neighborhood.

Geena pushed the manila folder she'd brought with her across the table toward Angie. Inside was the copy of the written report of the exam Angie had performed on Janey. "Do you remember this girl?" she asked. "The kit seems to be lost."

"Why doesn't that surprise me? They're either lost or sitting on a shelf somewhere and never processed." Angie shook her head in disgust and opened the file, read the report. When she finished, she pushed the folder back toward Geena. "I had no idea she was the first victim, not until I saw her face on the news."

"What can you tell me about her?"

"On the record, I'd tell you exactly what's in the file," Angie said. "Off the record, I'd tell you that her mother was a piece of work. She made it very difficult for me to do my job. She didn't want me touching her daughter and, I quote, 'in her most intimate of places.' She insisted her daughter was a virgin, a good Catholic girl. I don't question Janey was a good kid. She was, how shall I say, immature for her age. I believe she was eighteen or nineteen years old at the time, but her worldview was more like that of a fourteen-year-old kid." She shook her head. "It broke my heart to see what was done to her."

Geena reached for Angie's hand, squeezed it. After a moment she asked, "Is there anything else you remember?"

Angie took her time before responding. She turned the cup around in her hands. When she finally spoke, her voice had transformed into the soft, tender one she used with victims and with parents of victims. "Janey didn't talk much during the exam, but that's not uncommon. I explain the steps, what I'm doing. I answer any questions they may have." She paused. "You know, now that I think about it, she did ask what the chances were that she was pregnant. She said she refused, and I'm quoting here again, 'the abortion pill.' I told her there was always a chance, but I didn't find semen. But then again, the exam didn't take place for more than forty-eight hours after she was admitted to the hospital. She'd been cleaned up by then. But you read the report. I did find evidence of sexual assault. There was some trauma, abrasions."

Geena nodded.

Angie continued. "I don't think anyone was sure what happened to her. I think they thought at first it was an attempted suicide by drowning. They assumed she jumped from the bridge. And I remember she didn't have any defensive wounds. But the marks on her neck, wrists, and ankles were big clues something else was going on. Add to the fact she wasn't talking to anyone, not even to her parents. I think someone from the psych department got her to open up. Once they learned she'd been abducted, they looked closer at her injuries and suspected she may have been raped too. They got her to agree to the exam."

Geena had seen in the file that Janey had talked to someone in the psych department during her hospital stay. But Janey hadn't included the psych evaluation with the other medical records.

"Why do some girls fight back and others don't?" she asked.

Angie sat back in the chair. "What are we talking about here?"

"You've examined hundreds of girls. What do you think makes certain girls victims?" she asked.

"The conversation we should be having is what makes certain men rapists. What we as a society should be concentrating on is changing *their* behavior. We need to stop looking at the victim and asking what they did or didn't do wrong."

"You're right. In a perfect world, you're absolutely right."

"But it's not a perfect world, is it? And to answer your question, I don't know why certain girls become victims and others don't. But I can tell you this. It doesn't mean they're weak. They get mixed up with the wrong guy. Or they could just be at the wrong place at the wrong time. Maybe the bastard lives under the same roof with them. There are endless scenarios. As to why some fight back and others don't? People respond to fear, to trauma, in their own way. It's what makes us human. It's what makes *you* human. And there's no shame in that either way."

Angie had a gift for understanding how a victim thinks and feels. It wasn't just a violation of their bodies but of so much more. The price they paid went deeper than broken bones, cuts and bruises, humiliation.

They were robbed of ever feeling safe again, stripped of the freedom to move around in the world without the fear of being attacked.

It was no way to live.

But so many women were living it anyway, the survivors. Janey.

Outside the shop window, a man hopped off his bicycle. He fiddled with a lock, wrapping the chain around a no parking sign. A line had formed at the counter eight people deep. Most of them were staring at their phones. A few wore earbuds, gym gear, fueling up before their big workout.

"I have one more question for you," Geena said. "Did Janey give you any indication that she had any idea who might've done this to her?"

"Are we still off the record?"

She nodded.

"There was nothing she said outright. Maybe she knew him. Maybe she didn't. But my guess is that she was familiar with him. Maybe he was someone she'd seen around somewhere. Most victims are assaulted by someone they know, but you know that." Angie picked up her coffee and took a sip before setting it down again. "The news report was right? Janey was pregnant, then? She had the baby?"

"It seems so," Geena said.

CHAPTER THIRTY

Janey found Christian sitting in the grass in the backyard with the rabbit in his lap. She stood on the small patio, gazed at the back of his head. His one ear stuck out farther and was slightly lower than the other one. Something about the little imperfection pressed against her heart. She was overcome with a fierce urge to throw her arms around him, protect him from the cruelties of the world. She wondered if any of his classmates had noticed his lopsided ears. Had they made fun of him? Would some girl break his heart one day because of it? No mother wanted to see their child hurt, made fun of, which reminded her of poor little Bella falling off the slide and breaking her arm. No mother wanted to believe their child was capable of being the one who could hurt someone else.

Another thought crossed her mind. If Christian had pushed the little girl off the slide, was he also capable of doing something much worse to the rabbit, beyond putting her on top of a hot stove?

"Who do you have there?" she asked, and she rushed to where he was sitting in the yard.

"Bunnie." He looked up at her. "I think she likes me," he said, beaming.

"Of course she does," she said, scolding herself for thinking badly of him. Everyone else seemed to think of him in this way. Even she had her moments, while confessing her darkest fears to Helen during therapy. And she hated herself for it. It didn't feel natural to entertain such thoughts about her child. She sat next to him. The ground was damp from morning dew and all the rain they'd had in the last few weeks. She scratched behind Bunnie's ear.

"She makes a funny noise," Christian said.

"She's grinding her teeth. It's her way of purring," she said. "It means she's happy."

"She's happy being with me?" He phrased it as a question.

"She wouldn't be purring otherwise," she said, and she hugged him, the first hug of the day. She couldn't wait to tell Carlyn about this moment, what was happening right now with Christian and Bunnie. Carlyn would be so proud of how far he'd come with the rabbit. But she remembered Carlyn wasn't coming to see Christian anymore. Well, she would just have to tell Helen.

"Janey," her mother called, marching into the backyard from the side of the house. Father Perry was with her. "There you are," she said, and she stopped, taking in Janey and Christian sitting on the wet grass. "What on earth are you doing?"

"Nothing," Janey said, and she stood, brushed the dirt from her jeans. She offered a shy hello to Father Perry. Christian stood, Bunnie in his arms, and went into the house. They followed him through the back door leading into the kitchen. Janey motioned for her mother and Father Perry to sit at the table. She put Christian and the rabbit in front of the TV in the family room.

"Can I get you something to drink?" she asked when she returned.

"I'd love a cup of tea," her mother said.

Janey heated water on the stove. After a few minutes, she set two steaming cups on the table. "I didn't know how you take yours," she said to Father Perry. Her mother took hers extra sweet with three spoons of sugar.

Janey sat across from them and tucked her hands between her thighs.

Outside, car doors slammed. The reporters were returning for another shot at her and her son. She'd made sure the doors were locked. She'd pulled the blinds on all the windows so no one could see inside her home, so their accusing eyes couldn't reach them. And their questions couldn't penetrate the brick walls, no matter how loudly they shouted.

"I brought Father Perry to see you." Her mother smoothed her skirt, one that dropped to her ankles, a modest length, prudent. "I thought it might be a good idea for you to talk with someone."

"I already see someone," Janey said.

"Yes," her mother said. "What's her name again?"

"Dr. Watson. Helen." Someone at the hospital had given her Helen's information. She didn't remember who. Much of her memory during that time was blurry. Her stay in the hospital and then the weeks and months that followed drifted in and away, a fog that had never lifted. It wasn't until January, when Christian was born, that she'd snapped out of whatever trance she'd been under. But then she'd slipped into a different kind of half consciousness, up all night with a colicky baby. She'd spent the next several months sleep deprived. Then the next few years had become long, never-ending days of dirty diapers and tantrums.

Janey turned away from her mother and said to Father Perry, "I'm afraid she brought you here for nothing." Anything she had to say to the father would not be said in front of her mother.

"Janey!" her mother snapped.

"I see." Father Perry put his cup down. "Well, maybe some prayer would be in order before I go."

She looked away. "I don't feel like praying," she said.

Her mother clutched her chest. "Janey Montgomery, I did not raise you to be rude. You will do exactly what Father Perry asks you to do. Or, or . . ."

"Or what? What will you do, Mom?" She didn't know where the defiance was coming from. She'd never talked back to her mother before, and definitely not in front of other people, a priest no less.

She'd always been the good daughter, the good girl. But her mother must know she wasn't that girl anymore.

For a moment her mother was stunned into silence. Her neck and cheeks were flushed. Something crossed her mother's face, sort of like a light bulb appearing above her head. She turned to Father Perry. "It's all the pressure she's under, which is exactly why I brought you here in the first place. The media and the police, asking questions that are really none of their business. I mean, if Janey knew anything about who's done this to us—" She caught herself. "That's right, to *us*," she said, and she spoke directly to Janey when she asked, "Do you know how hard it's been for your father and me? Seeing you hurt? Seeing you struggle and not knowing how to help? We don't know what to do, how to handle it all. And I thought maybe Father Perry could help us. Isn't that right, Father? Father?" Her mother's hand flitted about her chest, finally resting in her lap.

Father Perry turned toward Janey. "Perhaps your mother is right. But maybe you would be more comfortable talking in private? We can schedule something at my office if you'd like."

"I'd really like to be there," her mother said.

"Would you rather we schedule a family session?" he asked.

She didn't answer. She stared past the father to the entranceway of the family room, where the television was turned down low, the cartoon's beeps and buzzers a muffled sound.

"Mommy!" Christian called. "It doesn't work." He was talking about the remote control. They'd been having trouble with it for a while now. Maybe the batteries were dying. "Mommy," he called again. "Change the channel!"

"Excuse me," she said, and she got up from the table. She was sorry for the pain she'd caused her parents. She never wanted to hurt them. But she couldn't go back to being the daughter she was before the attack. The open, bright-eyed kid they'd raised had shriveled up and withered away. The new woman she'd become was the best they were going to get.

CHAPTER THIRTY-ONE

"Brassard," Sayres called as he walked past her desk on his way to the conference room at headquarters.

She pushed her chair back and stood, followed him into the room, where photos of the Spring Girls covered the wall. She had to force herself not to look over his shoulder at their faces. She caught herself peeking while he sipped his coffee and stared at the paperwork in his hand. She couldn't help it. Something about the girls' eyes drew her in. It was as though they were pleading with her to make it stop, to catch him. She wanted to tell them she was trying, but it wasn't easy. He wasn't leaving them much evidence, packing up his tent and taking it with him.

"We got the DNA on the kid." Sayres passed the report to her. "According to this, there's no question Christian is the son of our guy."

She scanned it. "And Josh Wheeler's DNA?"

"We didn't get that back yet," he said. "Let's get a facial composite on the son with an age-progression feature."

Parker walked into the conference room. "There's a call for you," he said to the lieutenant.

Sayres left to take the call.

"What did I miss?" Parker asked.

"Janey's son is a match," she said. "Do we have photos of Christian? Anything from her social media pages we could use?"

"I checked Facebook, Instagram, Twitter, you name it," Parker said. "Most of the posts were dated seven years ago. There are some recent ones where she was tagged by some coworkers, but nothing of her son."

"Seven years ago. That was right around the time of the assault," she said.

"And if she's been trying to hide her son's identity, she wouldn't post photos of him," Parker said. He added, "We could always ask her to text some over to us."

"I think it's something we should ask for in person," Geena said. "She's going to need to understand we want to show it to the public. And after the latest leak, she may be a little reluctant to just hand them over."

Geena and Parker left headquarters and drove straight to Janey's house and parked. Geena got out of the car and noticed an empty coffee cup lying in the gutter, the rim smeared with lipstick. She bent down, picked it up.

"What do you want to bet this belongs to the redhead on the evening news?" she said to Parker as they made their way to Janey's front door. She tossed the cup in the outside trash can.

She knocked. Twice. Waited. There was movement inside, someone shuffling around. She knocked again. When she didn't get an answer, she called, "Janey, it's Detective Brassard and Detective Reed."

"It's okay, Janey," Parker added. "We're alone. There's nobody else out here."

Geena looked at him, marveled at his sensitive tone.

After another few seconds, Janey opened the door. Her hair was in another braid, but it looked unwashed and slept on. Flyaway strands stuck out in every direction. Her eyes were swollen, possibly from crying, but there was also something panicked, frantic about them. She invited them in. When Geena passed her, she caught the faint scent of body odor.

"Sorry to drop by so early," Geena said. It was midmorning, and for a mother with a small child, it didn't seem likely it would be too early. Didn't young kids tend to wake up at the crack of dawn?

"Everything okay?" she asked once they'd sat in what was becoming their usual positions, with Geena sitting on the edge of the chair, Parker sitting on the arm of the chair at her side, and Janey perched across from them on the couch, her hands folded in her lap.

"Yes," Janey said. "Everything is fine. I didn't get much sleep is all."

Parker held up the new answering machine he'd picked up when he'd been off duty and that Geena had only found out about on the car ride over. "I got you a new one, just like I promised," he said. "If you want, I can set it up for you."

"Thank you," Janey said. "But I think I'll wait to hook it up, if that's okay."

"Sure," Parker said, and he placed it on the coffee table.

"I want you to know we never talked with the media about your son," Geena said.

"If it wasn't you, then who?" Janey asked.

"We're still looking into it."

Geena noticed the crayons and coloring books on the floor, the television turned to some kid's program, the volume too low to be heard, but no Christian. It looked as though he'd been here a few moments ago.

"Where's Christian?" she asked.

"In his room," Janey said.

"Does he want to come out and say hi?" she asked. It seemed to her as though Janey tucked her son away every time they dropped by.

"He's in a time-out," Janey said. "Why are you here again?"

"We got the DNA test results back," Geena said. "It's a match. He's his son."

Janey nodded. "Is that all?"

"No," she said. "We're here because we need something else from you. We need a recent photo of Christian."

"Why?" Janey asked.

"Have you ever heard of age-progression software?"

"Yes."

"Then you know if you provide us with a photo of Christian, the software will let us see what he might look like as he ages."

"But why do you need to know what my son will look like when he's older?" she asked as understanding swept across her face. "You think he looks like his father."

"Don't you?"

"I think he looks like me. He looks like *my son*."

Parker remained quiet during the exchange, possibly waiting for the right moment to step in if needed.

"I understand what you're saying," Geena said. "I do see a resemblance to you. But with the software we have today, it might help us get an idea of what his father might look like. We can show it to the public, see if someone recognizes him or knows someone who resembles the image."

"And you think this is going to help you catch him?"

"Yes, we think it could." Honestly, she had no idea at this point. It didn't sit right with her, relying on an image of a six-year-old kid to solve a case. But what choice did they have? They were running out of options.

"You're only going to use Christian's picture for the software? You're not going to share the picture I give you with anyone else?" Janey asked.

"We're only going to share the age-progression photo," Geena said.

Parker picked this moment to speak up. It was that indescribable, indefinable thing that either clicked with a partner or didn't. You were in sync with someone or you weren't. Albert had been the yin to her yang. Who knew it could happen with more than one partner? "If you want to call Christian from his room, we can take a picture with our phone, save you the trouble of looking for one," he said.

"I put him in his room for a time-out," Janey said. "He had a tantrum over the remote control not working. He needed to cool down."

"Why don't I just go and get him," Geena said. She stood and headed for the hallway. "Is it this door?" she asked, and she pulled open the first door on the left without waiting for permission.

Christian was sitting on the floor amid torn magazines, the pages with images of wild animals strewn about among Matchbox cars and dinosaurs. His wavy bangs were matted with sweat and stuck to his forehead. His cheeks were flushed. He looked up at her with what she could only describe as anger. Janey drifted in behind her. Parker stayed in the family room, as Geena knew he would, to take a look around.

"Detective Brassard would like to take your picture," Janey said. She reached her hand out, prompting him to take it. "Why don't we get you cleaned up?"

Christian stared at his mother as though he wasn't sure if he wanted to listen to her and do what she'd asked. Eventually, he put his hand in Janey's. Geena stepped back to let them through the doorway. They disappeared inside the bathroom down the hall.

Geena rejoined Parker in the family room. He was walking around, looking about. He shrugged, which she took to mean he didn't see anything out of the ordinary, nothing in plain sight, anyway.

Another minute later, Janey and Christian returned. Christian's hair was combed, parted to the side, but still damp with perspiration. Parker held up his phone and snapped a couple of pictures before either Janey or Christian could protest.

"That will do," Parker said, bending over Christian, ruffling his hair. "See, and I didn't even ask you to smile. I'm not so bad after all, am I?"

Christian gazed up at Parker, but rather than the same blank expression that usually covered his face, the one Geena had noted when she'd first met him, his eyes were darker somehow, as though he'd understood why they were here, what they'd wanted from him all along.

~Helen Watson, Psy.D.
Patient: Janey Montgomery, ID 27112

Janey sits in the chair. Her clothes are disheveled. Helen can smell Janey's unwashed body. When Janey called earlier, she was distraught, mumbling about the detectives and the investigation. But then she mentioned the rabbit. They might as well start there.

"Tell me what happened with the rabbit," Helen says.

Janey seems to perk up, visibly straightens her posture, leans forward. Her eyes are brighter, clearer, happy to share whatever has happened. "I'm not sure where to start," she says.

"Describe the event to me," Helen says.

"Okay, well, I found him in the backyard with the rabbit in his lap. In his lap! He was petting her. He was so gentle with her," Janey says. She is unaware of the tears rolling down her cheeks as she talks.

"Is this the first time he's held the rabbit?" Helen asks.

Janey's tears come faster. She lets them drip from her chin, staining the front of her shirt and pants. "Well, he did pick her up before, you know . . . the stove." She pauses. "But he's never held her. I just think maybe he didn't know what to make of her at first, you know? He followed her around the house. He tried to pet her once in a while, but mostly he ignored her."

"I see," Helen says. "What do you think brought about his sudden interest in her?" she asks.

"I have no idea," Janey says. "I mean, I thought maybe it was something you said to him."

"No, it wasn't me. I didn't say anything."

"You didn't talk with him about Bunnie?"

Helen scribbles circles in her file. She looks up at Janey. "No," she says.

"Do you think it has something to do with when Carlyn was working with him? I should tell her, shouldn't I? It was her idea to get him the rabbit. And it seems to be working. He's showing affection. He seems to be bonding with her."

Helen continues scribbling in her file, drawing slash marks through the circles. "I don't see any reason to contact Carlyn at this point."

"Oh," Janey says. "You don't think this is a big step for him?"

"After what happened at the school with the little girl, I'm not so sure it's as big a step as you seem to think it is."

"Okay," Janey says.

"You trusted Carlyn, yes? Enough to follow her suggestions? Or were you following her orders?"

Janey's brow furrows, her mouth twists. Helen waits. It seems as though Janey is taking her time to think before answering. When Janey finally does answer, a trace of irritation has made its way into her tone. "I trusted her enough to do whatever she asked of me. Anything to help Christian."

"Do you trust me like you trusted Carlyn?" Helen asks.

"Yes." The rocking starts, slowly at first, but it picks up speed the closer Janey comes to saying what's on her mind.

Helen waits her out again, knowing by now that Janey will eventually continue on her own without prompting.

"I just want my son to be a normal boy," Janey says.

"I can make that happen."

"How?" Janey asks.

"Leave him to me."

CHAPTER THIRTY-TWO

Geena dropped the DNA report on Josh Wheeler onto the table where Parker was sitting in the conference room. "This just came in. He's not a match. Safe to say we can rule him out." She walked over to the board and removed Josh's name as a possible suspect.

"He's got to be in here somewhere," Parker said about the Strangler as he scrolled through the file on the computer.

She didn't have to look at the screen. She'd memorized the file, snapshots taken of each page on a slide inside her mind. Sayres was going to be pissed they'd hit a dead end. What they needed was the age-progression photo on Christian to be completed so they'd have something to show the public, an image of what the Strangler might look like. It was their best shot at finding him at this point.

Bill walked into the room carrying a laptop. His tie was thrown over his shoulder, most likely to keep it out of his coffee. His eyes looked tired, a sign he'd been staring at the computer screen for hours. He sat next to Parker. "I think I've got something. At least, I think it's worth looking into."

"We'll take whatever you got," she said.

"I've been looking for other possible connections between the girls and the colleges. And I've been going through the faculty and staff directories I found online for the campuses. It hasn't been easy. There are over three hundred and fifty part- and full-time employees at one of the small campuses and seventeen hundred at another. And that's just two of them. The school in New Jersey, the one where Amy went, has three thousand faculty and staff. And that doesn't include janitors or cafeteria workers or volunteers."

"A needle in a haystack," Parker said.

"You would think so. But I might've found something. A guy who was employed on two of the three campuses in the last couple years. He's about the right age according to our profile. And he has access to students." Bill pulled up a faraway image of a man in his mid- to late thirties in a shirt and tie, wavy dark hair, leaning back in a chair at a desk. His title: academic adviser.

"Worth a look," Parker said.

"Definitely," she agreed. "Do we know who the girls' advisers were when they were students?"

"I'm still working on it. The colleges aren't keen on releasing information up front about their staff or their students. We're going to need a warrant."

"We're going to need a little more on this guy to get a judge to agree to a warrant." Geena wrote down his name: Robert Harms. "We could contact the girls' parents, see if they know who their daughters' adviser was or if they recognize the name."

"Let's not contact them just yet. Now that I have a name and I know what I'm looking for, I can run a search in their emails and see if his name pops up. Any chance you remember seeing messages from him in their emails?" he asked her.

She took a minute to think about it, to stare into space, so to speak, while she searched her memory. Did she have an eidetic memory? Did such a thing even exist? Neuroscientists would answer no. She tended to agree with the science to a point. All she knew was that she could recall large amounts of information, pages of text, images of a crime scene, in more detail than the average person.

"What?" she asked when she caught Parker shaking his head.

"How does this memory of yours work exactly?" he asked.

She thought about the best way to describe it to him. "It doesn't happen automatically, like people think when they hear someone has an eidetic memory. At least it doesn't for me. I have to study what I'm seeing. It's like when you study for a test. You read over your notes or the textbook for so long that the pages become pictures in your mind. Then, when you take the test, you flip through the mental pictures you've created of the pages to find the answers to the questions. It works the same with case files and crime scenes."

"That has never happened to me when I was taking a test," he said.

"Call me lucky." But was she? There were certain images she wished she could scrub from her memory permanently. Albert had been right. She'd had to choose how she'd processed the information she'd seen and where she'd put it. She'd managed to keep most of the disturbing images behind a dark curtain, only peeking behind it when it was necessary for the job.

"Nothing is jumping out at me," she said finally, but there were thousands of emails. Sure, she'd memorized the file, but not every email or text message the computer-crime lab had collected had imprinted in her mind.

"Anything on the leak?" she asked.

"Nothing yet," Bill said.

Sayres entered the room. He looked at the board, the lack of suspects. "You saw the report on Wheeler? What else do we have?" he asked. "I'm meeting with Jonathon in an hour."

Bill spoke first, filling Sayres in on the recent update on the possible connection he'd found between the victims and an academic adviser. While Bill talked, she picked up her phone, texted the computer-crime lab, asked about more intel from Valerie's computer and phone, and to look for any emails or text messages from a Robert Harms and to put a rush on it.

CHAPTER THIRTY-THREE

Janey returned home from her appointment with Helen. Pop had watched Christian for her while she was out. She found them sitting in his pickup truck outside her house. Several reporters were hanging around. Pop got out of his truck and approached her car. The media converged on him like a flock of pigeons pecking at crumbs.

He opened her car door, holding off the crowd at the same time. "Come on," he said.

She pulled the hood of her sweatshirt over her head and got out. They were pushed and shoved as they made their way through the mob. The throng of reporters shouted questions at them, prying for information about Christian and the Strangler.

Janey slid into the front seat of the truck, hiding as best she could. She kept her head down, her face hidden from the cameras. Christian was wedged in the front seat between her and Pop, breaking Pennsylvania's child passenger safety laws. His hood was also pulled over his head and covered much of his face. The police officer who had been sitting outside her house had gotten out of his car, tried to maintain some semblance of order.

Pop rolled his window down and said to the crowd, "Shame on you, harassing a woman and child. Don't you think they've been through enough?" Then he pulled from the curb and drove away.

She removed her hood once they were several blocks from Eighth Street. "Thanks, Pop," she said.

"Let's hope they take what I said to heart and leave you alone."

"Where's Mom?" she asked.

"Running errands."

"Is she still mad that I wouldn't talk with Father Perry?"

"She's pretty upset," he said.

"Why aren't you mad at me?"

"It serves no purpose. There's no point in arguing about it now."

"Pop, can I ask you something?"

"Anything," he said.

"Do you think I made the right decision?" She'd never asked him back when she'd first learned about the pregnancy. She'd been in a deep state of shock, self-pity, and an overwhelming sense of shame. She'd blamed herself, believed she must've done something to provoke the attack, like worn the wrong type of clothing or given off the wrong signal: things her mother had warned she shouldn't do.

Janey had always thought she'd supported the church's belief in the right to life. But a person's view could change when presented with the kind of situation like the one she'd found herself in. And yet her beliefs hadn't changed. Keeping her baby had felt like the right thing to do. Her parents had pushed for her to consider adoption. But once Janey had felt that first kick, she'd known she could never give him up. He'd become a part of her that she wasn't willing to let go of, not when so much of herself had already been ripped away.

"You made a decision," he said now. "And it was the right one."

Janey stared out the window for the rest of the ride. The sun was shining. The trees were full of new green leaves. Flowers were opening. The beauty of a spring day, the cheerfulness of it, always came with mixed feelings. She could never look at spring the same way again. It wasn't the promise of a new beginning, the fresh start she'd always thought it could be. Instead, it had morphed into something else: an end of something, her sense of self, her safety, her innocence, the pieces of her that had been shredded, discarded as carelessly as trash.

Pop parked in the driveway and hit the garage door button. He got out of the truck and started tinkering in his woodshop. Janey led Christian into the house and sat him at the kitchen table. She got him a plate of cookies and a glass of milk and sat across from him. He'd been so quiet on the ride to her parents' house. He had to be confused about what was happening.

"You must be wondering why all those people have been outside our house," she said.

He shrugged.

"Well, they think I have information about something, but I don't. And once they realize that, they'll go away. Okay?"

"Why do they think you have it if you don't?" he asked.

"That's a very good question," she said, but one she couldn't answer. One day when he was older, she would have to tell him everything. But today, she was worried about how this was affecting him right now. "Do you have anything else you want to ask me?"

He shook his head, intent on eating his cookies. He didn't seem upset. She wondered if he was holding it in and if it would manifest itself in other ways.

While he finished his snack, she joined Pop in the garage. "Maybe you and Christian could work on your special project for a while. I think it would be good for him to keep busy and do something normal."

"About that," Pop said. He seemed anxious, wiping off sawdust from the top of a workbench, fidgeting with a piece of sandpaper in his hand. "I wasn't going to bring it up, with everything else that's going on, but now that you're here . . ."

"What is it?"

"It's over there." He pointed to the corner of the garage. "Underneath the sheet."

She pulled the sheet off, stepped back to get a good look at it. It was a wishing well but oddly shaped, elongated to look more like a trough with a roof.

"It was Christian's design," he said. "I didn't want to stifle his creativity. He said it was a gift."

"A gift for who?"

"For a girl at school. Something for her horseface to drink from."

"He said that?"

"Yes. And then he ran out crying. Where would he have learned such a thing?"

"I don't know. Maybe the cartoons he watches," she said. "Do you know what girl from school he was talking about?"

"Emma, I believe. The girl with the broken Easter eggs."

"Right," she said, telling herself this was a little thing compared to everything else they were dealing with. She shouldn't get worked up about it. She threw the sheet back over the piece. "Maybe we should play a game with him instead."

※

After playing several games with Christian, Janey's father dropped them off at home. The reporters were nowhere to be seen. It was possible Pop's shaming words had chased them away for now.

She dropped her purse on the counter. Christian ran to the family room, where his toys were scattered on the floor. There was a knock at the front door. She looked out the window and saw Helen, grateful she was here to work with Christian. She unlocked the door and let her in. Once the doctor was inside, she immediately locked the door again.

"I brought your mail in," Helen said, and she walked into the kitchen. "It was piling up. The mailman couldn't close the box." She dropped the stack of envelopes and magazines on the countertop.

Janey picked through the pile absently, finding the water and sewage bill as well as the electric and phone bills. How was she going to pay them now that she wasn't working? She stopped on a manila envelope. There wasn't an address or even a stamp. It wasn't sealed.

"What's this?" she asked, but Helen had already left the kitchen for the family room, where Christian was sitting on the floor, drawing on a piece of notebook paper with his crayons.

Janey reached into the envelope and pulled out a printed article titled "The Murder Gene." She looked over her shoulder to make sure no one was there, something you did when you didn't want anyone to know what you were reading. She reached for the chair at the table and dropped into it, reading and rereading every word about the theory behind the genes *MAOA* and *CDH13*, predictors for violence, case studies involving some of the most violent criminals in the last three decades. A particular paragraph stuck out, a family of men in the Netherlands with a long history of violent behaviors. The men possessed a mutation on their X chromosome, a flaw in the *MAOA* gene.

The article cautioned against accepting biological factors as the sole precursor to violence. Environmental factors played an important role in how genes were expressed, the age-old nature-versus-nurture argument. But she had stopped processing information by this point. She'd read enough. She desperately wanted to cling to the idea that her son was good. And kind. He wasn't the disturbed little boy the school was making him out to be. And yet, the article's theory wrapped itself around the doubts she'd been having about his behavior, cracking the very foundation under her feet.

Christian's voice shook her from her thoughts, bringing her back to the kitchen, pulling her from the place she'd drifted to, a dark place where she'd felt little hope. Helen stood next to her and placed a hand on her shoulder. Janey wasn't aware her body was rocking, back and forth, hard enough for the chair to scrape the floor.

"Is everything okay?" Helen asked.

Christian stood in the doorway. It seemed to Janey that he was always watching, listening, as though he was looking for signs, indications of her disloyalty.

She pulled herself together and slipped the article back into the envelope. "Is there something I can get you?" She stood, made her way to the refrigerator, dropped the envelope on top of the counter with the rest of the mail.

She searched for some cheese and crackers, celery sticks, and peanut butter. Where was all the food? When was the last time she'd gone grocery shopping? It had been before the news had broken about her connection to the Strangler. She'd avoided running errands, feared the way people would look at her, the pity, the accusation in their eyes, the silent judgment against her. Most people wouldn't say what they were thinking about her out loud, how she should've been able to identify the man who had attacked her. She should've gotten him off the streets, out of their community, secured behind bars.

It was her fault the other girls were dead.

Maybe they were right, and she was to blame. Because she had seen something, something she hadn't told anyone, not her parents or Helen or the detectives.

CHAPTER THIRTY-FOUR

Geena was sitting at the conference room table using the keyword search on Jessica Lawrence's emails, looking for anything from Robert Harms. Bill did the same with Mia Snyder's emails. Parker searched text messages, and the crime lab worked on Valerie Brown's laptop.

Geena was thinking about Albert and how he'd searched Janey's computer and mobile phone. She wondered how thorough he'd been. She'd placed several calls to the rehab center, but no one had called her back. The last call she'd made was to Albert's house. Pearl had answered. She'd told Geena that Albert was home, but he was resting.

Geena was upset at Pearl for deliberately keeping Albert away from her. But she understood Pearl was acting from a place of love, protecting her husband from any further stress while he recuperated. Still, she was hurt.

She took a break from staring at the computer screen, mentally flipped through the pages of notes she'd personally taken or notes Parker had taken during the times they'd interviewed Janey.

After a minute, maybe two, she found what she was looking for. She turned to Parker, who was sitting at the table next to her. "Janey said she struggled at the end of the semester her freshman year in college."

"Okay," Parker said.

"She went for a walk to clear her head. Is it possible she spoke with Robert Harms before she headed out? Isn't that what advisers are there for, to help with scheduling classes, choosing careers, adult life decisions?"

"I guess so."

She looked at her watch, contemplated heading to Janey's house, then picked up her phone and punched in Janey's number. She asked who her academic adviser had been when she'd been in college. Janey said it was a woman, but she no longer remembered her name. "Her adviser was a woman," Geena said to Parker after hanging up.

"Found one," Bill said. "Mia Snyder sent an email to Robert Harms asking about switching a class."

Her phone went off, a text from the computer-crime lab. They'd found a couple of email exchanges between Robert and Valerie.

Now they were getting somewhere.

Sayres walked into the conference room and dropped the age-progression photo of Christian onto the table.

Geena picked it up, examined it. It was as though she were looking into Christian's future, what he'd look like as a grown man. There was something unnerving about it, something about his eyes.

She pulled up Robert Harms's profile at the college, but photos of the staff weren't available online. Next, she put his name into a search engine to see what images came up. She found the one Bill had pulled up earlier, but it had been taken from too far away to make a good comparison.

"What is it?" Sayres asked, looking over Geena's shoulder at the computer screen.

"Trying to find an image of Robert Harms to compare it to."

Bill filled Sayres in on what they'd found out about Robert Harms and his connection to at least two of the girls.

"Couldn't hurt to talk to him," Parker said.

Sayres checked his watch. "Go. And send a copy of the photo to Janey to see if she recognizes him. We've still got two hours before it hits the five-o'clock news, and then I want you back here covering the tip line."

Geena took a picture of the photo with her phone and texted it to Janey; then she slipped on her suit jacket, gray to match her pants. She wore a white oxford shirt underneath, sensible shoes. She checked her pockets for her phone and badge.

Parker picked up the car keys. The college was a forty-minute drive over the mountain. They'd better get moving.

CHAPTER THIRTY-FIVE

After Helen's session with Christian had ended and they'd had some crackers (because it was the only food left in the cupboards), Helen went home. It was now late afternoon. The sun was out, and the temperature was a delightful sixty-eight degrees. The news media still hadn't returned. Janey imagined the pretty redheaded reporter and her cameraman sitting outside at a bar somewhere sharing a drink, planning their next ambush, strategizing how to get Janey to talk to them.

Detective Brassard had called, asked about Janey's old college academic adviser. The detective had been in a hurry to get off the phone and had never told Janey why she'd wanted to know. And then, soon after she'd hung up the phone, the detective had sent Janey a picture of the age-progression photo of Christian. Janey had been shaken, but the only thing she'd recognized about it was that it looked like a much older version of her son. She'd texted the detective and let her know.

Christian ran into the family room. She was right behind him with the new batteries her father had given her for the remote control. Christian lay on the couch, waited for her to turn on the TV. He seemed more tired than usual. He wasn't a boy who napped regularly. But the last few days hadn't exactly been normal around here, not with the reporters hanging around and the detectives continually dropping by unannounced.

She changed out the batteries and turned on the TV. "You can watch cartoons for an hour while I'm cooking dinner," she said. She should limit how much television he'd been watching lately, especially after learning from her father the name Christian had called Emma. Now that she thought about it, Emma did kind of have a horseface, just like her mother.

But that wasn't a very Christian thought, and she chided herself, told herself she was better than that. Emma was a child. Janey was the adult. She needed to act like one. Just then her cell phone rang. The elementary school's number showed on the screen. No doubt Mrs. Delacorte calling to reprimand her for keeping Christian home from school. She had half a mind to let it go to voice mail again, but she picked up the phone and put it to her ear. She was an adult.

"I hope I'm not catching you at a bad time," Mrs. Delacorte said.

"No, it's fine," she said, and she walked away from Christian, entered the kitchen to talk in private.

"I noticed Christian wasn't in school today. Is he okay?" Mrs. Delacorte asked.

"He was feeling under the weather," Janey lied.

"Well, I'm sorry to hear that. I hope he's feeling better soon. The reason I'm calling is that I'd like to schedule a meeting with you. It would be with the principal and a member of the disciplinary board. We'd like to discuss the recent developments concerning Christian's behavior."

She had expected this. Both her parents were teachers, although her dad was retired now, and she'd heard plenty of discussions at the dinner table about troubled kids and disciplinary actions. "Okay," she said to Mrs. Delacorte, noticing Bunnie wasn't in her cage. That was odd. She didn't remember letting the rabbit out.

"What about Monday morning?" Mrs. Delacorte asked.

"Fine," she said. It wasn't like she'd have to be at work, since she'd been let go for an undetermined length of time. She'd have to get her father to watch Christian for a few hours again, since her mother was teaching classes, and Janey wasn't about to send Christian back to school until she'd heard what they had planned.

While Mrs. Delacorte continued to explain what the meeting would entail, Janey walked around the house looking for Bunnie. The rabbit wasn't in her usual hiding places. She wasn't under the kitchen table or under Janey's bed.

Mrs. Delacorte rambled on, but Janey wasn't listening. "I'll have to call you back," she said.

"But we're on for Monday?" Mrs. Delacorte asked.

"Yes, fine," she said again, and she hung up. She was about to ask Christian if he'd seen Bunnie, but he was asleep on the couch. She walked back into the kitchen. Since it was such a nice night, she decided she'd cook hot dogs on the grill. She opened the refrigerator drawer and found the pack. She checked the hot dog rolls. They were moldy. She really needed to go grocery shopping and decided the best thing for her to do was to ask her mother to pick up a few things for her tomorrow. She'd use sliced bread for the hot dogs tonight. She had no idea if Christian would eat a hot dog without the normal roll. She'd have to find out.

After starting the grill, she walked around the backyard searching for Bunnie, wondering if maybe she'd gotten out somehow. She called for her, listened for stomping or thumping. Rabbits often stomped or thumped when they were nervous or afraid. She didn't hear anything. She went back inside, locked the door, and heated up a can of baked beans.

When the hot dogs were done grilling, she called Christian in for dinner. He didn't answer. "Wake up, sleepyhead," she said, and she walked into the family room, where she'd left him sleeping on the couch.

He wasn't there.

"Christian," she called, and she hurried down the hall to his bedroom. "Christian," she said. She stopped inside the doorway to his room. His back was to her. She knew right away something was wrong. "Christian. Honey."

He turned to face her, but he wouldn't look at her. Instead, he kept his head down, his gaze on the floor by his feet. She stepped closer. He moved to block her view of something on the rug behind him.

"What is it?" she asked, and she gently nudged him out of the way to see what he was hiding. She covered her scream with her hands. "What have you done?" she yelled, and she dropped to her knees. Bunnie stuck out from under the bed. She was on her side, panting, clearly in distress. "Oh, Bunnie." She didn't know what to do, how to help. She turned on her knees toward Christian, grabbed his shoulders, shook him. "What have you done?" she yelled again.

He was shaking his head. "I didn't do it," he said.

"Why are you lying to me? Why?" she asked, pleading, her mind reeling, wondering about all the other lies he must've told and she'd believed.

"Mommy, I'm not lying," he said.

"You're standing here trying to hide the rabbit from me. Don't tell me you didn't do it." She was trying to reason with him, get him to just please, please tell her the truth. If he told her the truth, then she could deal with why he'd done it in the first place.

"I'm not lying," he said, and he stepped out of her reach. "I found her here under my bed like this." He pointed to the floor close to where the rabbit lay.

"What do you mean you found her like this?" Her mind raced. Maybe the rabbit had eaten something that had made her sick. Or . . . or maybe it was him, the man who'd attacked her. Maybe he'd broken into their home. She jumped up from the floor and ran to the front door. It was locked. It didn't look tampered with. She'd used the back door to grill the hot dogs, but it had been locked when she'd first opened it. She was certain. Nothing appeared out of place. Still, she raced from room to room, checked that the windows weren't broken.

Everything was secure, exactly how she'd left it.

She found Christian standing in the hallway. Was he playing her for a fool? Manipulating her? Did he think it was funny watching her panic and run around the house like a madwoman? This was the second time he'd hurt Bunnie. What was happening to him?

He held his arms out to her, holding the rabbit's limp body in his hands. He was crying. "Take her, Mommy. Please, take her."

She took the rabbit from his hands, cradled her in her arms. Her vision was blurry, her cheeks wet with tears. She couldn't send him to his room, not until she'd cleaned the rabbit's poop from the rug.

"Go to the bathroom and wash your hands," she said. "Then I want you to go in the kitchen and eat your dinner."

"I'm not hungry," he said.

Well, of course he wasn't hungry. How could he be hungry after this, this mess that was now on her hands? "I don't care if you're not hungry. You're going to the kitchen after you wash your hands, and you're going to eat your dinner."

She couldn't look at him. She couldn't believe his lies, not this time, not after he'd done this horrible, awful thing.

Janey sat underneath the dogwood tree in the small backyard. The sun was setting, dropping behind the mountain. The moist earth soaked her bare feet. A cool breeze rustled the branches, spraying white flower petals onto the grass. Christian was in the house, in his bedroom, with the chair against the outside of his door, locked inside, away, for his own safety as well as hers.

After the shock of what he'd done to the rabbit had worn off and she'd called Pop to take Bunnie to the vet, she'd become angry. She was angry at Christian, angry at the media for harassing them, angry that her secrets were out in the first place, and, most of all, she was angry at her attacker and the power he still had over her life. She'd scrubbed Christian's carpet until the sponge had fallen apart in her hand. She'd stomped around the kitchen and slammed cabinet doors. Christian had sat at the table and watched her, eating his hot dog in silence, but not the sliced bread that was supposed to have made up for not having rolls. At one point, he'd asked for a "real" roll. She'd tossed the loaf of bread across the kitchen, screaming, "There's your roll!" The terror on his face had stopped her from throwing the plates too. She'd known then that she was out of control. She'd had to separate herself from him. She'd locked him in his room.

Now, she sat outside, trying to calm herself down, clear her head. Pop had called. The vet was keeping Bunnie overnight. She'd been stabilized. They were hopeful. She'd told Pop to tell them to do whatever they had to do. She didn't care about the cost. She'd find a way to pay the bill.

She bowed her head, said a prayer. How had he done it? Had he poisoned the rabbit? Smothered her? Held her too tightly? A sob caught in her throat. She bent down and picked up the scattered petals, watched as they blew from her hand in the breeze. She looked over her shoulder at the house. In spite of what Christian had done, he was still her son, and the overwhelming, unconditional love she felt for him brushed up against her heart.

CHAPTER THIRTY-SIX

It was hard to describe the feeling Geena had upon meeting Robert Harms for the first time. He had the wavy hair like Christian's, but Robert's was darker. His smile was easy, even charming. But she couldn't deny the physical response she suffered sitting across from him in his small office in the Academic Enrichment and Learning Center. It was as though she was drawn to him and repulsed by him at the same time. She could understand how these mixed signals might confuse a younger girl, one with less experience than she had. Sometimes certain men were so smooth that you questioned your judgment and, in turn, dismissed that first sense of unease. You opened the door, so to speak, allowed them inside your personal space, and only then did that inkling of doubt you'd had initially resurface. It started in the back of your mind, a question about whether or not you could trust this person. It worked its way into your stomach, a gut reaction, until the instinct to run, to get out of there, tightened your chest, squeezed your throat, stifled the scream that would come much too late.

She sat up straight, her hands at her thighs, ready to reach for her weapon. Sweat had collected underneath her arms. Parker sat in the chair next to her. He seemed to pick up on her body language, but he didn't show it outwardly, maybe not having the same physical reaction to Robert Harms as she was having.

"Does this have anything to do with a student?" Robert asked, leaning back in his chair, crossing his legs, his posture relaxed, unaffected by the presence of two homicide investigators in his office.

"You could say that, yes," she said. He wasn't a big guy, more like average in size, trim, nothing remarkable about his appearance. From her position, she couldn't get a good look at his shoes, but it was possible he wore a size eleven.

"I'm not sure how I can help you," Robert said.

"There's one student in particular that we're interested in. Valerie Brown." She watched Robert's face closely. If she hadn't been paying attention, she might've missed the small twitch of his mouth. But there was no mistaking the flash of recognition in his eyes.

"It doesn't ring a bell," Robert said, lacing his fingers together in his lap. "I see many students throughout the day."

She put a photo of Valerie on Robert's desk. "Does she look familiar to you?" she asked.

"Oh yes, I recognize her. I heard something about her on the news," Robert said. He stopped short of saying anything about it being a tragedy, a terrible loss, a horrifying act.

Geena's heart rate accelerated, pounded inside her chest, thumped between her ears. Adrenaline heightened her senses—the echo of voices outside the office, the click of heels on tile floor, the birds singing in the trees in the courtyard, and Parker shifting his body weight in his seat ever so slightly.

"What was your relationship with her?" Geena asked.

"I don't recall speaking with her specifically. I might've advised her on her class schedule. We may have exchanged emails." He shrugged.

"Did she ever visit you in your office?" she asked.

"Maybe. I can't say for sure, though. Some of the students come in regularly, others sporadically, and only when they're desperate and need help."

"Why would they be desperate and need help?" Parker asked.

"Oh, the usual. They're failing a class and need to transfer out of it. Or they added the wrong class, and they're worried about screwing up their schedule and not graduating on time. Those sorts of concerns that seem momentous to young people."

"Did Valerie come to you with any of these concerns?" she asked.

"Not that I recall, no," Robert said.

"You mentioned advising students on their academics, but I imagine some of the students come to you with more personal problems," Parker said.

"Sure," Robert said. "Some do, but not that often."

"Did Valerie mention anyone hanging around her, bothering her, perhaps an old boyfriend?"

"No, not to me," Robert said.

"Did she talk to you about any other concerns she was having?" Geena asked.

"No, she didn't."

She nodded.

"I'm sorry," Robert said, "but what does any of this have to do with me?"

"We're talking to everyone who had contact with Valerie in the last few weeks," Parker said. "And we noticed she exchanged some emails with you recently."

"Well," Robert said, and he unlaced his fingers, pulling his chair closer to the desk. "I don't recall every student that emails me with questions."

"What about this student?" Geena asked, and she put Mia Snyder's photo on the desk next to Valerie's. "Does she look familiar to you?"

He picked up Mia's picture, seemed to consider whether he recognized her, then set it down. "No, not really."

"Her name is Mia Snyder. You were her adviser."

He tossed his hands up. "I advise hundreds of students. I can't be expected to remember all of them." He held up his finger, made a big

212

deal out of checking his phone. "Now, if that's all, you'll have to excuse me. I have a meeting I need to get to." He stood and walked out the door.

Geena and Parker watched him walk down the hallway. It was strange the way he'd just gotten up and left abruptly. She wasn't exactly sure what to do.

"Tell me you felt it, too, that something isn't right about him?" she asked.

"Yes," Parker said. "He looks a little like Christian if Christian's hair was darker."

"There *is* a slight resemblance to the photo we had done." She picked up the images of Valerie and Mia that she'd laid on Robert's desk and put them back in the folder. She had a strange feeling, as though she'd seen him somewhere before. And then it came to her. "He was there," she said. "At Minsi Lake. He was the guy I talked to when they were removing the fish with the nets. He was taking pictures with his phone. He was wearing a baseball cap; that's why I didn't recognize him right away."

They hurried down the hall to catch up with him. They found him near the elevators.

"Mr. Harms," she called.

He looked over his shoulder. And then he took off for the stairwell. Parker didn't hesitate and ran after him.

Geena followed, racing down the steps. She lost sight of them as they turned the corner. She jumped the last few stairs to the landing, pushed open the lobby door still clutching the folder with the photos. She ignored the stares from faculty and students as she burst through the double doors that led outside.

A bunch of students with backpacks stood in the walkway of the quad. They were looking at their phones, earbuds stuck in their ears, avoiding having to interact with each other. She pushed her way through the pack of kids, saw Parker sprinting across the open stretch of grass, heading in the direction of what appeared to be an academic hall.

Geena turned and ran for the car. Students walking the path darted out of her way. She jumped into the cruiser, tossed the folder onto the passenger seat, and circled around the parking lot to the back of the building to try to head them off. She spotted them at the far end of the lot. Parker was on top of Robert after knocking him to the ground. She pulled the car close to where they were lying. The car was half in the grass and half in the lot. She threw it in park and jumped out, leaving the driver's side door wide open.

Parker held Robert down while Geena cuffed him. Then Parker pulled him to his feet, kept a firm grip on Robert's upper arm. There were grass stains on the knees of Robert's khakis. His elbow was bleeding from a brush burn from when Parker had tackled him.

"Why did you run?" Parker asked. He was breathing heavily. Beads of sweat covered his brow. His suit jacket was rumpled. There was a smudge of dirt on the pant leg of his right thigh.

Robert shrugged. He wasn't complaining or trying to convince them of his innocence. He didn't even ask why he was being detained. If anything, he seemed resigned to the fact he'd been caught.

A crowd of students had gathered, their phones out, recording the incident.

Geena slipped her hand underneath Robert's other arm. She gripped him tightly, her entire body humming with the possibility she was touching the Strangler. "Come on," she said, and she led him to the cruiser. She opened the back door. "Get in. We can talk at headquarters."

He got in without saying a word.

She closed the door, immediately wiping her thigh with the hand that had touched him. Then she closed the driver's side door, which had been left open when she'd jumped out of the car. She rejoined Parker on the sidewalk, where he was talking to some of the students. Her muscles twitched. Her skin vibrated with what this could mean. She had to keep her cool. It was possible they were still being videotaped on someone's phone. Every movement they made was subject to public scrutiny.

"What did Mr. Harms do wrong?" one of the students asked.

"Nothing for you to worry about," Parker said. "I need you to put your phones away."

"You're fast, bro," one of the boys said. "You like shot out of nowhere and took him down. Bam." The boy made a gesture like he was throwing something to the ground. His hair was long and tied back in a ponytail. He had gauges in his ears. They looked painful. Geena didn't understand the whole body piercing craze. She'd had her ears pierced back in high school but had let the holes close after two months. She couldn't stand having something stuck in her lobes.

"All right, everyone back to class or wherever it is you were going," Parker said. The students dispersed.

"You okay?" she asked as they made their way to the car, where Robert sat in the back seat waiting.

"Fine," Parker said.

"You're fast, bro," she said.

He flashed one of his infrequent smiles and got in the car. She opened the rear passenger-side door and looked down at Robert's feet.

"Size eleven?" she asked.

CHAPTER THIRTY-SEVEN

Robert Harms was sitting in the interview room while Lieutenant Sayres and the entire team watched him on the closed-circuit TV. They'd removed his handcuffs and had left him sitting there for the last thirty minutes and had just watched him. It was as though they were trying to find something about him that screamed psychopath. The problem was that he looked so normal. Geena could even say Robert was attractive. If she'd seen him in any other circumstance, say a crowded bar, she might've thought he was good looking, someone she'd be willing to chat with if he'd approached her and was taller than her, which he was not.

But that was how these predators got you, by their somewhat good looks and their sheer ordinariness.

Robert kept checking the brush burn on his elbow. He touched it and made a pouty face. He seemed so childlike. What grown man made a fuss about such a small scrape?

Parker passed the age-progression photo around. Everyone agreed that if the hair were darker, you could make the argument that Robert resembled the image. He was about the right age, based on their profile. They knew he was connected to two of the girls, Mia Snyder and Valerie Brown.

"Bill, find me a connection to all five girls. Not three or four. All five," Sayres said. "And let's get a warrant for his DNA in case he won't give it up freely."

"I'm on it." Bill left the group still huddled around the screen.

Geena checked her phone, saw a missed text from Janey about the age-progression photo. "Janey got back to me about the photo. She didn't recognize him."

Sayres nodded. "Does he know why you brought him in?"

"Nope," Geena said. "He never even asked."

"Really?" Sayres said. "What exactly happened out there?"

"We talked to him in his office. I got a bad feeling about him. I think we both did," she said.

Parker nodded.

"We kept the conversation casual. He said he had a meeting and just got up and walked out on us. After he left, I remembered seeing him at Minsi Lake on one of the days we stopped when they were salvaging the fish. It seemed like a big coincidence. We went after him to ask him about it. When he saw us, he took off running. Parker chased him down and tackled him."

"That explains a lot," Sayres said, referring to Parker's rumpled jacket and dirt-stained pants.

"I admit that it felt good to knock him down. But you're not going to like what I have to say next," Parker said. "Some of the students were around. I think they videotaped it with their phones."

"Well, that's just great," Sayres said. "How long until it's posted all over the internet?"

No one answered, because the truth of the matter was that it was probably already circulating the sites as they stood there.

Robert inspected the small brush burn on his arm again, or, as Geena now thought of it, his boo-boo. "We brought him in," she said to Sayres. "We get first crack at him."

"All right," Sayres said. "Let's hope he feels like talking."

Geena got an antiseptic wipe and a Band-Aid from the first aid kit. "Ready?" she asked Parker.

"Lead the way," he said.

They entered the room together. Robert was still looking at his arm.

"I thought you might want to clean that up." She handed him the wipe. When he'd finished cleaning his cut, she passed him the Band-Aid. "It looks pretty sore," she said. An outright lie, but her goal was to put him at ease and make him comfortable. Anything to get him talking. It was also the reason they'd removed the handcuffs. Let him think they were agreeable, they were on his side.

"Can I get you anything to drink? Water? Soda?" Parker asked.

"Water would be nice," Robert said.

Parker left the room in search of a water bottle, leaving Geena alone with Robert. She felt that immediate sense of unease.

"Thank you for the Band-Aid," he said. "Can I tell you something? Just between us?" He leaned forward, the small metal table the only thing separating them.

"Of course," she said.

"You're much too pretty to be a cop."

He surprised her. She couldn't decide what an appropriate response would be. *You're a creepy dickhead* came to mind. But that wouldn't have gotten him talking. Before she could come up with anything suitable, the interview room door swung open, and Parker walked in. He set a water bottle on the table in front of Robert.

"Here you go," Parker said, and he sat next to Geena. "Before we get started, I want to remind you of your rights." He read him his rights. "I also want you to be aware that this interview is being recorded. Do you understand?"

"Video or audio?" Robert glanced up at the camera mounted in the corner of the ceiling.

"Both," Parker said.

"So it wasn't just between us," Robert said to her.

"Anything you say in this room will be recorded," she said.

"Please state your full name for me," Parker said.

"Robert Harms," he said, and he twisted the cap off the water bottle and drank. His demeanor hadn't changed since they'd spoken to him in his office. He appeared relaxed. Or was he relieved? She wasn't sure which one it was.

"What's the significance of spring?" she asked.

Robert seemed to understand what she was asking, and nothing in his expression looked surprised by it. "Springtime is the best time. It's about transformation. New beginnings."

"Is that what you think you do? Transform them?" she asked.

"Are we talking about the Spring Girls?" Robert asked. "I saw it on the news. I like the name they've given them."

Geena's mouth was slick and warm. It was as though he was dying to tell them what he'd done. She'd read about this happening in other cases with serial killers, how they liked the attention, how they wanted to relive their crimes over again because it was all about them, their egos, their needs.

"Answer the question," she said.

"Do you take everything so literally?" Robert asked.

She didn't like the feeling of his eyes on her. There was something cold about his gaze, something ruthless.

Parker stepped in. "Why don't you tell us about Valerie Brown?" he asked. "Tell us what happened."

Robert looked Parker over as though he was assessing him in some way. "Is that the one that does it for you?" he asked.

Parker's face remained stoic, but like Geena was, she knew he was taken aback by Robert's boldness. He was cocky, but he wasn't admitting to anything. He also seemed to think he was smarter than them.

"Let me tell you what I think happened," she said. "I think you were walking the trails when Valerie happened to come along. You decided to grab her. You couldn't pass up the opportunity in front of you. There wasn't a whole lot of planning on your part. In fact, there wasn't any planning at all, was there?"

Robert didn't say anything.

She continued. "I mean, come on, dumping her body in a lake that's being drained? Doesn't sound like someone who thought things through. Doesn't sound like someone who's smart to me."

"You got it wrong." Robert appeared agitated suddenly. It was obvious he didn't like her challenging his intelligence.

"Oh, I don't know. I think I got it right. Don't you think so?" she asked Parker.

"Sounds right to me," Parker said.

"She liked to go for a walk after dinner," Robert said.

"So you stalked her," Geena said.

He shook his head. "I wouldn't put it that way."

"How would you put it?" she asked.

"Not that way," he said.

"Is it fair to say you got to know Valerie's routine?"

He didn't answer.

"Did you know all the girls' routines?" Parker asked.

There was something unnerving about the way Robert's eyes lit up at the mention of the other girls. But he still didn't answer the question. He still wasn't admitting to anything.

"Okay, let me put it to you this way, Robert. We found semen," she said. "And we're getting a warrant right this minute to get a sample of your DNA. Unless you'd like to give it to us voluntarily, of course. Either way, you're not going anywhere. So it's up to you. If you're smart, like you seem to want us to think you are, you'll talk to us and give us what we need. But maybe you're not as smart as you want us to believe. Maybe you're just really stupid. So tell me, which is it? Are you smart or stupid?"

Robert stared at her.

"It's like she told you," Parker said. "We've got DNA. You're not going anywhere."

Robert seemed to be thinking things over, and then he said, "Ask me another question."

"How did you knock Valerie out?" Parker asked. "What did you use? Was there something on the rag? Some kind of chemical maybe?"

Robert turned to Parker. "Did you know chloroform actually takes time to work?" He talked as though he was giving him nothing more than a logical explanation. "You can walk for about ten minutes or more before it takes effect."

"You held the rag over Valerie's nose and mouth and had her walk somewhere?" Geena asked.

"I could more or less get where I needed to be."

"To your campsite," she said.

"Very good, Detective," Robert said, seemingly impressed she knew this detail.

"What did you do next?" she asked. Parker sat remarkably still beside her. She was playing with her pen, clicking it and tapping it on the legal pad in front of her. She had to do something. Playing with the pen released some of the energy building inside her.

"That's an open-ended question. You can do better than that," Robert said.

"Did you tie her up?" she asked. "Like this?" She held her hands together in front of her, palms up. The girls' being tied had never been released to the public, but with all the leaks in the case, she was trying to get him to show her how he'd done it, prove that he was there so he couldn't say later that he'd heard about it elsewhere.

He seemed annoyed she hadn't gotten this right. He put his arms behind him to show how Valerie's wrists had been tied behind her back. She could almost hear Sayres barking orders to get a search warrant for Robert's residence and car. Robert looked directly at Geena; then he said, "You would look good tied up."

She came out of her seat. She was about to leap across the table and punch him when Parker put his hand on her arm, kept her in her chair.

Robert looked at Parker with a little more interest.

"Who are we talking about here? Just Valerie? Or were there others? What are their names?" Parker asked.

Geena calmed herself, told herself to play Robert's game if it would keep him talking. She wanted nothing more than to put him behind bars for the rest of his life and to do it using his own words.

Robert sat back in the chair, crossed his legs, scratched his head.

"We have Valerie Brown," Parker said. "Who else?"

Robert scratched his head again. For the first time since they'd brought him in, he looked uncomfortable. Of course he did. He didn't see his victims as human beings, as girls with names, lives, families, and friends. They were just tools to him, something he used to act out his fantasies, to satisfy his own selfish, twisted needs.

"Give us their names," she said. *Say their names, you coward.*

He shrugged.

"You knew their routines, but not their names? I find that hard to believe," she said.

When Robert didn't answer, Parker said, "Okay, we'll let you think about it. Let's go back to what you did after Valerie was tied."

They waited for him to answer, but when he didn't, Geena jumped in. "Did you have to wait for the chloroform to wear off?" she asked. "Because you wanted to see the fear in her eyes. Because you wanted her to know you were in control." She paused, thinking about how the girls didn't have defensive wounds. "But that's not your style, is it? You raped her while she was unconscious."

Robert checked the Band-Aid on his elbow as though he was suddenly bored.

"Tell me their names," she said.

Robert raised his hands and mimicked like he was choking someone. Then he dropped them to his lap. "You know it's incredibly hard to strangle someone. It takes a lot of effort."

"Is that so?" Parker asked.

"I didn't always get it right," Robert said.

"Which one didn't you get right?" she asked.

"The first one," Robert said, and he leaned forward, once again closing the space between them. "So you see, Detective, I am smart. Because I learned."

CHAPTER THIRTY-EIGHT

Janey stood in the hallway outside Christian's bedroom. The chair was still pushed against the door. She'd stayed up late into the night researching articles on the internet about the murder gene. It was just a theory, she'd told herself over and over again. *Just a theory.* She'd gone to sleep sometime after two a.m. She'd slept in fits and starts. Her dreams had been plagued with images of the rabbit's limp body in Christian's hands as he walked around the house, leaving the rabbit's entrails behind him. In dreamland, Janey had been frantically trying to clean up the stains before the detectives discovered her son was a monster too.

Now, this morning, she removed the chair from Christian's door and set it aside. She poked her head into his room. His blinds were closed, keeping the sunlight from entering his lair.

He turned his head toward her. "Mommy," he said. "Is that you?"

"Hi, baby," she said, and she entered the room. She sat on his bed, brushed the bangs from his forehead. "How did you sleep?"

"Good," he said.

She closed her eyes momentarily, breathed deeply. He'd slept with a guilt-free conscience. How was that possible after what he'd done?

"Mommy, can I ask you something?"

"Sure. You can ask me anything." She braced herself.

"Is Bunnie going to be okay?" he asked.

"Yes," she said. Pop had called earlier with the good news. They'd agreed he'd take the rabbit home with him. He'd already stopped by and picked up the cage. "She's going to stay at Nana and Pop's while she gets better."

"Are you going to tell Helen what happened?"

"I . . ." She hesitated. "Do you want me to tell her?"

"No, I don't want you to tell her."

"Well, that settles it then. It will be our secret." She was being a coward. She was afraid to tell Helen, worried about what the doctor would think of him. It was obvious he was also worried about what Helen would think of him.

"What if she asks where Bunnie is?"

"We'll tell anybody who asks that she's in a nice home. It's not lying, because Nana and Pop's place is a nice home."

Christian nodded. "I think that's a good answer," he said.

It took everything she had not to shake him and ask him why he'd done it in the first place. And now she was teaching him how to lie about it, how to get away with it. She stood from the bed. "How about breakfast?" she asked.

Janey cleaned up the breakfast dishes. Christian was coloring in the family room. She turned on the small TV on the counter and sat down at the kitchen table with her second cup of tea. The mug wasn't even halfway to her lips when Detective Reed appeared on the screen, tackling someone on the lawn of the college campus.

Her hand shook as she slowly set the cup back on the table. The video was of poor quality and jumped around. The sound was muted. Detective Brassard appeared in the shot. Somewhere off screen the redheaded reporter was talking. The detectives led the man toward their car. The screen froze on the man's face. She inhaled sharply. The image was blurry, his features undefined.

And still, he looked familiar.

She felt dizzy. The pretty redhead was talking again. Robert Harms had been taken into custody. He was an academic adviser at the community college, and the state police had apprehended him fleeing from campus late yesterday afternoon. He was being charged with one count of murder and two counts of rape. The investigation was ongoing. More charges were pending the outcome. According to the district attorney, the Spring Strangler had been caught.

Somewhere behind her there was knocking. She turned toward the back door. It was as though she were moving in slow motion, her mind trying to sift through a dense fog. The knocking was louder.

"Janey, it's Mom."

She got up from the table, stumbled, banged her leg against the post, spilling the tea. She unlocked the door and flung it open. She blurted, "I'm sorry about not talking to Father Perry. Don't be mad."

"Oh, honey, I'm not mad at you," she said. She stepped inside, setting a plate of muffins on the countertop. "Did you hear the news?"

She nodded and fell into her mother's outstretched arms. For the first time since yesterday and finding the rabbit injured, whatever strength that had been holding her together disintegrated.

"It's over, baby," her mother said. "They caught him. It's over."

It was the end of looking over her shoulder, checking if she was being followed, wondering if one day he would come for her, or worse, if he would come for her son. She'd feared running into him, seeing his face and not knowing who he was.

But all that was behind her now. Her horrible story was coming to an end.

She and her mother separated. She wiped her eyes and nose with her sleeve.

It was over.

But it was the start of something else she couldn't name. Something elusive.

Something unwelcoming.

She held on to the counter, feeling unsteady, weak in her knees. Her head was heavy. Her vision blurred. A thousand black dots merged in front of her eyes until they were one big mass of complete darkness.

"Janey, honey. Wake up," her mother said, tapping the back of her hand against Janey's cheek.

Janey's eyes opened. She was staring at her mother's round face. "What happened?" she asked.

"You fainted," her mother said.

She tried to get up.

"Slowly," her mother said, and she helped her sit up.

She touched her face where it was hurting.

"You're swelling up." Her mother stood and put some ice in a towel before holding it against Janey's cheekbone. "You hit it on the counter-top on the way down. I tried to catch you."

"I'm sorry."

"Don't apologize. You've been under a lot of stress. Hold this," her mother said. "Let's stand you up."

Janey held the towel with ice against her face while her mother helped her to the table and sat her in the chair. Christian was standing in the doorway of the kitchen. His head was down.

"How's my grandson?" her mother said, and she ushered Christian to the table. "Would you like a muffin?"

Janey turned toward the TV. A mug shot of Robert Harms filled the screen.

For the second time that morning, everything went black.

CHAPTER THIRTY-NINE

Geena stood in the driveway of a small Cape Cod on Sullivan Trail in Forks Township. It was made of brick with an attached single-car garage. The grass was cut. The shrubs in front of the house were trimmed. There was nothing extraordinary about it. It blended in with the other homes in the neighborhood, just like its owner once had.

The garage door was open. From what Geena could see, it looked as though it could have been anybody's garage, with old paint cans lining the shelves. A push lawn mower was shoved against the far wall, along with a ladder and a small snowblower. The car was not there. It had been towed from the college campus parking lot to one of the station's garages to be combed for evidence.

They'd obtained search warrants for both the car and the house late last night, not long after Robert had started talking. They'd gotten a lot of information out of him during that first interview, including his DNA. They'd learned he'd carried Valerie's body to Minsi Lake and that he'd struggled. It hadn't been easy. They were assuming it had been the same with the others.

Geena still had a lot more questions for him, like what was the significance of the tiny braids on the crowns of some of the girls' heads? Why had he untied their wrists and ankles after he'd strangled them?

But Robert had said he'd needed a break, that he'd grown tired of them, and he was done talking. He'd asked them to leave, as though they were his guests and he wanted them to go home. Then he put his head on the desk and engaged in what Geena and the other investigators called the sleep of the guilty. The ones who were innocent tended to be too anxious and ramped with worry to ever fall asleep in the interview room.

Parker walked up the driveway to where she was standing, watching the forensic unit. He'd stepped away moments ago to take a personal call.

"Is your girlfriend upset you didn't make it home last night?" she asked.

"Becca? No, it's fine," he said.

She didn't press him for more information. He didn't like to talk about Becca. In Geena's experience, guys didn't talk about the girls they really cared about. And she suspected that Parker was in deep where Becca was concerned.

The forensic unit continued searching the garage. They'd been processing the scene for several hours. It was now close to noon. So far they had collected a tent, fishing gear, size eleven hiking boots with lug soles, a stockpile of cotton rags, and a bottle of chloroform. But where were the tiny rubber bands he'd used to tie the braids in their hair? Where were the ligatures?

They were missing something. She could feel it.

"No clothing or personal items?" Parker asked. He was referring to the victims.

"None yet," she said. They were hoping to find evidence of the girls' clothes or perhaps the personal items they'd had on them when they'd been abducted. Geena made a mental catalogue of every personal item missing for each girl, in the belief that the Strangler would have kept something small for a trophy. Mia Snyder: silver necklace with a white daisy pendant. Amy Kaplan: gold hoop earrings. Jessica Lawrence: three silver rings and a belly button ring with a pearl drop center. Valerie Brown: emerald earrings and ring to match. And Janey Montgomery? Well, Geena just didn't know.

Her phone went off, a text from the lieutenant requesting she and Parker return to headquarters at once.

"Do you want to tell me what's going on?" Sayres asked the second Geena stepped into the conference room, with Parker right behind her.

"Sure, if I knew what we were talking about," she said.

"Harms is ready to talk again, but he says he'll only talk to you," Sayres said. "Not you, Reed. Or me. Or anyone else on the team. He doesn't want anyone in the room with him but you, Brassard, and only you. Why do you think that is?"

"I have no idea, unless . . ."

"Unless what?"

"Unless it's because I'm a woman."

"I think we covered this before," Sayres said. "Explain."

"He thinks he can intimidate me," she said. "He thinks he has the upper hand when he's talking to me. But he doesn't."

"What are your thoughts, Reed?" Sayres asked.

"I think he's playing games," Parker said. "But she can handle him."

She appreciated the vote of confidence but was annoyed Sayres felt as though he needed her partner to confirm she was capable of doing the interview on her own, when her word should've been enough.

"All right," Sayres said. "We'll give him what he wants, as long as he talks. But if he refuses to answer your questions, I want you to get out of there. Immediately. Are we clear?"

She nodded and turned to leave, Sayres calling after her, "And Brassard. You've got one chance to do this right. Don't blow it."

"I've heard that before," she mumbled, and she headed to the interview room, where she found Robert sitting in the same plastic chair behind the same desk as the night before. His hair was messy, as though he'd been running his hands through it for hours. His khaki pants were rumpled. His shirt was wrinkled. But what did his clothes matter when soon he'd be wearing a state-issued wardrobe?

She sat across from him. "How are you doing?" she asked.

"I could use a drink of water," he said. His breath smelled stale with what she could only describe as hungry breath.

"Of course." She glanced at the camera. "Someone will bring that in for you. Maybe something to eat too? And just to be clear, this interview is being recorded." She reminded him of his rights.

He sighed loudly. "Yes, I agreed to talk to you. Only you."

"Why me?" she asked.

He didn't answer. Instead, he picked at the Band-Aid on his arm.

"Would you like to clean that again?" she asked.

He shook his head. He was sulking.

"Tell me about Mia Snyder," she said, and she waited, but he wasn't talking. "Or do you want to start with Amy Kaplan?" When he didn't answer, she said, "Robert? Are you with me?"

He nodded.

"I need you to speak for the recording."

"Yes, I'm with you," he said.

"I'm curious about something. Why did you weigh Amy's body down and not the others?" she asked.

"I was wondering when you were going to get around to that," he said.

"What does that mean?"

"Things were different."

"Different how? You didn't plan on taking her? You didn't know her routine?" Amy had been on the side of the road with an apparent flat tire. It seemed he'd acted on opportunity and not careful planning.

He wouldn't look at her.

"Tell me in your own words. What was different? Why did you weigh her body down?"

"I'm done talking about it."

He didn't want to talk about Amy because she had to have been the one who had fought back. He hadn't been in control. He hadn't been organized. "All right," she said. "Then why don't you tell me why you untied them? What was the purpose?"

"I said I'm done talking about it."

"I'm here because you said you wanted to talk."

"I wanted to see you."

"Why?"

"I just wanted to."

"You're wasting my time. I'm out of here." She stood and turned for the door.

"Wait," he said. "I know you."

She should have walked out and not given him the satisfaction of playing along with his games. But something about the way he'd said he knew her had her turning around. She was on the defensive. It wasn't where she should be, and she knew it. "What do you mean you know me?"

"I know your type. You're not as tough as you think you are. In fact, I don't think you're tough at all. I think you're weak. You're weak because you're desperate to be liked."

"You don't know anything about me," she said. She was suddenly aware the lieutenant and her partner were hearing this.

"I'd pick you out of a hundred girls."

"Go to hell," she said.

Robert stood. "You do what you're told because you want everyone to like you."

"Sit down."

"Deep down, you want *me* to like you."

"I said sit down."

He lunged at her.

She was quick to react and blocked his arm from striking her. Then she grabbed it, twisted it behind his back, and slammed his body into the desk. His foot caught the leg of the metal chair, pulling them off balance. They toppled to the floor. She landed on top of him. Her leg tangled with his. She was blindsided by rage, a pulsating infestation deep inside her core that had started ever since the first girl had turned up. She was about to deliver a body blow when the door to the interview room flew open. Parker raced in and held Robert down while Geena pulled herself up. She pushed her knee between Robert's shoulder blades and cuffed him. She stood. Parker lifted Robert to his feet, sat him back in the chair that hadn't been knocked over.

"Sit and don't move," he warned.

Geena stepped out in the hallway. Parker joined her. Back inside the interview room, Robert cradled the same arm where he'd gotten the original boo-boo from when Parker had tackled him. "You hit me," he whined.

Parker slammed the door, locking Robert inside.

Sayres was yelling for her to get in his office. She turned to go. Parker followed her.

"What happened in there?" Sayres asked. "We've got everybody's eyes on us on this one. The last thing I need is for the media to get ahold of this, thinking we roughed him up and violated his rights." He poked his head out of the office door and called out to anyone and everyone on the floor, "Someone go check and make sure that asshole is okay." He turned back around. "Now get out of here. You're done for the day. In fact, you're done for the weekend. Go home and do something else for a while."

"What? You can't be serious," she said.

"I'm absolutely serious," Sayres said.

"Come on, I defended myself back there."

"You too, Reed. Out. Take some time and cool off. Let's see if anything comes of this. Go. I don't want anything to jeopardize this case."

Parker's face gave nothing away as he strode out of Sayres's office. Geena sauntered out behind him. She caught up to him at their temporary desks.

Parker pulled open desk drawers, slammed them closed, possibly searching for personal items to take home with him. He didn't seem to find anything and stood there awkwardly.

Bill walked up to them, lowering his voice when he said, "There's something you need to know."

"What is it?" She checked that her phone was still in her pocket, and she hadn't lost it when she'd knocked Robert down.

Bill lowered his voice even more. "Janey Montgomery's mom, Margaret Montgomery."

"Yeah, what about her?" she asked.

"Margaret's maiden name is Eugenis. She's Albert's sister."

She couldn't believe it. She could hardly get the words out when she asked, "What are you saying? Janey is Albert's niece?"

"It seems so. And that's not all," Bill said. "I know who the leak is."

"You don't think Albert . . . ?"

Bill was shaking his head. "Pearl," he said.

CHAPTER FORTY

Geena pulled into Albert's driveway and parked. She'd told Parker that since they'd been given unwanted time off for the rest of the weekend, she was going home. But she didn't go to her condo. Instead, she'd ended up here.

She gazed at the house, white with black shutters and a picket fence. It seemed to sag at the edges where a person's shoulders would be, its roof hunched, weighed down from years of hard use, much like Albert himself. He'd raised his kids here, his family. In all the time she'd worked with him, he'd often talked about Theo and Megan but never about his extended family. He'd only ever mentioned once, in passing, that he had a sister, Margaret. Geena had never made the connection.

She got out of the car. The grass in front of the house needed to be cut. Weeds sprouted in the flower beds. Since his stroke, she imagined Pearl didn't have much time for yard work. She devoted all her attention to taking care of him. And Theo had since returned to Colorado. Megan had gone back to work.

Instead of knocking on the door like she'd planned, she headed in the direction of the small barn where Albert kept the lawn mower and all his gardening tools and supplies. He preferred to think of the dilapidated barn as his toolshed. Like it or not, she thought, he was a farmer, and this was his barn.

She slid the door open and found the old push lawn mower sitting in the middle of the dirt floor, as though someone had dragged it out and then forgotten about it. It had been a long time since she'd cut grass in the yard where she'd grown up. Her father had taught her when she was in high school. He'd shown her how to change a flat tire, balance a checkbook, fix a leaky faucet, lay shingles on a roof. Her father had given her the gift of independence. She could still hear her mother balking during these father-daughter lessons.

"Look at her," her mother had said. "She's gorgeous. She'll never have to change a flat tire in her life. Men will be fighting over who gets to change it for her."

"That's not the point," Jean-Pierre had said; then he said to Geena, "You don't need a man to do the things you can do yourself."

"Oh, please," her mother had said after hearing his every word. "I could change a flat tire if I had to. How hard can it be?"

"This from a woman who doesn't sweat. She perspires," he'd said, and he lifted her mother in his strong arms as she pretended to fight him, laughing, telling him to put her down.

Geena got the mower started. Thirty minutes later her shoes and the hem of her pants were covered in grass. Her white blouse stuck to her back with sweat. She finished the front yard and shut off the mower as the door to the house opened. Pearl stood in the doorway with a glass of iced tea. Geena approached her. Pearl handed her the glass and walked back inside without saying a word. She gulped the tea down and followed her.

"Albert," Pearl said, and she opened a door to a room on the first floor that had been made into a bedroom. "You have company," she said, and then disappeared down the hall.

Geena stepped into the room. A twin bed took up much of the space. Several gardening books were piled on the small table next to him. His left eye sagged. His hair stuck up in different directions. He was wearing a striped pajama top.

"Hey you," she said, and she sat in the chair next to the bed.

"Was that you mowing the lawn?" he asked. His speech was slurred, but he was able to talk. Theo had told her before he'd returned to Colorado that Albert was working with a speech therapist.

"Guilty," she said.

"You didn't have to do that," he said.

"Think nothing of it. I would've come to visit sooner . . ." She stopped. She wasn't going to tell him how Pearl had tried to keep her from him. "We got him, Albert."

He closed his eyes. When he opened them again, he asked, "How?"

"Bill pulled his name off the college campus directories. We were able to connect him to two of the girls' emails. He was their academic adviser. We're still not sure if he was the adviser to all of the girls, but he had access to them." She swallowed hard. What she had to say next wasn't easy. "I know Janey is your niece," she said. "Why didn't you tell me when you first gave me her name? You knew I'd find out eventually."

"I couldn't bring myself to tell you. I wanted to, but I couldn't. I couldn't because I was afraid you'd think less of me."

"Why would I think less of you?"

"Because I'm a cop. Because I dedicated my entire life to protecting and serving my community. And I couldn't even protect my own family. My own niece. I failed her," he said. "And I was too proud to admit it. I know it's a poor excuse, but it's the truth."

He'd let his emotions, his pride, get in the way of doing his job. How could she fault him for it when she'd done the same where he was concerned? "I can't imagine how hard this must've been for you and your sister's family."

"Her boy," he said. "Is he the father?"

She nodded. "You didn't know?"

"I suspected as much. Even after I learned what happened, my sister insisted the boy's father was somebody Janey met in college."

"Until we had DNA. That's why you finally gave up her name, because now we could prove it one way or the other." Just as the words left her mouth, Pearl entered the room.

"That's a long enough visit for now," Pearl said. "You two can catch up another time."

Geena wouldn't argue with Pearl, not in front of him. "I'll see you soon," she said, and she left, made her way to the kitchen. She put her dirty glass in the sink and waited for Pearl. A minute or two passed. She could hear the murmur of Pearl's voice, then the click of her shoes on the hardwood floor. Pearl started at the sight of Geena leaning against the counter.

"I thought you'd gone," Pearl said.

"I want to have a word with you." Geena crossed her arms. She was certain her right hip was bruised where she'd banged it on the table when she'd fallen on the floor in the interview room. Her forearm ached where she'd hit it on the chair.

"I can't imagine about what," Pearl said, and she plucked the glass from the sink and put it in the dishwasher.

"Why were you leaking information to the media?"

Pearl took her time to answer. Eventually, she said, "After the first girl was found, Margaret confessed to me that Janey had been attacked and that she hadn't become pregnant by some boy while she was in college, like she'd told Albert. She made me promise not to say anything to him. She begged me for the sake of the family's privacy, and I agreed, against my better judgment. I went along with the lie. But then the second girl turned up, and I felt I had to do something. I thought by telling Albert and asking to be anonymous, I wasn't breaking Margaret's confidence. Not really anyway. It wasn't easy. But he still had a hard time accepting the fact that his niece was . . . well, you know, one of them. He wanted proof. Needed it in a way that I had never seen before."

"And he got it when we had DNA," she said. "Okay, but that doesn't explain the leaks to the media."

Pearl didn't say anything.

"Does Albert know?"

"That I leaked information? No," Pearl said. "That he doesn't know."

"Why did you do it?"

"I wouldn't expect you to understand," Pearl said. "But if you must know, I did it for Albert. I did it for him *and* his sister's family, although I doubt she'd see it that way. When Albert finally learned what really happened to his niece and that . . . that man, that *strangler*, could be responsible . . . you're a cop. You can imagine how he felt. He was devastated that he wasn't able to protect his own niece from some lunatic. And then his sister continued to beg him not to tell anyone. What was he supposed to do? Keeping it a secret was tearing him apart." There was a catch in her voice. "It was killing him. I love my sister-in-law and my niece, but I love my husband more. He couldn't say anything. But I could."

Geena nodded. She'd seen the changes in Albert. Not being able to do his job the only way he knew how had destroyed him. And then there was Janey. Geena had been so centered on collecting evidence and securing a confession from Robert that she'd never thought about what the news might do to Janey and her son.

"Have you talked to Albert's sister today? Or Janey?" she asked.

Pearl shook her head.

Geena checked her phone for the time. It was too late to go to Janey's house. Sayres wouldn't be happy if she did, anyway. She wasn't on the clock for a reason.

"Call them," she said. "Let them know it's going to be all right. Let them know they can call me anytime and that I'm here if they want to talk." Sayres couldn't get mad if Janey was the one who reached out to her.

"Why can't you call and tell them yourself?" Pearl asked.

"Let's just say the lieutenant is not exactly thrilled with me at the moment."

"And why is that?"

"Our suspect stepped out of line. I ended up knocking him off his feet."

Pearl's eyes gleamed. She said, "I'll tell Janey to call you."

⚡

Geena stepped out of the shower. She slipped on a white robe and dried her hair with a towel. The ten-o'clock news was turned down low on the flat-screen TV hanging on the wall in her bedroom. Codis was curled at the bottom of the bed, his snoring intermingling with the murmur of the weather report. She dropped down next to him and put her head in her hands. What if Robert filed a complaint, said he was attacked in the interview room? They'd been under scrutiny all the time lately. Every step they'd made had been under the watchful eye of the public defender's office and, more recently, the media.

The doorbell rang. She hopped off the bed, hoping it was Parker. He hadn't said a word to her since she'd left headquarters. She felt bad after she'd gotten them both sent home like a couple of misbehaved kids.

"Who is it?" she asked.

"It's me," Jonathon said.

She probably shouldn't let him in, but even as she was thinking it, she knew she would. She opened the door. He followed her to the kitchen, although this wasn't their usual routine. Four months ago, she would've led him directly to the bedroom, their clothes dropping to the floor along the way.

"Something to drink?" she asked.

He shook his head.

She poured herself a glass of wine, leaned against the counter. "Does your wife know you're here?"

"Don't do that."

"Sorry. Sorry. You're right." She swirled the wine in the glass. "Why are you here?"

"I heard what happened today," he said.

"Word travels fast."

"How did it feel to take him down?"

"I'm not going to lie. It felt pretty good."

He nodded. Codis sniffed him out and came bumping into the kitchen. Jonathon bent down to pet him. Codis grunted and farted in appreciation. She would've been embarrassed by Codis's free-flowing bodily functions in front of anybody else, but it showed how familiar she was with Jonathon in her life. Or at least how familiar she had been with him at one time.

When he finished with the dog, he stood. "Sayres is going to have to take a hard look at the videotape. He might be forced to take some form of disciplinary action if there's any kind of complaint from our suspect."

"Do you think it will come to that?" she asked.

"I hope not," he said.

The way he was looking at her told her everything she needed to know. He missed her as much as she missed him. She gulped some wine.

"You know Parker tackled him too," she said.

"I saw."

"On the internet?"

He nodded. "How do you like working with him? I noticed he doesn't talk much. A bit of a loner, if you ask me."

"True, he's quieter than most. He'd rather listen than talk. Nothing wrong with that. He's a good guy."

"A good guy? High praise coming from you."

"Don't tell me you're jealous?"

He shrugged and stepped toward her. He touched the collar of her robe. "Maybe a little." He moved in closer.

She rested her head on his cheek. He smelled so good, and it reminded her of the way his cologne had lingered on her sheets after he'd spent the night. But he couldn't stay here with her, not with his wife waiting for him at home. He had to go. She couldn't do this again. She couldn't be the other woman. She'd given him up once, and it had hurt like hell. She couldn't give him up a second time. And she would have to. Maybe not today or tomorrow but someday. There was no future for them.

"You shouldn't be here," she said.

"I know."

"You should go."

"She left *me*," he said.

"You took her back."

"We have kids. A long history."

"Yes."

"I'm sorry," he said.

"Me too." She closed her eyes. It was dangerous being this close to him, having his breath in her ear.

"I should go," he said.

"Yes, you should go."

He kissed her cheek, his lips lingering there. Then he stepped back. "There's nothing on the videotape that I need for the trial. We got everything I need from the first interview. All you have to do is say the word, and it could disappear."

She was touched by his offer, to put himself at risk for her, but she couldn't take him up on it. She wouldn't take him down with her, if it came to that. "I couldn't ask you to do that. It's not right. I defended myself. And if anybody says differently, if Sayres feels differently, then I'll accept whatever is coming to me."

"Are you sure?"

"I'm sure."

"Okay," he said. "You know the rules. I never offered to help. And I was never here."

She nodded. He knew how to cover his ass, she thought as he walked away. And what a nice ass it was. She listened to his footsteps, and then the front door opened and closed. She could still smell him in the room, all around.

"But you were here," she said, and she downed the rest of the wine in the glass.

~Helen Watson, Psy.D.
Patient: Janey Montgomery, ID 27112

"Thank you for seeing me," Janey says.

"It was me who called you, remember? In fact, I tried calling you yesterday. I left several messages. I was worried about you and Christian."

"Yes, I know. I got them. I was with my mother." Janey doesn't say anything after that, as though being with her mother is explanation enough, and Helen is annoyed by this.

"Tell me," Helen says. "How do you feel after seeing his face? Is anything coming back to you? Do you recognize him?"

Janey shakes her head. "I still don't remember seeing his face during . . . that night. It's still a blank. Except now that I know what he looks like . . ." She breaks off.

"Go on," Helen says, staring at Janey. She doesn't blink. When Janey doesn't continue, she asks, "Does seeing his father change how you feel about your son?"

"No," Janey says. "Of course not. I love my son."

"Yes, I understand that. But after all the trouble Christian has gotten into lately, you haven't once thought he was like his father?"

Janey doesn't answer right away. And then she says, "That's an awful thing to say."

"Maybe that was out of line. I apologize," Helen says, but she doesn't mean it. She knows from previous sessions that Janey has entertained these thoughts about her son, and on more than one occasion. "Why don't you tell me what happened to your face?"

Janey's hand immediately goes to the bruise on her cheekbone. "I fell," she says. "I hit it on the countertop."

"How did you fall?"

"I'm not sure, really. I think I fainted."

"I see. When is the last time you ate something?"

"I . . . I can't remember. Yesterday, I think," Janey says.

"You need to start taking better care of yourself," Helen says. "If you can't take care of yourself, how can you expect to take care of Christian? Are you feeding him at least?" she asks. This is the first time she's being tough on Janey. It's now or never.

"Of course I am."

"I'm glad to hear it," Helen says. She gives them both a minute. Then she says, "Tell me what was inside the manila envelope."

"How did you know about that?"

"I saw it when I brought in your mail. It seemed to have upset you."

"It's strange," Janey says. "It must've been put inside my mailbox by someone other than the mailman. There's no return address, or address of any kind. I don't know who it's from."

"That is strange," Helen says. "What was inside the envelope?"

"An article."

"What was the article about?"

"The murder gene," Janey says, closes her eyes.

"Do you believe in the murder gene?"

Janey doesn't answer.

"Do you know who might've sent it to you?" Helen feels a chill up her spine. She can't help it. Although her face remains neutral, she can't control

her body's physical response. The only thing she can do is mask it. She takes a moment, gathers herself, asks again, "Who do you think sent you the article?"

"I don't know," Janey says.

"Any guesses?" Helen asks.

"Someone is playing with me. Someone is trying to hurt me. Someone is trying to hurt my son."

Helen asks, "Why do you think someone is playing with you or trying to hurt you and your son?"

Janey doesn't acknowledge Helen's question. Instead, she redirects the conversation in her usual way of circling around the things she finds hard to talk about. "The school called me," she says. "They want to meet with me tomorrow to discuss Christian's behavior."

"I see," Helen says.

"I'm worried. They're talking about in-school suspension. That can't be good for him."

"No, I wouldn't think so." This is news to her. She wasn't expecting this. But she supposes it shouldn't have come as a big surprise, since he did hurt that little girl. "Tell me," she says, "how're Christian and the rabbit getting along? Any progress there?"

"She's no longer with us. She went to a nice home," Janey says without missing a beat.

"She went to a nice home?" She can do nothing but repeat what Janey is telling her.

"Yes," Janey says. "I gave her away. I thought it was for the best. It wasn't working out."

Helen regards Janey for a moment. For the first time in almost seven years, she wonders if she's misdiagnosed her. It's true, Janey has lied to her before, small white lies that meant nothing. But this feels different. There's something about this particular lie that feels calculated. She leans forward so her face is the closest it has ever been to Janey's face. It's time she calls her out. "You're lying," she says.

CHAPTER FORTY-ONE

"Thanks for coming over, Pop." Janey closed the door behind him and locked it. Although the media had left her alone since the Strangler had been caught, she'd relied on the ritual of locking the house up tight for far too long to feel comfortable any other way. Even the police officer was no longer in front of her house. It was a sign that things were going back to normal. She should be relieved. Why didn't she feel relieved?

She'd watched the replaying of the press conference late last night after Christian had gone to bed. She'd sat at the kitchen table with a bottle of wine and watched the small television she'd placed on the countertop, which was meant to keep her company most nights while she washed dishes. Robert Harms had been transported to the county jail. The DA rattled off the charges against him. Someone asked the DA if he would be pursuing the death penalty. She hadn't followed the discussion after that: something about the death penalty and the current governor's request to stay executions. She pinched her eyes closed when the photo of Robert Harms appeared on the screen. But the trace of fear that her son was like his father that had slithered around in the dark shadows of her mind had pushed its way into the light. She screamed, the sound so primal it frightened her. She'd finished off the rest of the bottle, swallowed a pill, and passed out in bed.

And then this morning she'd gotten the strangest text from her aunt Pearl. Call Detective Brassard if you need anything. That was it. That was the entire message.

"Christian is still sleeping. I didn't have the heart to wake him," she said to Pop. It was more like she didn't have the kind of energy she needed to get him up and fed, not when she had to get ready for the school meeting. She was nursing a wine headache. She'd taken her first shower in days.

"Go to your meeting," Pop said. "I'll get him up."

Within minutes Janey was pulling into the parking lot of the elementary school. The sun was out even though it was raining: a spring shower. It wouldn't last more than a few minutes, but it was enough to soak her hair and shoulders. She hurried to the front doors of the building and pressed the buzzer. "Yes," the tinny voice said.

"I'm here to see Mrs. Delacorte," she said. In the next second, the door was unlocked and she stepped inside. The hallway smelled like sour milk and sweat but not like adult sweat. It was more like that funky kid smell, a mix of dirty hands and unwashed hair. It was the same smell Christian would come home wearing on his clothes and skin.

She entered the office. The secretary told her to take a seat; Mrs. Delacorte would be with her shortly. She sat in a small chair facing the tall front desk. She felt like a child who had done something wrong and had been sent to the principal's office.

She didn't have to wait long. Mrs. Delacorte appeared. She was wearing a long skirt. Her small nose and lips were pinched tight on her flat face.

"Hi, Janey," she said. "Follow me."

She followed Mrs. Delacorte into a small classroom Janey had never been in before. Mrs. Delacorte directed her to sit in a lone chair at a long table opposite a woman she didn't recognize. The woman looked polished in her dark suit and short hair. It occurred to Janey that the woman was here representing the school district. Mr. Ward, the principal, walked in and greeted Janey; then he shook the woman's hand and sat next to her. Mrs. Delacorte shut the door and sat next to Mr. Ward.

"This is the specialist's room," Mrs. Delacorte said. "It's mostly used by our reading specialist, Miss Eileen."

Janey nodded.

"And this is Connie Labarre. She's the supervisor of special education for the district."

"Special education?" Janey asked. "My son doesn't have an IEP. He doesn't have special education services."

"We're aware of that, but I think you can agree he does need some kind of behavioral support," Mrs. Delacorte said.

Janey didn't know what to say. He was already in therapy. He was getting help, no thanks to them. She felt ganged up on with the three of them sitting on one side of the table and her all alone on the other side. She suspected the setup was designed to make her feel isolated and outnumbered.

"Well, let's get right to it," Mrs. Delacorte said. "We came up with a plan we think is suitable for everyone involved."

"You mean suitable for the school and the other parents," Janey said.

"I mean for the school and for Christian," Mrs. Delacorte said.

Janey was sitting back in the chair, arms folded. Her legs were pressed together. Her sweatshirt, which she now realized was far too casual for the meeting, was wet from the quick shower that had started the second she'd gotten out of her car. Even the weather was against her.

"We think it would be best if Christian finished out the school year in a different classroom. We'd like to place him in Mr. Schlegel's class."

"Okay," she said. That didn't sound so bad. Separating Christian from Claire's daughter, Emma, and the other little girl, Bella, who had broken her arm, would probably be for the best.

Mrs. Delacorte continued. "I'd also like to meet with Christian during lunch and recess. He can have lunch with me in my office and stay with me during recess. I have a couple of students who do this daily. It's a way of teaching certain students who are struggling how to manage free time."

"I don't see how this will help socialize him. I mean, that's what I've been sending him to therapy for, and it's been working, I might add." Or it had been working before the news about his relationship to the Strangler broke. Now, she wasn't sure what was happening with her son.

"It's not forever," Mrs. Delacorte said. "Let's try it for a couple weeks and see how it goes."

"In other words, you're going to be his babysitter," Janey said. "You're going to babysit him when he's not in the classroom. You're going to keep him away from the other children to appease their mothers."

"I don't believe that's what I'm suggesting," Mrs. Delacorte said. "I prefer to think of it as time I'll get to spend with Christian to get to know him better."

Mr. Ward spoke up. "It's a way of satisfying all parties involved."

She looked at Connie Labarre. "I suppose you came up with this plan?"

"I think it's a good solution to a difficult situation," Connie said. "We can reevaluate the plan of action over the summer and see if we need to make any adjustments for the next school year."

Mrs. Delacorte pushed a stack of forms across the table. "This is your copy. Look it over. If you agree, I'll need you to sign at the bottom of the last page."

Janey picked up the packet and scanned it. The writing was formal and all very clinical and *legal* sounding. The school district was covering their ass on this. But even as she was reading it over, she thought she'd sign it. There were only eight weeks left of the school year. She picked up the pen but hesitated to write her name.

"We really need you to sign the forms. I didn't want to have to bring this up, but we've received some new information, and if you don't agree to these terms, I'm afraid we'll have to move forward with a more formal hearing."

"What new information?"

"Christian's therapist faxed over a report to me first thing this morning."

"I didn't authorize her to send you anything."

"I have the release right here," Mrs. Delacorte said, and she passed Janey the paper. "Is that your signature?"

It was her signature, but she had no recollection of signing it. "May I see the report?" she asked.

"Of course." Mrs. Delacorte handed it to her.

Janey noticed it was signed by Dr. Carlyn Walsh. She'd written that Christian was deeply troubled, and she'd recommended removing Christian from his home. Child Welfare Services had been contacted. Dr. Walsh had written that soon after she'd given her recommendation, she'd been promptly terminated. She went on to state that she was unaware of the current conditions in the home, as Christian was no longer under her care. Janey stopped reading. What was going on? Why would she say that? Why would she tell the school these lies about Janey and her son?

"Janey?" Mrs. Delacorte said.

"Yes, I'm sorry, did you say something?"

"Is Christian seeing another therapist?"

"Yes, and it's going . . . it's going really well," she said. But was it? Was it really? Her son had hurt the rabbit. Or had he? Was it an accident, like all the other incidents could've been—the cracked Easter eggs, the hot stove, Bella's broken arm?

"In light of this," Mrs. Delacorte said, and she pointed to Carlyn's report, "we're still willing to work with you and Christian, but only if you'll agree to the terms we discussed. And we'll need you to sign."

Janey signed the form, even though she believed separating her son from the other children wasn't going to help him and could possibly set him back. But what other choice did she have?

She left the meeting shaken. Her legs weak and clumsy as she made her way to the car. Once she was behind the wheel, she pulled her cell phone out and called Carlyn's number. She was sent to voice mail.

"This is Janey. Christian's mom." Her voice was full of emotion. "Why would you say such horrible things about me and my son? Why? Why would you do something like that?" She quickly hung up the phone when she noticed Claire getting out of her car a few feet away. Claire reached into the back seat and pulled out a tray of cookies. Maybe the class was having a party: a party Christian hadn't been invited to.

Maybe everybody was right where Christian was concerned— Mrs. Delacorte, Claire, Carlyn. Even Dr. Watson, *Helen*, was apprehensive. And maybe, just maybe, Janey was right. Maybe he was deeply troubled, disturbed. But something inside her wanted so badly to believe he hadn't done the things he'd been accused of doing.

Then she thought about last night, watching the news, the horrible feeling she'd had that he was like his father. And what about all those therapy sessions she'd had with Helen, where she'd entertained that very idea?

Enough was enough.

She had to find out the truth about him, whatever it might be.

She was his mother.

It was her job to take care of him the best way she knew how.

There was only one thing left to do. She sent a text to Detective Brassard. Meet me at the county jail.

CHAPTER FORTY-TWO

Geena sat at her old desk at headquarters. Parker was in Albert's seat, working on the computer and catching up on paperwork. She was tapping her pencil on her leg. The station was quiet, with most of the patrol out on the road. The phones weren't ringing. The lieutenant was in his office. He hadn't spoken to either one of them since they'd come in this morning. His silence was enough to make her crazy.

"Did you get to see Becca over the weekend?" she asked.

"Yes," Parker said, his eyes never leaving the screen.

Okay, so he didn't want to talk about Becca. She was reminded of what Jonathon had said about how Parker didn't talk much. She'd replayed her conversation with Jonathon over and over again in her mind, knowing she'd done the right thing by asking him to leave Saturday night. "Relationships shouldn't have to be so hard. At least not the right ones," she said, thinking out loud.

Parker looked her over. "Who are we talking about here?" he asked.

"No one," she said. "Forget I said anything."

"Did you see the latest press conference?" he asked.

"No, I missed it." She never turned on the TV, avoiding having to see Jonathon's face after she'd sent him away.

"They moved Harms to county," Parker said. "I wonder if they got anything more out of him."

She continued tapping the pencil, but rather than tapping it on her leg, she tapped it on her desk. She was restless, much like she'd been yesterday, Sunday, lying in bed, hiding under the covers, Codis curled up at her feet. Something about her conversation with Robert troubled her, and it wasn't just that he'd accused her of being weak. She'd gone through the entire interview in her head, turning over every word they'd exchanged.

The evidence they had against him so far lined up. But they hadn't found the little rubber bands that were used to tie the braids in the victims' hair; they hadn't found ligatures.

She was certain they were missing something.

She checked her phone. She had a couple of texts. The most recent one was from her mother, asking about taking Codis to the dog park. She typed a reply. Sure, you can give it a try. Codis couldn't see or hear, but maybe he'd enjoy the change of smells. Or maybe not. Sometimes if Geena walked him too far from home, he'd start shaking, nervous in unfamiliar surroundings.

The other text was from Janey.

Geena pulled into the county jail parking lot. Parker had insisted on coming with her. Anything was better than sitting around doing paperwork. She parked next to Janey's car. Janey was standing by the driver's side door, waiting for them. Her hair was damp. The shoulders of her sweatshirt wet. She looked as though she'd gotten caught in the rain they'd had earlier that morning.

"Listen," Geena said to Parker before they got out of the car. "Sayres may not like that we're meeting her here."

"She contacted us," he said. "Let's just see what she wants."

They both got out. Janey's eyes looked as though she'd been crying.

"What's going on?" Geena asked.

"I want to see him," Janey said.

"See who?" Parker asked.

"Christian's father," she said.

"I'm not sure that's a good idea," Geena said.

"Did you see him on the news? Did you recognize him?" Parker asked.

"No," Janey said. "I still don't remember anything. I just need to see him," she said, and she wiped her nose. "Can you understand that?"

Geena thought she could. Janey wanted to confront the man who had attacked her, left her for dead. And who had also given her a son. She imagined Janey had questions for him. Geena certainly did. But she wasn't sure it would be good for Janey's mental health to let her see him. "What do you want to say to him?"

"I don't know," Janey said.

She wondered if Janey had thought this through. "Are you sure about this? It's not going to be easy."

"I can't explain it. I have to look him in the eyes. I have to know."

"What do you have to know?" Parker asked.

"I have to know if my son is anything like him."

CHAPTER FORTY-THREE

Janey didn't know how else to explain it to the detectives. She had to see Christian's father for herself. She was afraid. Of course she was. How could she not be? But what could he do to her now that he hadn't already done, and from behind bars? She was terrified for a much bigger reason. She was scared she'd see her son reflected in his eyes. What was she going to do if she did? She didn't know. She didn't know anything other than she had to do this. She'd never get any rest until she knew for sure.

"Can you get me in?" she asked.

Detective Brassard looked at Detective Reed. It seemed to Janey as though they had an entire conversation between them without having to speak. She wondered if it was like that with all cops and their partners.

"You have five minutes," Detective Brassard said.

Janey said, "I'll only need two."

Janey sat in a metal chair in a small cubicle in front of a glass partition. She slowly breathed in and then out, relaxing her diaphragm like she'd done in the bathtub when she'd prepared to hold her breath underwater.

You can do this, she told herself. She had to do this, for her son as much as for herself. She concentrated on her breathing, tried to relax and center herself. But when the door opened and Robert Harms appeared, it took all her strength not to jump out of the chair and run.

He was escorted into the room by an armed guard. He sat across from her on the other side of the glass. The guard stayed in the room with him, near the door. She breathed in, tried to manage her fear and calm the panic seizing her chest. She breathed out. He picked up the phone and nodded for her to do the same. When he realized she wasn't going to, he set his down. All those nights in the tub had prepared her for this. It was now or never. She took a deep breath and held it. It was her way of feeling as though she was the one who was in control.

She wouldn't meet his eyes. Not yet. She had five minutes, her personal record for denying her lungs air, although she'd told the detectives she'd only need two. She searched his face, the thin lips and square jaw, the nose that wasn't too big or too small. His hair was dark and wavy. There were things about his features that were familiar and things that were not. Christian's lips were fuller, his hair blonder, his complexion lighter than this man's.

Nothing about seeing Robert triggered memories of the attack.

But she still hadn't done what she came here to do. She squeezed her hands together as though she was bracing herself for an extreme kind of pain, and then she looked Christian's father in the eyes. She didn't see a trace of emotion inside of him. There was no remorse or even curiosity as to what she was doing here. She didn't see anger or fatigue. There was no love or hate or fear. There was just . . . nothing. She found herself trembling under his empty gaze.

She stood abruptly. The chair kicked back at her sudden movement. She rushed to the exit. The door was locked. She had to wait for it to be opened. She hurried down the hall and through the doors that led outside. She opened her mouth and swallowed a large gulp of air.

The detectives were leaning against their cruiser in the parking lot.

Janey fumbled for her keys while she filled her chest with oxygen.

"Are you okay?" Detective Reed asked.

"Yes," she said. "I'm okay."

"Did you remember anything after seeing him?" Detective Brassard asked.

"No," she said. "It's still a blank."

"What did you say to him?" Detective Brassard asked.

"Nothing," she said. "I didn't say anything to him. I never picked up the phone."

Detective Reed motioned with his head to an area across the parking lot. "We got company."

Two important-looking men got out of a black luxury sedan. Janey recognized the face of the one man. He was the DA for the county. She'd seen him on TV talking about the case.

"You better go," Detective Brassard said.

Janey didn't understand what was going on, and she didn't care to know. She got in her car. She couldn't wait to get home.

"Pop," Janey called, and she tossed her purse and car keys onto the kitchen counter.

"In here," he said.

She found him sitting on the floor with Christian, an array of colored pictures scattered around them.

"He's quite the artist," Pop said.

She sat next to her son. He didn't acknowledge her. He acted as though he didn't know she'd left the house and that she'd been gone much of the morning. She picked up a drawing of a stegosaurus. She could tell what it was by the armored plates along its spine. Christian continued coloring.

Pop got up. "I better get going," he said. "Your mother is going to be home soon."

She walked him to the door, thanked him for looking after Christian for her.

"How did the meeting with the school go?" he asked.

"They want to put Christian in a different classroom until the end of the school year," she said.

"That doesn't sound so bad, does it?"

"No, it doesn't," she said.

He kissed her forehead. "Try not to worry," he said, and he left.

She closed the door and locked it. She returned to the family room and knelt in front of Christian. She lifted his chin, stared into his eyes. It was there, the kindness and goodness she was looking for. And somewhere in his gaze, she also saw compassion and curiosity and, finally, confusion. Relief moved through her, overtook her, filled her heart.

"Mommy, why are you looking at me like that?"

"You're a good boy," she said, and she wrapped her arms around him. "A very good boy. And don't let anyone tell you differently."

CHAPTER FORTY-FOUR

"What are you two doing here?" Sayres asked. He stood across from Geena and Parker in the parking lot. His hands were on his hips, pulling his suit jacket away from his body, accentuating his lean waist. The sunlight showed the lines on his face, the tiny hairs growing on his shaved head.

"Janey texted me," Geena said. "She asked us to meet her here."

Jonathon managed to stand slightly to the side of Sayres and out of direct contact with her. She might've been able to pretend he wasn't there at all if it weren't for the wind carrying his cologne.

"Well, are you going to tell me what she was doing here, or do I have to guess?" Sayres asked.

"She wanted to see Harms," she said.

"And did she?"

"Yes."

"And you let her?" he asked.

"Legally, there's nothing standing in her way," Jonathon said.

"She didn't say anything to him. She didn't remember anything new. She just wanted to look him in the eye," she said. "And after what she's been through, I didn't think it was too much to ask."

"She can do that at the trial," Sayres said. "And the sentencing."

"We should tell them," Jonathon said to Sayres.

"Tell us what?" she asked.

"The DNA's a match. No question he's our guy," Sayres said. "But there's something else. While you two were cooling off over the weekend, the team found some women's clothing, makeup, and some feminine products in his house. You know, that kind of stuff. None of the items belong to the victims."

"Maybe he likes to dress up as a woman," Parker said. "It's not unheard of."

"But why would he need feminine products to play dress-up?" she asked. "Maybe the stuff belongs to a family member or possibly a girlfriend."

"Bill's already looking into Harms's relatives," Sayres said.

"Has anyone talked to the neighbors?" she asked. "Maybe someone has seen a woman hanging around. Maybe they know who she is."

"One step ahead of you," Sayres said. "I've got Craig making the rounds."

"Let us help him," she said.

"It's not a bad idea," Jonathon said. "Speed up the process."

"Fine," Sayres said. "Help him out. But Brassard, tread lightly. Internal Affairs is looking at that videotape. I had no choice but to turn it over to them."

Geena nodded and got in the car. The lieutenant hadn't removed her from the case, which she'd taken to mean he'd watched the video and was on her side.

"Remember the braids in the girls' hair?" she asked Parker once she'd pulled from the lot. "You said it was an odd thing for a guy to do."

"Yeah, what about it?"

"When you add in the fact that he'd also untied them, it just doesn't seem to fit with what we know about him. Maybe we were right from the start, and he's not smart. Maybe he's not the brains behind the crimes."

"You're thinking he had an accomplice?" Parker asked.

"I'm thinking we need to find out. Where are the rubber bands? The ligatures? It doesn't sit right with me that we didn't find them with what was most definitely his murder kit."

"I agree," Parker said. "We need to find this woman."

✵

Geena leaned against the car. It was a pleasant enough day, maybe a little muggy from the rain earlier. She fidgeted with her ponytail, ended up tying it in a topknot. She was restless again, waiting for Parker to return. He was knocking on doors up and down Sullivan Trail, while Craig worked the other side of the street. She'd already checked the homes behind Harms's Cape Cod.

A car slowed and pulled into the driveway directly across from Harms's house. She watched a young woman get out of the driver's side. She lifted a small child from the back seat. With the other hand, she picked up a plastic bag from a local grocery store.

Geena looked down the street where the guys were standing before she made her way over to the mother. "Excuse me, do you live here?" she asked.

The woman turned toward Geena, balancing her little girl in her arm. "Yes. Can I help you?"

"I'm Detective Brassard." She held up her badge. "I was wondering if you could answer a few questions for me."

"Is this about the man across the street?" she asked.

"It is."

"Come inside," the woman said.

Geena took the grocery bag and followed her into the house through the garage. The house was much bigger than the other homes in the neighborhood. This one had an open concept that gave Geena a good look into the family room and dining room. The kitchen was immaculate, with white cabinets and gray countertops. On closer inspection, she could see the greasy fingerprints around the knobs on the lower cabinets and the splatter of milk or juice on the stainless steel appliances. The woman put the little girl in a high chair with a bowl of Cheerios, and then she introduced herself as Holly.

"I didn't know him," Holly said. "As you can see, our yard has arborvitae lining the street. They were planted to keep out the noise of traffic as well as for privacy."

Geena had noticed the trees. "We're talking to everyone in the neighborhood," she said.

"I saw the news, and I have to say I'm a bit freaked out to learn I was living across the street from a serial killer." Holly was smoothing the hair down on her little girl's head. Geena didn't think Holly realized she was doing it.

"Have you ever seen any women going in or out of his home?" she asked.

"Oh God, there's not another girl missing, is there?"

"We're just trying to gather information."

"You know, now that you mention it, I have seen a woman in the driveway once in a while. She was older, or should I say she wasn't young, like the girls' photos I saw on TV. She was maybe around my age or a little older than me."

"And how old would that be?"

"Maybe mid- to late thirties," Holly said. "She was average height, dark hair. Nothing special about her that stuck out, other than her car."

"What was special about her car?"

"It was a white Jaguar, an older model. Not like ten years older, but more like a model from the seventies. I think it might've been a convertible, but with a hardtop. You can tell she really took care of it like it was her baby." Holly shrugged. "That was my impression, anyway, from across the street and standing in my driveway."

"Any other identifying features about her other than her age and dark hair? Or her car?"

"No, not that I can think of."

"Okay, thank you. You've been a big help." She took out a card and set it on the countertop. "Call me if you think of anything else or if you see her around again."

She waved to the little girl in the high chair before she showed herself out. The guys had converged in front of Harms's house. Police tape blocked off the driveway and front door. She joined them.

"I was just telling Parker the cadaver dogs were here on Sunday," Craig said. He was bald, and the top of his head glistened with sweat. His skin was getting red under the sun. "I guess they figured it was possible they'd find something in the house or yard."

"Did they?" Parker asked.

Craig shook his head. "But we still don't know if there are any others. He lawyered up minutes after you knocked him around," he said to Geena.

"Did you get anything from the neighbors?" Parker asked.

"Yeah, from the lady across the street," she said. "She noticed a woman in her thirties, average height, dark hair, coming and going from the house. She only saw her from her driveway and couldn't give a better description than that, but she noticed the woman drove a vintage white Jaguar. Thinks it was a convertible with a hardtop."

"Vintage? How old are we talking about?" Parker asked.

"She thought maybe seventies," she said.

"It shouldn't be hard to spot," Craig said. "Let's drive around, see if we can find it."

~Helen Watson, Psy.D.
Patient: Janey Montgomery, ID 27112

"I went to see Christian's father," Janey says.

"You did what?"

"I went to see Christian's father."

Helen is stunned into silence. She didn't expect this. She's been concentrating on Janey and her son this entire time and hasn't given much thought to the father. How stupid of her. "Did seeing him help you to remember anything?" she asks. She is breathless, waiting for Janey to answer.

"No. But it made me realize that I have to stop living in the past, not only for my sake but for my son's sake. We need to move forward. And in order for me to be able to do that, I do need to remember. I need to know what happened to me. I want to be hypnotized."

"We talked about this, and you know I don't think it's a good idea. There's a potential for it to bring about false memories," Helen says.

"If you won't do it, then I'll find someone who will."

Janey shocks her for the second time. Where is all this defiance coming from? This strength? Helen has always known Janey to be meek, submissive. This development is new. Perhaps she went too far, pushed Janey in a direction that she didn't want her to go in. "I don't think it's wise to change doctors in the middle of treatment," she says.

"So you'll do it?" Janey asks.

Helen sits back in the chair, thinks it over. If Janey is determined to be hypnotized, then Helen should be the one to do it. She can't risk anyone else poking around inside Janey's head. She's worked too hard on her. They've come so far together. "Okay," she says.

"Then let's get started," Janey says. "I don't want to wait."

It's been a long time since Helen has researched this method. She's not confident it will work. She was being honest with Janey when she told her the pitfalls of such practices. She has Janey lie on the couch. She places a pillow under Janey's head. "Are you comfortable?" she asks.

"Yes," Janey says.

"I want you to look up," Helen says. "Keep looking up as you close your eyes. You'll feel your eyelids flutter. I'm going to count down from ten to one; each time I count, you'll take a step down the stairs, going down, deeper and deeper inside yourself." She continues the process, counting down until Janey reaches the bottom stair. She then has Janey go through some arm motions, getting her to relax her muscles. The neck muscles are typically the first to tense and the last to relax. All the while she's talking to Janey, relaxing her, she's taking her deeper inside her memories. She touches Janey's forehead, feels her neck is loose. Then she takes Janey back to that night, supplying the few details Janey has provided in their many sessions together.

Janey relives the events over again—the rag over her nose and mouth, waking up with her wrists and ankles tied. She gives only vague details of the assault. She's disoriented. There's something covering his face, so she's not able to see the man on top of her. She's crying and fighting for air. She can't breathe. She's choking. She's left for dead. But she's not dead. She hears voices. He's talking to someone. He's fumbling around. It's hard to do, he says. It's his first time. Then she's falling. Her body hits concrete, but it's not solid and fills all around her, over her, under her, swallows *her. It's water, and it's bitter cold, rushing over her head, pulling her downriver. Her head breaks through, she gasps, takes in water, looks up and sees the bridge. There's someone on the bridge. Someone familiar.*

It's him. My God, it's him.

No, it's not him.

It's a woman. And she's looking down at her.

CHAPTER FORTY-FIVE

Janey's head didn't feel right. She was having trouble focusing. Her thoughts drifted up and away as if they were attached to balloons. And yet, her skull was as heavy as the bolts of fabric she used to lift at work. Her body ached. Her muscles were sore, as though she'd spent hours swimming against the current. The last time she'd felt this way, she'd woken up in the hospital after they'd pulled her from the river.

She didn't remember driving home late last night after she'd left Helen's office. Christian had been with her. He'd fallen asleep on a sofa chair in Helen's waiting room, if that was what one could call the space. It was more like a foyer with a coatrack, if you didn't count the sofa chair. Janey had never seen anyone in the waiting room. Helen scheduled patients so they didn't bump into each other.

Janey should not have driven home in her condition. It had been poor judgment on her part. She was lucky they'd gotten home safely. But what if they hadn't? It could've given Child Welfare Services another reason to take her son from her. She'd forgotten to mention to Helen about Carlyn's interference, siccing a caseworker on them. She'd have to tell her. Maybe there was something Helen could do to stop it.

Janey moved around the kitchen tentatively. Any jarring motion caused her head to throb. Helen hadn't mentioned the side effects of hypnosis, if that was what this was. She wondered if the doctor had known there could be side effects. When Janey had come out of the trance, she'd been calm, although her throat had been raw.

Her dreams through the night had been very different, though, far from the relaxed state she'd felt in Helen's office. An image of a woman standing on the bridge, watching her drown in the river, had replayed in her mind's eye over and over again until she'd screamed. It had been so vivid, except for the blurriness of the woman's face.

She'd known all along there had been a woman on the bridge that night. She hadn't mentioned it to the detectives. This was the secret she'd kept from everyone. She'd tried to convince herself that it was something she'd made up in one of her dreams, because it hadn't made any sense. A man had attacked her. Christian was proof.

But now it seemed the woman on the bridge had been real. *Too real* for it to have been a false memory.

The toast she was making for Christian's breakfast popped up. He was seated at the table with a banana that he refused to peel himself. She plucked the bread from the toaster. It was darker than he liked, but it wasn't burnt. She worried he wouldn't eat it, but she buttered it anyway.

"It's burnt," he said when she set it down in front of him.

"It's not burnt. It's toasted."

"Burnt," he said, and he pushed it away.

She didn't have it in her to argue with him. She peeled his banana and handed it to him. She put more bread in the toaster. Her phone went off. Carlyn was finally returning her call. She picked up the phone from the counter and walked into the family room. She had every intention of answering, but something held her back. She realized she didn't want to hear Carlyn's explanation as to why she'd sent that awful report to the elementary school.

What good would it do now, anyway?

She shut the phone off and tossed it on the couch.

She smelled something burning.

She raced into the kitchen. Smoke poured out of the toaster. She rushed to unplug it. The two slices of bread were black.

"Burnt," Christian said.

There was a knock at the door.

Now what? She looked at the clock. Eight a.m. Who could be here at this hour? She went back to the family room, peeked out the window. There was a woman on her stoop. She held a folder in her hand. The caseworker from Child Welfare Services. It had to be. She was trying to catch Janey early, unaware. Off guard. She wanted to see Christian in his natural surroundings, the way he lived day to day. She didn't want the house cleaned if it normally wasn't. She didn't want him bathed, his clothes washed, if only for the sole purpose of her visit. And wouldn't she want to see the state Janey herself was in?

She wouldn't let the caseworker take her son from her. She'd fought too hard to keep him. She wouldn't give him up now. The hospital had wanted to give her a pill to abort any chance of pregnancy. She'd refused. Her parents had urged her to consider adoption. She hadn't.

She'd wanted her baby then. And she wanted him now.

Christian was hers. *Hers.* And no one had the right to take him away from her.

She crept back to the kitchen, put her finger to her lips. "Shh," she said to him. She had to get him out of the house. She had to take him somewhere safe. Her parents' house no longer felt like an option. Would the caseworker think to track him down there? And she definitely wasn't dropping him off at school. She'd go to Helen, something she should've talked about with her in the first place. She was certain Helen would know what to do.

The woman knocked harder. "Janey Montgomery?" she called.

Janey led Christian to his room, grabbing his shoes along the way. "Let's get you dressed," she whispered. He seemed to sense her urgency, or more like her panic. For once he didn't argue.

Janey put him in jeans and a T-shirt. She ran her fingers through his hair. He didn't pull away or throw a tantrum. She was still wearing the same clothes she'd worn yesterday. She didn't have time to change. She caught a glimpse of herself in the mirror. Her hair was wild around her face, having been rained on and then slept on. It was a mass of knotty waves.

The woman banged on the door a third time. "Hello?" she called, murmured something Janey couldn't make out. The house was silent after that.

She waited a few more minutes. When she thought it was safe, she said to Christian, "Let's go . . . hurry," and rushed him to the car. She strapped him in the seat and then pulled from the curb, drove down the street, checking the rearview mirror repeatedly to see if she was being followed.

CHAPTER FORTY-SIX

Geena and Parker and the rest of the team huddled around the conference room table. They'd spent much of yesterday driving around Harms's neighborhood, but they hadn't found the vintage white Jag.

Currently, Bill was tapping away on the keyboard, searching for the owner in the system. He was going on the notion there couldn't be many classic Jags registered in the state of Pennsylvania and, specifically, Northampton County.

"Sifting through paperwork is making me nuts," Geena said. "I need to be moving."

"Uh-huh," Parker said, obviously distracted. He was looking over the list of evidence they'd already collected. "He was prepared with the tent, the rags, and the bottle of chloroform. His fishing gear was packed and ready to go. His hiking boots were right outside the door."

"That's what makes it so odd that the ligatures and rubber bands weren't in his kit," Geena said.

"We have enough to nail him without the ligatures and rubber bands," Craig said.

Sayres walked into the room, addressed the team. "Harms won't give up the woman's name, not even to his lawyer, so I hear. Are we any closer to tracking down this Jag?"

"Still working on it," Bill said.

"What are you two doing sitting here?" Sayres said to Geena and Parker. "Take another drive around, see if you can locate it."

Parker drove down Sullivan Trail and all around Harms's neighborhood. Geena checked every driveway and passing car, not that the Jag would be hard to spot. When they'd covered the entire area as best they could, Parker took Route 191 into Bangor. He wove his way through the one-way streets starting with First Street, then climbing the hill to Eighth Street where Janey lived.

"Harms lived pretty close to Janey," Geena said. "What do you think? About fifteen minutes?"

"Give or take," Parker said, and he pulled over in front of Janey's house. "Who's that?" he asked. There was a woman on Janey's front stoop. Janey's car wasn't parked anywhere on the street.

Geena and Parker got out of the car.

"Hi there," Geena said as they approached the woman. "Can we help you?"

The woman looked skeptical.

"I'm Detective Brassard, and this is Detective Reed." She held up her badge.

"Oh, sure. I'm Marie Cruz, Child Welfare Services. I'm looking for Janey Montgomery. I have the right house, don't I?"

"You do," Geena said.

"This is the second time I've stopped by this morning, but she still doesn't seem to be home."

"You're a caseworker?" Geena asked.

Marie Cruz looked them over as though she was trying to decide what, if anything, she should tell them. "Are you handling the Strangler case everyone's talking about?"

"We are."

"Yeah, well, then you know all about Ms. Montgomery's unusual situation."

"We do," Geena said. "But may I ask what you're doing here?"

"I got a call from the elementary school asking me to check on her and her son. It's customary for the school to call us in certain circumstances if they suspect some form of neglect or abuse."

Geena exchanged a look with Parker. It seemed to Geena that Janey may have struggled sometimes with taking care of Christian. She knew it couldn't be easy for a single mom. But she'd never noticed signs of neglect or abuse, not even when Janey had sent him to his room for a time-out. It was typical punishment for bad behavior.

"What were the school's concerns, exactly?" she asked.

"Apparently, they received a report from the boy's therapist telling them there were some problems in the home."

"What kinds of problems?"

"Well, that's the strange part about this whole thing," Marie said. "This therapist didn't give us much information, just demanded we take the boy from his mother."

"That is strange," Geena said.

"Yeah. And I've worked with her before on other cases. Some of those cases were hard, and I was glad to be working with her. She's good. And always professional." She shook her head. "That's why it doesn't make sense the way she's handling this one."

"What's this therapist's name?" Parker asked.

"Carlyn Walsh. She's got some fancy degree, and I'm telling you the woman is good with kids. It just doesn't fit, her handling a boy and his mother this way. But hey, here I am. We all have a job to do, right?"

Geena's interest was piqued at the mention of Carlyn's name. She was a witness they'd interviewed last December in the "Cold Woods" case, which was also Geena's and Parker's first big case together after she'd been transferred to the field station. Decades-old bones had been found not far from the Appalachian Trail. They'd questioned Carlyn when they'd discovered she'd been friends with their suspect.

"Well," Marie said. "It looks like I'll have to come back for a third time." She headed to her car.

Geena and Parker got back into their car.

"Maybe we should find out what's going on," she said.

Parker started the engine. "I don't suppose you remember Carlyn's address, with that memory of yours?" he asked.

"Of course I do."

"Point the way," he said as they pulled from the curb.

CHAPTER FORTY-SEVEN

Janey pulled into the driveway and parked behind the doctor's fancy car.

She got out of her car, helped Christian out of his seat. They followed the brick path that led to the back door of the house. Grass had started growing between the bricks, and the tops were covered in moss. She'd walked this path so many times over the last seven years that she knew which bricks were loose, which were cracked. The last brick she placed her foot on before she stepped onto the stoop had been engraved with the year the farmhouse had been built: 1920.

She stepped through the door (which was never locked for patients) and stopped in the foyer. The cushion on the sofa chair was still indented where Christian had slept the night before, while she'd been hypnotized. Christian climbed onto the chair, clutching a stegosaurus in his hand. She bet the *T. rex* was hiding in his pocket, waiting to strike.

"Wait here and play with your dinosaurs. I won't be long." She pulled in a deep breath before pushing open the office door. She was still feeling the effects of last night's session. She was a little dizzy. Her thoughts, hazy.

Helen looked up from whatever she was working on at her desk. "This is a surprise," she said.

"I need your help," Janey said.

Helen seemed to consider Janey's request. She put her pen down, and then she got up and closed the door. "Please, have a seat."

Janey sat in the chair designated for patients. The cushion formed to her butt as though she was the last one who'd sat on it, which she probably was.

Helen lingered by Janey's side before taking her seat back behind the desk. "Does this have something to do with our session last night?" she asked.

"It's about Christian," she said. "Carlyn contacted Child Welfare Services."

"Yes, I know."

"What do you mean, you know?" She didn't remember telling her, but she'd been mixed up about so many things lately.

"It wasn't really Carlyn who requested they be contacted."

She was confused. If it wasn't Carlyn who had made the request, then Helen had to know who had. Something inside of Janey seemed to break, scattering her into a million pieces. "It was you. You forged Carlyn's name. You copied my signature on the release. But why? I don't understand. Why are you trying to take my son away from me?"

Helen sat back in the chair. "It was only a matter of time until you figured out who I am."

"What are you talking about?" She was struggling to make sense of what was happening.

"You still don't know?" Helen asked. "Take a closer look. You still don't recognize me? You don't remember anything about who you saw last night? About what you remembered, what you've always known?"

There was something about the shape of Helen's face, the pointed nose and chin. It was the face she recognized from her dreams, the blurry face she remembered when she'd been hypnotized. She looked into Helen's eyes. The pieces were starting to fall into place. "You're the woman on the bridge."

"Yes," Helen said.

There were so many questions racing through her mind. Nothing made sense, and yet, everything did. The puzzle that had been her life these last seven years was coming together. "You're not a psychologist, are you?"

"Am I licensed? No. But I did take a couple of classes in psychology, enough to be convincing to a small list of clients. It's not much, but I get by."

"But the hospital gave me your name. They would've checked your credentials."

"Actually, it was me who visited you in the hospital. I was the one who gave you my card. I admit it was a big risk. I didn't know if you'd recognize me. But you were pretty out of it. They had you on some strong medication."

"I . . . I don't understand. How did you know I'd contact you?"

"I didn't. And then, a few weeks after you were released, you called to schedule an appointment. And what a surprise to learn you were pregnant."

Janey struggled to comprehend the full magnitude of what Helen was telling her. There was only so much she could take in at one time. She'd placed her trust in this woman. She'd confessed her secrets to her, cried, agonized over her darkest fears about her son. She gazed at the framed degree on the wall.

"It's a fake," Helen said.

"The publications in psychology journals?"

"A lie."

"Who are you?" she asked. Slowly, it was sinking in, how Helen wasn't who she said she was, how she'd never wanted to help her, how she'd been lying to her.

"My real name is Mary Harms. I'm Robert's sister. He's Robbie to me, but no one knows that, do they? I changed my name several years ago to Helen Watson when things got complicated."

"You're . . . you're his sister? You knew what he was . . . was doing to them? To me? You . . . you were there?" Her hand touched her throat. She pulled at the collar of her shirt. This wasn't happening.

"Well, I couldn't expect him to do it on his own now, could I?"

"I don't understand." *Breathe,* she told herself. *Breathe.* But controlling her breath wasn't going to help her now. The door behind her, the one she needed to escape through, felt far away and out of reach.

Helen sighed. "My dear brother is sloppy. He lacks discipline. And sadly, this last time, he didn't listen to me. He went out on his own, even though I told him it was too risky with the lake being drained. It wasn't the right time. But he got greedy, and now he's in jail." She stood from the chair and walked around to the front of the desk. "There's nothing I can do to help him now. I really did try to temper him." She leaned against the desk, her knees nearly touching Janey's. "But I have my nephew, thanks to you. And I'm catching him much younger than Robbie. I have a better chance of shaping him. He'll have more discipline. He'll do exactly what I want him to do."

"What are you saying?" *Christian!* If her emotions had color, they would have been the color of ice, of cold terror. She'd made a terrible mistake by bringing her son here. Helen wanted him. She wanted to . . . to *groom* him. She couldn't let Helen have him. She wouldn't. How was she going to get them both out of this? But Helen didn't know she'd brought him with her. Helen probably believed he was in school. She had to think, use this to her advantage somehow. She had to remain calm. She wasn't aware she'd started rocking until her knees knocked into Helen's.

"I really don't want to hurt you. I know you may not want to believe this, but I've grown to like you. That's why I contacted Child Welfare Services. If you could've just left well enough alone, they could've taken Christian for me, and we wouldn't be here right now. They would've left his care in my capable hands. And you could've gone on with your life, freed from the burden of motherhood. But you kept pushing. Then you wanted to be hypnotized. You insisted. I couldn't take a chance on your going to someone else. I mean, how was I supposed to keep my eye on you, on what you remembered, if you stopped coming to see me? You didn't leave me a choice. And now here we are, and I'm forced to take more drastic measures."

"You're delusional. They'll never let you take my son," she said. "They'll never let you have him. My parents wouldn't let that happen."

"Your parents?" Helen laughed. "They wanted you to give him up for adoption, remember? They won't fight me. They never wanted him."

"That's not true," she said, although they had pushed her into giving Christian up for adoption right up until her delivery date. But no. She wouldn't let Helen twist her thoughts where her parents were concerned. She wouldn't be manipulated by her again.

"Even if that is the case," Helen said, "it's easy for a child to get lost in the system, especially with a little help."

"I won't let you take him from me." The panic, the fear she was feeling was shifting, turning into something else, something hot and fluid.

"You're not fit to be his mother. Christian is special. He has a gift most people don't understand," Helen said.

A gift? The feeling moving through her was taking shape and form, spitting and popping. "It was you who sent me the article. You wanted me to believe in the murder gene."

"Don't you?"

"No," she said. "You're wrong."

"Then how do you explain what happened to the rabbit?"

"What do you mean what happened to the rabbit?" Janey had never told her what had really happened to Bunnie. Then it occurred to her. "*You* hurt her."

Helen smiled. "A little poison in her food. It really was easy."

"You're . . . you're crazy." A sense of relief cycled through her. Christian hadn't hurt Bunnie. This horrible, awful woman had poisoned their pet.

"What about the school?" she asked. She wanted the truth. She wouldn't be lied to again. "And the little girl who hurt her arm? Did you have something to do with that too?"

Helen leaned back. She seemed content with talking about it for now. "Oh, that was all just a coincidence. But it really worked in my favor. And you and that guidance counselor were so eager to believe Christian was involved. It was surprising to see how little faith you had in your son."

"I have faith in him. He's nothing like you. Or his father. You forget there's half of me inside of him. The good half. And there's nothing you can do to change that, not while I'm still alive."

Helen nodded. "Yes, I agree that is a problem." She rubbed her temples, and then she sighed heavily. "Robbie usually takes care of the messy parts for us. But I guess it's up to me now."

Janey tried to stand. She had to get herself and Christian out of there. Helen pushed her back down onto the chair. She loomed over her.

"How should we do this?" Helen asked. "You seem to like pills, given how easily you swallowed all those sleeping pills I gave you. You didn't think it was odd that I had a constant supply, that you never had to get a prescription filled? I mean, psychologists can't even prescribe medicine. I thought that was common knowledge. But you just took the pills blindly. I guess that just shows how really sick you are. Have you seen yourself lately? You've let yourself go. You really do play the part of victim so well. Now come on, up you go." She reached under Janey's arm to pull her up.

She smacked Helen's hand away.

She wasn't a victim. She was a *survivor*.

And she wouldn't let this evil woman hurt her son.

The next thing she knew, she was standing and pushing Helen away from her. She turned for the door, to run, to grab Christian and get away. But Helen reached out, grasped a handful of Janey's hair, and yanked her backward. She fought to free herself. Helen swung her around the room. Her hip banged into the chair, knocking it over. Then her head snapped back, and in the next second, her face slammed into the desk. And everything went black.

CHAPTER FORTY-EIGHT

Parker took North Eighth Street and several smaller streets before turning onto Garibaldi Avenue. They were at Carlyn's house in under five minutes.

"I don't see her car," Geena said.

"Let me guess. You remember the make and model too."

"Dark-blue BMW X5."

"You know, I think there's an alley behind the house," he said. "Maybe she parks back there."

"Let's see if she's home," she said.

They got out of the car and walked up to the front door. Parker rang the bell.

Within a few seconds, the door opened and Carlyn appeared. "I never expected to see you two again," she said.

They stepped into a large foyer that looked to have been some kind of storefront.

"It was a shoe-repair shop," Carlyn said, as though she'd read Geena's mind. "I don't get many people coming to the front door, and I haven't decided what I want to do with the space yet." She continued to lead them into an open family room and dining room. The hardwood floors were polished to a shine. A large-screen television hung on the wall opposite a black leather couch. It had a bachelor pad feel to it or, in this case, bachelorette.

Carlyn turned and faced them. She didn't ask them to sit. Instead, they stood in the middle of the room. There was a pile of board games on the table.

"Do you see patients here?" Geena asked.

"Not in my house," Carlyn said. "I have an office out back, but more often than not I work with them in their homes."

"Do you see Christian Montgomery in his home?" Geena asked.

"No. Not anymore. What's this about?"

"You don't see him anymore?" Geena asked.

"No. His mother wanted to try another therapist."

"That's interesting," Parker said. "We just bumped into Marie Cruz from Child Welfare Services outside Janey's house."

"I think I know what this is about. Christian's elementary school called me about a report I'd supposedly written and sent to them. But I didn't send them any reports, and I certainly didn't request Child Welfare Services be contacted."

"Do you know who did?" Parker asked.

"No, I don't. But I'd like to get to the bottom of it. I have no idea why my name would be attached to it."

"Do you know who Christian's new therapist is?"

"Her name is Helen Watson. She's been treating Janey for several years now. I guess Janey wanted her to take over Christian's therapy as well."

"Do you know where we can find this Helen Watson?" Parker asked.

"No, I didn't think to ask."

"Okay," Geena said. "Thanks for your help."

"What exactly is going on?" Carlyn asked.

"I'm not sure. We'll be in touch."

When they were back in the car, Geena pulled her phone out. She searched for any information on this Dr. Helen Watson on the internet.

Parker scrolled through his messages. "Bill got a hit on the Jag. He sent the address."

She said, "Sounds like an invitation to me."

CHAPTER FORTY-NINE

Janey's vision was blurry. Her head was heavy, fuzzy. Her face hurt. But she was alive. And as long as she was alive, there was hope. She tried to get her bearings and assess her situation. She was lying on her side on a bed. The sheets smelled fragrant. It took her a couple of seconds to place the scent. She must be in Helen's room. On Helen's bed.

Her wrists were tied behind her back. Her legs were tied at her ankles. Someone was sitting behind her on the bed. She felt their presence even if she couldn't see them. It had to be Helen. Robert was in jail. But where was Christian? Maybe he'd heard them fighting, hid somewhere safe. Maybe he'd gotten away. *Please, let that be the case.*

Helen tugged at Janey's hair. She was humming. Her voice sounded far away, although she was sitting next to her. She pulled Janey's hair again. She was fixing it, combing it, tying tiny braids around Janey's crown. She had a feeling of déjà vu. At the hospital, she'd ripped braids from her hair, tearing open her scalp right before they'd sedated her and put her on suicide watch on the sixth floor. No one had questioned why her hair had been braided then. They'd assumed she'd done it herself.

Helen stopped humming. She was talking. Janey tried to pay attention, to focus and figure out how she was going to get away.

"My mother used to braid my hair after my uncle came to visit us," Helen said, and she yanked Janey's hair particularly hard. Her head jerked backward.

"Every spring during fishing season, he took Robbie and me camping. We slept in tents. My uncle and Robbie in one tent and me in the other. When I was eleven, my uncle started visiting my tent. Sometimes he'd make me stay in there with him all day, and he'd make Robbie go fishing on his own." She pulled on Janey's hair again, much harder than necessary. "Then one year he started spending just as much time in the tent with Robbie as he would with me."

There was a long pause, as though she was waiting for Janey to say something.

"I'm . . . sorry," Janey said, and she pinched her eyes closed. *Where is my son? Please let him be okay.*

Helen's touch became softer as she ran her fingers through Janey's locks. "After his visits, my mother would comfort me by playing with my hair. Sometimes she'd tie it into these complicated braids. I think it was her way of apologizing. She knew what her brother was doing, and she did nothing to stop it." Then she yanked on Janey's hair again, harder than before. The pain was blinding. "But the last girl, Valerie— she didn't get the braids. And I do regret that," she said. "He did untie her, though. At least he gave her that."

This was madness. She couldn't make out what Helen said next.

Several minutes passed, or maybe it was mere seconds. She was fading in and out of consciousness. She couldn't be sure how much time had gone by. Helen was talking again.

"I won't have to worry about those things with Christian, will I? I'll always be there with him," Helen said. "Why didn't you tell me you brought him with you?"

No! she wanted to scream. Maybe she did scream. Her eyelids fluttered as though she might black out. She had to stay alert, strong for her son's sake. "Where is he?" she asked. "What did you do to him?"

CHAPTER FIFTY

Geena and Parker met Bill and Craig outside a colonial-style home in Upper Mount Bethel Township. A three-car garage was detached from the house at the end of a long driveway.

The front door opened. A man in his sixties wearing jeans and a gray T-shirt greeted them. "How can I help you?"

Bill flashed his badge. "We were hoping you could answer a few questions for us."

"What's this about?" the man asked.

"We're looking for the owner of a vintage white Jaguar. We think it could be connected to a case we're investigating."

"I'm the owner," he said.

"May we come in?" Geena asked.

They followed the man, Mr. Jacobs, to the kitchen. The wallpaper and carpeting were outdated. The furniture had seen better days. His wife was sitting at the table. She was wearing a matching gray T-shirt, like her husband's. Introductions were made.

"They're asking about the Jaguar," Mr. Jacobs said to his wife and then sat next to her.

"Are you the only one who drives the car?" Geena asked, thinking maybe they had a daughter who drove it. Since Mrs. Jacobs didn't fit the description of the woman, based on Holly's eyewitness account. These two looked to be retired.

"I'm the only one who drives it," Mr. Jacobs said. "The car's been sitting in the garage all winter. We haven't gotten it out yet this spring, not with all the rain we've been having lately."

"Do you have any daughters who might've driven it without your knowing?" she asked.

"We have three boys. They're grown and moved out. They wouldn't have taken it without permission."

"Okay," she said.

"May we see the car?" Parker asked.

"Sure." Mr. Jacobs got up from the table. His wife got up too.

They followed the couple to the garage, where there was an SUV and a silver sedan. The Jag was under a dusty tarp. Mr. Jacobs pulled the cover back to reveal the white convertible underneath.

Craig whistled. "She's a beauty," he said.

Mr. Jacobs smiled. "She's a bit dirty. I'll have her cleaned up before I take her out."

Mrs. Jacobs rolled her eyes and said to Geena, "She's his baby."

Bill ran his hand over the ragtop. "Do you have a hardtop for her?"

"No, no, just the ragtop."

It was quickly becoming apparent this wasn't the Jag they were searching for.

Parker walked around the car. "Do you know anyone in the area who has another one like this?" he asked.

"No one that I know of," Mr. Jacobs said.

"Do either one of you know this man?" Geena showed them a picture of Robert Harms.

They both shook their head. "Only from the news," Mr. Jacobs said. "Is this about the Spring Strangler?"

They ignored his question. Craig handed him his card. "If you see another car around like yours, give us a call."

"Thank you for your time," Geena said.

They exited the garage, waved to the Jacobses, and returned to their cruisers.

"Anything turn up on Harms's family?" she asked Bill.

"Father split when he was a kid. Mother's deceased. He's got a sister, Mary, I haven't been able to locate yet."

"Okay. What's next?" she asked.

Bill and Craig said they were going back to headquarters. They'd let Sayres know it wasn't the Jag they were looking for. They got into their car. Parker was staring at his phone.

"What is it?" she asked.

"A message from Carlyn asking us to contact her. She said it's urgent."

CHAPTER FIFTY-ONE

"Christian is fine," Helen said, and she got up from the bed. "He's in the kitchen having a snack."

Janey wanted to cry. *Thank goodness.* But he was still in danger. If anything happened to her, his life would be in this woman's hands. If she could just keep Helen occupied while Janey figured out how to get to him, tell him to escape, to run, to find help. And she had to stay awake to do it. She could not black out. She tried pulling her wrists apart to see if there was any give to the rope. None. Next, she tried her ankles. She could move them slightly.

"You didn't finish your story," she said. "Whatever happened to your mother?" She tried working her ankles a little farther apart.

Helen's voice came from across the room. "She's dead."

"I'm sorry. That must've been hard." She continued trying to work her ankles free. Her head ached.

"Don't be sorry. I'm not." Helen was standing in front of a dresser. Janey couldn't see what she was doing.

Should she try screaming? Would anyone be able to hear her? Probably not. The only other house she'd passed on her way to therapy was at least a mile away. But she had to do something. She kicked her feet harder, but not hard enough to draw Helen's attention. She had to keep talking, distracting her, and maybe she could kick herself free. "How did your mother die?" she asked.

"Heart attack." Helen's back was to her.

"Whatever happened to your uncle?"

"I ran him over with the convertible out there," Helen said. "It was his car. We lived in Jersey then. I kept the tags, kept it exactly how it was. I don't know. Maybe I'm just sentimental that way." She shrugged. "Anyway, he was teaching me to drive, or that was his excuse to get me alone. The cops thought it was an accident."

"It wasn't an accident?"

"No," Helen said, and she moved to the side of the bed. She was holding a glass of water and a bottle of pills. "This was fun, you asking me questions for a change. But I'm afraid our little session has to come to an end. It's time you take your pills now."

Janey heard what sounded like a car engine idling outside the house. Helen must have heard it, too, because she turned toward the window. Janey wriggled her legs harder, trying to work the rope at her ankles free.

Helen whipped around. Water splashed from the glass. "What do you think you're doing?" she hollered.

The bedroom door flew open.

Christian stood in the doorway.

"Run, Christian!" Janey yelled. "Run!"

CHAPTER FIFTY-TWO

"Do you see what I see?" Geena asked Parker.

A vintage white Jag sat underneath a carport in Helen Watson's driveway. Janey's small economy car was parked behind it. Parker had called Carlyn after she'd messaged him. She'd told him that she'd tried to find information on Helen Watson after they'd left but hadn't been able to locate anything about her being a licensed psychologist. She'd thought it was more than strange and asked them to look into it. She'd given them Helen's address, which she'd found online.

Parker picked up his phone. "Yeah, Bill, we found the Jag." From their angle on the street, they could see the license plate. Jersey tags. No wonder they hadn't found it registered in Pennsylvania. He read off the number, and then he gave Bill the address for Helen Watson's residence, requested backup. He turned off the engine.

"How far are we from Minsi Lake?" Geena asked as she reached for the door handle.

"About two miles, give or take."

They got out of the car and headed up the porch steps to the front door of the small farmhouse. She knocked. There wasn't an answer. She was about to turn away and check for a back door when she heard what sounded like someone hollering. "Did you hear that?"

Parker nodded.

She heard it again. It sounded like a scream. She tried the door-knob. It was locked.

"Stand back," Parker said. He slammed his foot into the door, but it didn't budge. It was made of a thick solid wood.

"Back door," she said.

They ran around the side of the house, followed a brick path. They reached the back door. It was ajar. It didn't look tampered with, so probably not a break-in. Maybe someone had forgotten to close it on their way inside. Or perhaps someone had left in a hurry.

They stepped into what looked like a foyer that doubled as a waiting room. The house was quiet. Too quiet. Whoever had yelled a moment ago was suddenly silent.

The office door was cracked open. Geena pushed it all the way open with her foot. A chair had been knocked over. A notebook was on the floor. Blood was splattered on top of the desk. They reached for their weapons.

They continued through the downstairs, clearing each room before moving on. Nothing looked out of place. An empty glass of milk and a plate with cookie crumbs were left on the kitchen table. Someone had been there recently. A child? *Christian?* They headed up the steps. Someone yelled, "In here! I'm in here!"

Geena and Parker raced up the remaining stairs, put their backs against the wall on either side of the bedroom door, guns drawn. Geena could hear her heart pound in her ears. She looked at Parker, nodded, signaling she was ready. He pushed the door open. Janey was lying on the bed on her side, her wrists and ankles tied. Tiny braids covered her crown.

"Is anyone here with you?" Geena asked, her eyes sweeping the room, taking in the white curtains, the small dresser, the black lamp on the nightstand, the dark area rug covering the hardwood floor.

"No." Janey shook her head. "She ran after Christian. Please find my son."

"I'll go," Parker said, and he rushed down the hall.

"Hang on," she said to Janey. "I'm going to cut you free." She found a pair of scissors on top of the dresser next to a bag of hundreds of small rubber bands. She holstered her weapon and picked up the scissors. She cut the ropes, noticed they were a diamond braid, and tossed them aside. The missing pieces of evidence. She'd been right about Robert's having an accomplice. "Try not to move around too much," she said. "Let me take a look at that gash on your forehead." It had stopped bleeding for the most part, but it was possible Janey had suffered a concussion.

Parker walked back into the bedroom, shook his head, indicating he hadn't found Helen or Christian.

"She's Robert's sister," Janey said. "She's crazy. She wants to take my son from me."

"Mary," Geena said, and she exchanged a look with Parker.

"I'm going to check the perimeter of the house," Parker said. "They couldn't have gone far."

Once Parker had gone, Janey said, "I want to get up. I have to find Christian."

"Let me help you." Geena slipped her hand underneath Janey's arm, helped her sit up.

Janey touched her brow. "I feel dizzy." Then she looked at her fingers. Geena imagined she was checking them for blood.

Geena helped Janey down the stairs and outside. "Wait here," she said. "I promise we'll do everything in our power to find your son."

Janey leaned against the car. "I want to help."

"You're in no shape to help. It's best you stay here. Let us do our job." She put Janey in the back seat, left the door open to give her air and a place to get sick. She knew she couldn't mess around with a possible concussion.

Then she called Bill to let him and the team know they had a missing child on their hands, filled him in on the details, requested an Amber Alert. Then she issued a BOLO for Helen Watson, a.k.a. Mary Harms. She shoved her phone in her pocket and went to search for Parker.

She found him in Helen's backyard. The grass was wet from rain, trampled on, marking a path that led into the woods. For once the rain had worked in their favor, pointing them in the right direction. The boy was on foot, and so was Helen. "They couldn't have gotten far," she said. "Let's go find Christian."

They headed into the woods, walking fast, calling Christian's name. Small branches whipped against Geena's legs. Her arms were outstretched, pushing the higher limbs away from her face. The air smelled damp, earthy, like worms after a rainfall. Parker was walking close by on her right. He stopped abruptly. She pulled up. He put his finger to his lips.

She strained to listen, then heard what sounded like crying. It was coming from somewhere to Parker's right. They moved in that direction, stopped again, listened. They didn't hear anything. They continued in the same direction. Twigs snapped underneath their feet. This time she heard something, someone sobbing. She grabbed Parker's arm. They stopped for a third time. The sound came from above them. They both looked up, searched the trees. It was hard to see through the branches and sprouting leaves.

"There he is," Parker said, pointing to Christian hugging a branch high in an old maple tree.

"What's he doing up there?" she asked.

"Hiding," Parker said. "Clever kid." Then he called to Christian, waved his arms. "Hey, down here. Are you okay?"

Christian nodded.

"Which way did she go?" Parker asked.

Christian looked at them, then pointed deeper into the woods.

"Go," Geena said. Parker had mentioned when they'd first discovered Valerie's body in Minsi Lake that he was familiar with the area. He'd have an easier time tracking Helen down, while she would try to get Christian out of the tree and to safety. "Be careful," she said to Parker and then watched as he disappeared behind the trees.

"Christian!" she called. "Do you think you can climb down?" He was up so high. She couldn't believe a small child could be that brave, considering the height. And, like Parker said, *clever*.

Christian shook his head. He clung to the tree.

"Can you try?" she asked. The last thing she wanted was to climb up after him. She'd never gotten over her fear of heights after she'd fallen that day in the park with her father. "I promise to catch you," she said to Christian now. The irony wasn't lost on her. Her father had said something similar right before she'd tumbled to the ground.

"I can't," Christian said.

"Okay. Well then, I guess I'm coming up." She looked around, unsure of what she was searching for, maybe another way to do this. Then she circled the tree to find the best place to start her climb. She grabbed on to a low-lying branch and hoisted herself up. *Don't look down.* Slowly, she picked her way higher and higher. Leaves and small twigs rained to the ground. The limbs were wet, slippery. But climbing up wasn't the hard part.

No, the hard part would be climbing down.

When she reached Christian, she put her hand on his shoulder. His face was dirty and streaked with tears. "I'm going to get us out of this, but I'm going to need your help. I need you to do two things for me. First, I don't want you to look down. Do you understand? Do not look down." She felt woozy. It was just the altitude. *Ignore it.*

He nodded.

"Second, I want you to grab on to me piggyback-style and hold on tight. I need you to really hold on to me. You won't hurt me. Lock your arms and legs around me. Do you think you can do that?"

He nodded again and without hesitation climbed onto her back, wrapped his ropy arms around her neck, his legs around her waist. She had a feeling he'd done this before, perhaps with Janey. Once he was secured around her, she carefully stepped off the branch, searched for a lower one with her foot, found it, and stepped down. She did the same thing on the next branch, gripping the one above her at the same time. Christian hung on tightly. She took her time, methodically working her way down the tree. She stopped once about halfway down to gather herself, focus, not throw up. Then she continued stepping onto a branch below while hanging onto a branch above. She was almost to the bottom when she spied Janey beneath them, looking up. When she was close to the ground, Christian reached for his mother and jumped into her outstretched arms.

Once Geena was out of the tree, she wiped her moist hands on her thighs. She was so happy her feet were on the ground she could have kissed the soil, bugs and all. And it was no secret she wasn't a fan of bugs. "I thought I told you to wait in the car," she said.

"I couldn't sit there, knowing my son was out here."

She understood, even if she wished Janey had listened to her. She was going to have to make sure mother and son got out of the woods safely before she could help Parker in the search for Helen.

Janey put Christian down, took his hand. "Mommy's a little unsteady on her feet," she said. "I can't carry you. You're going to have to walk." She wiped tears from his cheeks.

Geena checked her phone, but she wasn't getting a signal. Somewhere behind her she heard the sound of twigs snapping. She whipped around, peered at a small woman pointing a handgun at them.

"Isn't this cozy," the woman said.

Without thinking, Geena stepped in front of Janey and Christian, shielded them with her body.

"Don't even think about reaching for your gun," the woman said. Her hair was in tangles, her mouth open, spit dribbling onto her lips.

"You must be Helen," she said, feeling a rush of adrenaline.

"And you must be Detective Brassard."

"I am." She kept her hands where Helen could see them, trying to keep Helen calm, keep them all calm, in an attempt to control the situation that had crept up on them. "Let's talk about this. Okay?" Behind her, Janey and Christian were quiet.

The wildlife was not.

Squirrels scurried from branch to branch. Birds flapped their wings, scolded them with their high-pitched screeching. They were being territorial. Who could blame them? Humans were the outsiders here, disturbing them on an otherwise tranquil afternoon.

"All I want is Christian," Helen said. "Give me the boy, and no one gets hurt."

"Let's try to be reasonable about this. I can't just hand over an innocent child to a woman with a gun." She could feel herself sweating and wondered if Parker was anywhere close by.

"I really don't believe you're in a position to argue," Helen said.

"Maybe not. But you do see my point." She raised her voice slightly, trying to alert Parker or possibly the backup team to their location.

"Christian," Helen called. "I need you to walk over to me. If you come here to me, then your mom and her cop friend won't get hurt. Do you understand? It's up to you."

Geena could feel Janey at her back struggling to hold on to him. He must've pried himself away from her, because he stepped out from behind Geena before she could grab him, hold him back.

"Helen," he said.

"Christian, no," Geena said, reaching for his shoulder, trying to push him behind her again. "Put the gun down, Helen." Her voice was strong, commanding, but inside she was pleading with this crazy woman, *Please just put the gun down.* She had no idea if Helen was in any way skilled at shooting. If not, there was a good chance she'd miss hitting Geena and shoot the boy instead.

Helen ignored Geena. She seemed to have locked on to Christian. "Call me Aunt Helen. Did you know I was your aunt? We're family."

Janey reached for Christian, but he pushed her hand away. "Aunt Helen," he said, and he stepped closer to her.

"That's right, come here," Helen said. "I won't hurt them if you just keep walking."

Christian took another couple of steps and stumbled, falling. Geena reached her arm out to try to catch him, but he was too far away for her to grab him.

"Don't you move!" Helen yelled at her.

Geena saw a flash of something out of the corner of her eye—a dark jacket flapping open, a holstered gun, long powerful legs.

Parker.

He sprang from the trees. Helen saw him too late. He blindsided her, tackled her. The gun flew from her hand, disappeared in a patch of small plants. Birds flew from the branches. Crows. Their wings thundering in the air. Geena latched on to Christian, shoved him behind her and into Janey's arms.

Parker and Helen were on the ground in the mud and leaves. He was on top of her.

Geena raced to where they were lying on the woods floor. She tried to contain Helen's flailing arms. Her elbow came up and struck Geena's mouth. Helen kicked her legs. Then Parker was up, pressing his knee between Helen's shoulder blades, his hand on the back of her head. She writhed under his weight. It all happened quickly.

Geena grabbed her handcuffs. She pulled Helen's arms behind her back and cuffed her.

Then she stood and faced her partner. He was sweaty and covered in dirt. Helen was lying on the ground between them. She wasn't going anywhere. A dog was barking. Their backup team arrived, converging in the woods, moving in their direction, pressing in on them.

"You're bleeding," Parker said, and he motioned to Geena's lip.

She dabbed it with the back of her hand.

"Did you see where the gun went?" he asked.

"Somewhere over here." She swept the woods floor with her foot, finding a nine-millimeter hiding underneath a patch of small plants that she really hoped wasn't poison ivy. She reached for the rubber gloves she carried in the inside pocket of her jacket, slipped them on, and picked up the gun.

Zach and his dog emerged from the trees. The dog pulled on his leash, barking at Helen, who was still lying on the ground, twisting and cursing. Bill and Craig weren't far behind. Craig bent down and helped Helen to her feet, proceeded to read her her rights.

Geena had so many questions for Helen, but they stuck in her throat, making it impossible to speak without her anger getting in the way. *What kind of evil are you?* she almost asked, but maybe she knew the answer. Maybe she was the purest kind.

She walked away from Helen then, something she should've done in the interview room with Robert. She turned her attention to Janey and Christian, asked if they were okay.

Janey nodded. She was kneeling, crying, hugging her son. After they'd separated, Parker ruffled Christian's hair and said, "That was clever, climbing that tree."

"And brave," Geena added.

Janey laughed, cried, and said, "He likes to be up high so he can see."

CHAPTER FIFTY-THREE

The forensic unit swarmed Helen's small farmhouse, collecting evidence. They bagged not only the pieces of the nylon rope that had been tied around Janey's wrists and ankles but also a coil of the same rope—quarter-inch diamond braid—along with the plastic bag full of hundreds of tiny rubber bands. They'd found some of the Spring Girls' jewelry in a drawer in one of the bedrooms. Remnants of clothes and ligatures were found in the firepit behind the house.

Janey and her son had since been taken to the hospital by ambulance.

Geena and Parker briefed Sayres on what they'd learned about Dr. Helen Watson, a.k.a. Mary Harms.

"And how is it you two ended up here again?" Sayres asked.

"We were checking up on Janey," Parker said. "We learned from Child Welfare Services and Janey's son's previous therapist that something was amiss. We followed the lead here."

Sayres rubbed his brow where the deep creases in his forehead stretched toward his temples. "You two weren't supposed to make a move without my knowing about it."

"We didn't think it had anything to do with the case initially," Geena said. "We were just looking out for Janey."

The lieutenant seemed to consider her explanation. "Get me her statement," he said before striding away.

"We should get to the hospital," Parker said.

"Yup," she said, and she got into the car. Her lip was sore, a little swollen, but it had stopped bleeding. It was nothing more than a dull ache now. Despite ticking off the lieutenant and the possibility she might have to appear before Internal Affairs for striking Robert in the interview room, she couldn't help but feel pretty good, considering. Especially when she thought of Janey and how she'd proved there was a fighter inside of her somewhere.

She now believed there was a fighter inside all the Spring Girls, if only they'd been given a chance.

At the hospital, Geena listened as Janey told her and Parker what had happened in Helen's office, the things Helen had told her about how Helen had changed her name, poisoned Janey's rabbit, how she'd planned to take Christian away. Parker took notes. Janey talked about Helen and Robert's uncle and the cruel things he'd done to the sister and brother duo when they'd been kids, how their mother had known and had tried to comfort at least Helen.

"Now we know the significance of the spring season," Parker said.

"And the braids," Geena said. If she'd made the connection between the braids in the girls' hair and the untying of their wrists and ankles, both meant to comfort, something women were especially prone to do, she might have been able to figure out much sooner that the Strangler had had a female accomplice. If she had, maybe she would've been able to save at least one of the victims' lives. This would trouble her for many nights to come, the hindsight of such things, along with the images of the Spring Girls.

And she'd never forget how she'd let her feelings for Albert skew her judgment. *Loyal to a fault.* She'd have to work on that.

"Do you think it started with the uncle? Is that the reason they are like they are?" Janey asked.

"It's possible," Geena said. "We may never know for sure."

"I know I'm supposed to forgive them for what they've done. But I'm not sure I can. I'm not sure I ever will," Janey said.

"I don't think that's something you should be worrying about right now," Geena said.

Janey's parents stepped into the room with Christian. Christian looked past them to his mother, sitting up in the hospital bed. Janey held her arms out to him. "Come here," she said.

He walked over to her as though he wasn't sure. Then he climbed into her arms and buried his face in her neck.

Geena was moved by the sight of them. She wasn't the only one. Parker seemed touched by the scene as well. This was the reason Geena had chosen the job, or maybe the job had chosen her. Either way, it was an image she would cling to when the next case came up.

"I think we're done here," she said.

Geena and Parker walked out of the hospital and headed toward the parking lot. The sun was setting behind the clouds. The day was ending, but their work back at headquarters was just beginning. Helen Watson had been booked. They'd heard she was sitting in an interview room with Sayres. If Helen was anything like her brother, she'd be eager to tell him her side of the story.

They stopped when they reached their car, and they talked over the roof. "You know, I was thinking about the way you took down Harms," Parker said.

"What about it?" she asked.

"Your technique isn't bad, but it could use some improvement."

"You're joking, right?"

"I could give you some pointers if you want."

"Seriously?"

"I played a lot of football in my day."

"Get in the car, Reed," she said, and she smiled as she got into the passenger side.

Parker drove toward headquarters and a long night of work. She stared out the window and thought about Albert and his organic farm. He'd asked her once what kind of partner Parker was, whether she saw him as a companion plant.

She thought he very well could be.

EPILOGUE

Janey sat at the kitchen table, snapping the ends off string beans for a bean salad. It was the middle of August, and Christian would be starting first grade in a week in a new school in South Carolina. They'd moved to the new state at the end of June, when Janey's request for a transfer at the craft store had been granted. Josh had gotten her the position, pulled some strings with his uncle, and for that she was grateful. It had become apparent during Helen's and Robert's trials and afterward, when they'd been found guilty, that she could no longer stay in Pennsylvania, not if she and Christian were ever going to move on. Small towns had long memories. And they needed to be in a place where no one knew who Christian's father was so they could start to rebuild their lives.

Now, Janey wondered where the summer had gone.

Christian had finished kindergarten through an online program. Mrs. Delacorte had helped Janey with the process. As it turned out, it had been Claire's daughter, Emma, who had been arguing with Christian on the slide, something about who had been there first. They'd begun shoving each other when they'd bumped into Bella. Her falling and breaking her arm had been an unfortunate accident. And it had been Emma who had given Christian the plastic gun all those months ago at the beginning of the school year. And then Christian had smashed Emma's Easter eggs over a disagreement about who had found an egg first. Janey and Claire had eventually compared notes, apologized for their kids' behavior. It had become obvious Christian and Emma just didn't get along.

Janey put the trimmed beans in a bowl. Christian was in his bedroom, playing with his dinosaurs. She reached down and petted Bear, who was napping at her feet. The dog had been Carlyn's idea, since Bunnie was now living with Janey's parents permanently. Pop had become attached to the rabbit, building a large outdoor hutch for her in their backyard.

Two weeks before they'd left Pennsylvania, Carlyn had stopped by for her last session with Christian. She'd poked her head into the kitchen. "Ready?" she'd asked.

"Bring him in," Janey had said, and she'd rushed to the bedroom to get her son. "Carlyn's here, and she has a surprise for you."

"For me?" Christian had asked. "What is it?"

He'd followed Janey to the family room. Carlyn had been sitting on the floor next to a three-month-old puppy. Christian had dropped to his knees and petted the puppy without hesitation. It had been a very good sign.

"What kind of dog is he?" Christian had asked.

"I'm not sure," Carlyn had said. "A mutt of unknown breeds."

"What's his name?" he'd asked.

"I thought maybe you'd like to name him," Carlyn had said.

The puppy had nipped at Christian's fingers the way puppies do. "He looks like a bear," he'd said.

"He does look like a bear," Janey had chimed in. He was black and brown with a plump belly.

"Can we keep him, Mommy?"

"Only if you promise to help me take care of him."

"I promise," Christian had said.

Carlyn had also found Janey and Christian a therapist here in South Carolina. They saw Dr. James once a week. Sometimes their sessions were together and sometimes apart. Janey often felt hollowed out after their visits, but in a good way, like she was finally coming to terms with her thoughts and feelings about everything that had happened. Christian was also making progress. His tantrums had subsided to being weekly rather than daily.

Janey stood from the table, called the puppy to follow her outside to the backyard. He'd been house-trained, but he still had the occasional accident. Christian emerged from his bedroom and followed them out, carrying a tennis ball for the puppy to chase.

Janey's parents would be coming soon. They were visiting for the week. They were going to grill hot dogs and hamburgers. Her mother had made a pudding pie. Her parents hadn't told her about Albert's stroke until after the trial. They hadn't wanted her to worry. Last she'd heard, his speech was still slurred, but he was back working in his garden.

She sat in the lawn chair. Christian ran around the yard with Bear. She lifted her face to the sun and closed her eyes. She hardly ever thought about Helen or Robert anymore, although she'd written a victim-impact statement she would read in court during their sentencing. It would be hard, but she would do it for the Spring Girls. She would be their voice. Sometimes she could still feel them around her, hear their whispering words in the wind, see the shadows of their faces in the corners of her mind. But rather than feeling a deep sadness or the heat of their anger, she sensed a kind of peace in them and in herself. She was one of them. And she would always carry a part of them with her.

She opened her eyes to Christian's laughter, the puppy nipping at his heels.

He was her son. And he was going to be all right.

They were both going to be all right.

ACKNOWLEDGMENTS

In the spring of 2017, I spoke at the Bangor Public Library about my latest book. It was there that we discussed the draining of the community's beloved Minsi Lake. We played around with all sorts of ideas about what we might find once the lake had been emptied. It was at this event that the idea for *Spring Girls* started to take shape. Thank you to the Friends of the Bangor Public Library and the people who attended the event and brainstormed some fun ideas with me.

Thank you to my agent, Carly Watters, for being by my side since the very beginning. I couldn't have done any of this without you. And thank you to the team at the P. S. Literary Agency; your continued support is so much appreciated.

Thank you to Megha Parekh and the entire team at Thomas & Mercer, including but not limited to Sarah Shaw, Grace Doyle, Lindsey Bragg, and Dennelle Catlett. To my developmental editor, Charlotte Herscher, for knowing exactly what the story needed and for helping me shape it into the book it is today. Charlotte, your input is invaluable, and I can't thank you enough. Also, thank you to Shasti O'Leary Soudant for designing the stunning book covers for the series. And to Lauren Ezzo for her wonderful voice in the audiobooks.

A big thank-you to all the readers, bloggers, and librarians for reading and leaving kind reviews. A special thanks goes to Judith D. Collins and John Valeri for their powerhouse interviews and thoughtful reviews.

There is no greater feeling to an author than when someone "gets it," and these two do just that.

Although I didn't interview experts specifically for this book, I did use the knowledge from previous interviews and information they had so graciously offered in the past. Thank you again to the Pennsylvania State Police homicide investigators, especially Lieutenant Kreg Rodrigues. And once again thank you to Michael Ann Beyer for explaining forensic medicine. Any and all errors are mine and mine alone.

Thank you to the usual suspects—Tracey Golden, Mindy Bailey, Jenene McGonigal, Tina Mantel, Kate Weeks, Karin Wagner, and Laura McHugh.

To my husband, Philip, and our two daughters, my love . . . always.